The Ghost and Mrs. Fletcher

A Murder, She Wrote Mystery

OTHER BOOKS IN THE
Murder, She Wrote SERIES

The Ghost and Mrs. Fletcher

A Murder, She Wrote Mystery

A NOVEL BY JESSICA FLETCHER,
DONALD BAIN & RENÉE PALEY-BAIN

**Based on the Universal Television series created by
Peter S. Fischer, Richard Levinson & William Link**

AN OBSIDIAN MYSTERY

Doubleday Large Print Home Library Edition

This Large Print Edition, prepared especially for Doubleday Large Print Home Library, contains the complete, unabridged text of the original Publisher's Edition.

OBSIDIAN

Published by New American Library,
an imprint of Penguin Random House LLC
375 Hudson Street, New York, New York 10014

This book is an original publication of New American Library.

ISBN 978-1-62953-742-9

Printed in the United States of America

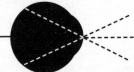

**This Large Print Book carries the
Seal of Approval of N.A.V.H**

In memory of Robert "Absolutely" Skow

Acknowledgments

Many thanks to the folks at Danbury Library, in particular John O'Donnell, information services, who gave us a personal tour of the wonderful Local History Room, and Maryellen C. DeJong, community relations, whose care and feeding of local authors are always appreciated.

We are also grateful to Wynne A. Whitman of Schenck, Price, Smith & King, LLP, and to our good friend, fellow author, and legal eagle, Ken Isaacson, for legal opinions; and to our crack agent, Bob Diforio, D4EO Literary Agency ("crack" in the old-fashioned use of the word, to mean "first-rate"); and to our patient and attentive editor at Penguin, Laura Fazio.

As always, we appreciate all who contribute their knowledge and expertise to the Internet, the virtual library that lives in our computers. While that library boasts convenience, its breadth is more than matched by our hometown libraries, which have the advantage of offering reliability and local treasures the Internet hasn't found time for yet. Both are needed. Both are precious.

The Ghost and Mrs. Fletcher

A Murder, She Wrote Mystery

Chapter One

"I'm dying and I know it." Cliff Cooper stretched out a hand to me. "Will you help me, Jessica?"

"Of course, Cliff," I said, taking his hand in both of mine. "But Seth Hazlitt says you still have plenty of good years ahead of you."

Cliff pulled back his hand and shook his head. "I know the truth." He pressed his body forward and coughed into the pillow he'd been hugging. His pale face turned crimson with the exertion. "See?" he said, falling back against the raised mattress. "Dr. Hazlitt's a crazy optimist."

"Can't say as I've ever been called that before, Cliff," Cabot Cove's favorite physician said as he folded the stethoscope he'd just used to listen to Cliff's chest. "If you'd take the medicines the nurses give you instead of tossing the pills in the flowerpot, you'd feel a lot better, and so would that plant." Seth gestured toward a drooping geranium next to vases of flowers lined up on the windowsill.

"You can't fool an old carpenter. I know when my sanding days are over."

Seth tucked his stethoscope into his black medical bag. "Probably breathing in all that sawdust instead of wearing a mask—which, by the way, I suggested to you years ago—landed you where you are. Too late to fix all the damage, but with your cooperation, we'd stand a chance of getting you out of here and back home into your recliner."

"Sounds nice." Cliff sighed. "Thanks, Doc."

Seth closed his medical bag and gave Cliff a pat on the arm. "I'll stop by later. In the meantime, try to be a good patient."

"I'll try." Cliff gave Seth a wan smile.

I accompanied Seth into the hall. "Is there really a chance for him to be able to return home?"

"I wish I could say for sure. There was a

good chance when he was first admitted, but he's refused to follow medical orders, rejected all the therapies we've recommended. And the longer he stays here lying on his back, the farther away his chances are of getting better. He's becoming weaker, getting frail. You have to use your muscles, or they atrophy."

"That cough sounds terrible. It must take a lot out of him."

"He has a bad cough, yes, but there's no underlying malignancy. In his case, getting well looks to be as dependent on willpower as it is on medicine. I hate to say that he's giving up, Jessica, but that's how it appears to me."

"Oh, Seth, that's terrible. What can I do to help?"

"Maybe you can talk some sense into him. He's turned away most of his visitors. Far as I know, you're among the few he's agreed to see."

"I am? I can't imagine why. We're only casual friends. Haven't Lettie and Lucy been here to call on him?"

"I don't believe so."

"That's odd. They've been friends for

years. In fact, I heard a rumor that he was about to ask Lucy to marry him."

"Mebbe so, but now he says he just wants to be left alone in the dark."

I returned to Cliff's room and took the chair next to his bed. A whiteboard hanging on the wall facing his bed said his nurse's name was Carolyn and the aide was Theresa. Cliff was a patient in the new one-story rehabilitation wing of Cabot Cove Hospital. Seth would never have put him there if he hadn't expected Cliff to get better. Hospice services were provided on another floor, or at home. The new wing had private rooms looking out onto the woods behind the hospital. A brochure extolling its amenities was on Cliff's bedside table.

"Each patient is afforded a prospect of Mother Nature's panorama," the brochure stated, adding, "Taking in nature's bountiful beauty each day—our unspoiled forest combined with delightful glimpses of wildlife—is conducive to the healing process."

Its flowery language aside, the brochure was correct that the view of the woods would be a pleasant sight if Cliff's nurse hadn't adjusted the blinds to keep out any light.

Cliff's eyes had closed, and he appeared to be sleeping. Once a strapping man, he looked as if his body had melted into the hospital bed, his shoulders no longer broad, his arms withered to half their previous size, his strong features softened with time. His large hands, now knurled with age, were the only evidence of his youthful vigor. I remembered how handsome he'd been, and how, after his wife died, so many of the single women in town brought him casseroles and cakes, hoping to impress Cliff Cooper. But he'd allowed only two people into his inner circle in those days and ever since: Lucy Conrad, his neighbor, and Lettie, her twin sister.

I waited for a few more minutes before deciding not to disturb Cliff's rest. I had begun gathering my things, intent upon leaving, when he called out to me in a rusty voice.

"Don't go yet, Jessica. I need to talk to you."

"I'm here, Cliff. What can I do for you? Are you in pain? Would you like me to call the nurse?"

He shook his head and cleared his throat. "Bunch of pill pushers in this place."

I laughed softly. "Most hospitals and nursing homes are like that. But if the pills will help you get better, don't you think you should take them?"

"Too late for me. But I want you to do me a favor."

"Anything that's in my power," I replied.

"I want Miss Simpson to sell the house before I die and give the money to my grandson. She knows. I called her. She said she'd get on it right away."

"Didn't you already provide for him in your will, Cliff?"

"Never got around to making one."

"Well, it's not too late. Would you like me to arrange a visit by your lawyer?"

"Don't have one of those either. Just put it down on a piece of paper, if you would."

I rummaged through my shoulder bag for a notebook and pen, scooted my chair closer to Cliff's nightstand, and used the book I'd brought for him to lean on as I took his dictation. "Okay, I'll write down what you say for now, but I'm bringing Fred Kramer with me tomorrow. He specializes in family law and estate planning. He probably has a simple form you can fill out with your instructions."

"Do I know him?"

"He was a colleague of Cyrus O'Connor Senior and took over his law practice when Cy's son gave it up to move to New York."

"Junior was a foul ball if I remember correctly."

"You do. But Fred Kramer is as upstanding as Cy Senior was. Will you talk with him if I can get him to come with me?"

"I suppose. I don't want anyone making a claim on my property. I promised it to Elliot."

"If you promised the house to Elliot, why do you want to sell it? Your grandson might like to inherit the home he grew up in."

"He's young and eager for adventure. The house would only tie him down. Knowing him, I figure he might feel guilty about getting rid of it, even if he wanted to. I don't buy the whole business about it being the family home for generations. I don't want anyone to put Elliot's head in a bucket and trick him into keepin' it."

"Who would do that?"

"You never know. I want the decision out of his hands."

"All right, but—"

"Don't argue with me, Jessica."

"No one's arguing with you, Cliff. I only meant you might want to think about the legal—"

"It's my house," he said, raising his voice, "and I can do with it what I want, can't I?"

He inhaled deeply, setting off a paroxysm of coughing. He ducked his head and hunched his shoulders, curling into the pillow as he attempted to muffle his spasm.

A nurse in a green uniform bustled into the room. I got out of her way and stood by the window. She roughly pulled my chair aside and made soothing noises as she began patting Cliff, making circles on his back with her hand. "Take it slow, Cliff. No deep breaths at first, just little soft ones. In through the nose, out through the mouth. That's better, sweetheart. Didn't I tell you what happens when you get excited? I could hear you yelling all the way down at the nurses' station." She aimed a stern look at me. "I've told him before that excitement isn't good for him," she said. "Maybe it's time to wind up your visit, and tell the others to stay away, too."

"Not her fault," Cliff managed to squeeze out between coughs. He took a few short breaths and knocked the nurse's arm away. "She stays."

"Only if you calm down," the nurse said, taking a step back and scowling, her gaze darting back and forth between Cliff and me.

Cliff made a circle with his finger, gesturing for me to take the chair again, and batted his hand at the nurse. "You can go now," he told her.

"If you insist, but if I have to come in again, she leaves." She walked out the door, rubbing her arm where Cliff's slap had connected.

"Yeah, yeah," Cliff said under his breath.

I couldn't tell if the nurse heard him.

"Always too bossy, that one."

I sat in the chair again.

"Where was I?" he asked.

"You were telling me you want Eve Simpson to sell your house and give Elliot the funds from it. There are going to be fees taken out for her commission, and taxes and other expenses. You know that, don't you?"

"That's okay. This way, he gets a lump sum and the freedom to do what he wants with it. No one can challenge him."

"Who could challenge him?"

"No one. That's the point. Did you write it down?"

"Yes. Is there more?"

"Yes." He leaned back against the mattress, his eyes searching the ceiling for the right words.

"I want Lucy to have whatever she wants of my things, not that there's anything valuable there. There are some bowls and such that my wife had. Glass things, I think. Or maybe they're crystal. Don't even remember when we got them. Might even've been wedding gifts. I never used 'em. Lucy can have them if she wants." He closed his eyes and lay quietly for a while.

"Why won't you let her visit you?" I asked

softly.

Tears welled up under his closed lids. He wiped the moisture away. "I don't want her to see me like this."

"Like what?"

"Like this." He looked down at the sheet that covered his body. "Like a beached striper, flopping and gasping for breath. She don't need to remember me this way. I'd rather she remember me in better days. Now, let me autograph that thing."

I gave him the paper I'd used to write down his bequests. He grabbed my pen with his right hand and signed his name.

"You give that to your lawyer friend. If he needs to get paid, there's some cash in a hollowed-out book of poems by Henry Wadsworth Longfellow. It's on a bottom shelf in the library."

"I didn't know you read poetry," I said.

"I don't, and no one I know does either. That's why I put my stash in there. If I'da used a Stephen King book, someone mighta borrowed it and I'd be out the money."

"I'll give this to Fred Kramer, but it may be wise to execute a more legal document.

It'll be much better if he comes to see you. Will you agree to see him?"

He nodded wearily. "If I'm still here. Give his name to the nurse. I'm not acceptin' too many visitors. Takes too much outta me." He heaved a sigh, then froze, his body stiffening.

"What is it?" I asked.

He let out a stream of air. "Whew! Was afraid I'd start it up again."

"The cough?"

He nodded. "Ever' time I try to take a deep breath. Doc is right. It's all them years of wood dust in the air. It's killing me now."

"Seth says if you worked at getting better, you might be able to get well enough to go home. Why won't you listen to him?"

"Not to say the doc don't know his business, but a man knows when he's dying, and I'm knockin' at death's door."

"In that case, you may not be up to reading my new book," I said, holding up the novel I'd brought as a gift. "Should I offer it to the nurse instead?"

"Put that back on the nightstand where you found it," he said, scowling. "I'll read it tonight. Good-bye, Jessica."

"Good-bye, Cliff. I'll be back. With the lawyer. You need a formal will, even though I expect you're going to live a lot longer than you think."

But I was wrong.

Chapter Two

1805 House for Sale

Charming historic colonial built by
a sea captain for his young wife

- Spectacular water views
- 8 bedrooms, 3 baths, kitchen,
  dining room, laundry, library
- Lots of period details
- Separate barn on the property
- Price on request
- An Eve Simpson exclusive

"If Cliff Cooper knew what we're doing, he would spin in his grave—that is, if he'd already been buried," I said to Eve Simpson.

To Seth's consternation and contrary to

my prediction, Cliff had succumbed within a few days of my visit, and I was never able to arrange for him to execute a more formal will than the makeshift one he'd dictated to me. Attorney Fred Kramer said Cliff's will would likely stand up in probate court, but he wished he could have made one with another witness's signature on it.

"I have to get rid of those books, Jessica. No one wants to buy a house where the bookshelves are overflowing. They're everywhere—on the floor, chairs, and on the steps going upstairs."

"That may be, Eve, but just throwing away all these books would be a crime."

"That's why I asked you to look through them. If there's anything of great value, I figured you'd recognize it."

Eve steadied the library ladder, on which I was perched five steps up, while I inspected one of the multiple shelves of books in Cliff's big seaside house, which she had recently advertised as on the market. With Cliff's encouragement, Eve had started the sales process right away, putting a notice in the local newspaper and planning improvements to the huge house. She billed herself as Cabot Cove's premier real estate agent, and I didn't doubt that she was. She didn't have a lot of competition. Even so, Cliff's home was the historic Spencer Percy House, the oldest house in Cabot Cove. Selling it would provide considerable bragging rights, plus a sizable commission, if Eve could find a buyer. But that was a big "if."

The house was much larger than the average family was likely to want. Cliff Cooper had been a widower with little interest in keeping it up, and with a tendency to save rather than throw things away. He was a hoarder, Cabot Cove's version of the compulsive Collyer brothers, who collected tons of items in their New York town house in the first half of the twentieth century. Thank goodness Cliff hadn't gone to the extremes of those famous siblings.

But he almost had.

Apart from two furnished bedrooms, other rooms in the Spencer Percy House had been repositories of cast-off furniture, old luggage, and piles of household items that were saved even though they no longer had a function in the lives of the occupants. Whether much of this had already been here when Cliff and his wife, Nanette, first moved in, or whether Cliff filled the empty spaces himself after her death, neither Eve nor I knew.

"Fred Kramer said he's officially the lawyer for the estate. I assume that means he's found Elliot," Eve said.

"Yes, but don't ask me how he discovered his whereabouts. He said Elliot was camping in Alaska with a friend who's a bush pilot. He's coming home, but he's coming by motorcycle, of all things. We'll have to hold off the funeral until he arrives."

"When was the last time he was in Cabot Cove?"

"No idea. I never saw Elliot after Cliff sent him off to boarding school."

"Well, at least Fred assured me that I'm free to do as I please with these books. What do you have there?"

"I'm no expert in antiquarian books," I said, pulling out a large cloth-covered volume missing its dust jacket, "but I have to say that most of Cliff's collection seems to be a combination of popular novels, outdated texts, old travel guides, and"—I flipped through the pages—"reference books from the last century. Hawaii isn't even a state in this 1956 atlas."

"Maybe I should call the junk man again," Eve said. "Herb carted away at least a ton of magazines and newspapers before Cliff died." She looked down at the faded carpeting. "That's how I found out that this is an oriental rug. You couldn't see the pattern with all the papers piled up on it. I didn't dare bring Cecil here. He's barely paper trained as it is."

Eve's Chihuahua, Cecil, was a canine senior citizen with dental problems and an occasionally weak bladder who'd belonged to an actress making a film in Cabot Cove. The actress had the misfortune of being killed on the set by someone with a grudge, and her grieving family wasn't willing or able to adopt the dog. But Eve generously took him in, much to my relief, because he'd been a temporary boarder at my home.

"You don't think Cliff's grandson will

want any of the books as a keepsake?" I asked.

"Fred says to do what I want with them, and that's good enough for me."

"Did you ask at the library?"

"They don't want anything published before the year 2000, and Doris Ann said that was stretching it. She said the library can't afford to hire the staff needed to sort through all the books people want to donate."

I returned the atlas to the shelf and stepped back down the ladder. "Well, that's a shame, but I doubt there's much of value here to salvage. If there is, it'll take greater expertise than I possess." I tried to shake the cobwebs and dust off my hands but only succeeded in smearing the dirt even more. "If I'd known I'd be scrambling around in this grimy house, I'd have worn my old painting clothes. Those shelves look like they haven't seen a vacuum or dust cloth in decades."

"I'm sorry, Jessica. I didn't realize it would be so bad."

Eve, of course, was pristine in a taupe suit with a silk scarf in a navy check artfully arranged around her neck, not a wave out of place on her carefully coiffed head. I, on the other hand, was afraid to use my grubby fingers to replace the lock of hair that had fallen down on my forehead.

"Well, what's done is done," I said. "Where's the nearest sink?"

"In the kitchen. Follow me."

Eve led me through the library's archway, down the main hall, and into a kitchen that had last been updated in the same decade as the atlas. Faded wallpaper with teapots on a yellow gingham background covered most of the walls, except where someone had pulled a section away to reveal even older wallpaper with stylized blue leaves surrounding bunches of cherries. The cast-iron sink was full of rust stains, but the cold tap worked, although it gave a loud groan before the water trickled out. I rinsed my hands, and Eve handed me a paper towel from a roll standing on the counter.

"If Fred Kramer said you're free to remove the books, what do you think about putting on a secondhand book sale?" I suggested. "If nothing else, you'll get a lot of people coming to see the house and perhaps attract a buyer. You might even sell as much as half the collection that way."

A soft thud sounded from somewhere in the house.

"What was that?"

"Oh, these old houses are full of random noises," Eve said.

"You're sure it's not Cliff Cooper back to haunt the place?" I said.

"Very funny, Jessica, but you're not the first to suggest that."

"That the house is haunted?"

"So rumor has it, but you can't prove it by me, even though every time I'm here, I hear something new. Yesterday, I was sure I heard someone walking around on the second floor. I raced upstairs, ready to threaten to call the police on the trespasser, but no one was there."

"I hope you don't have raccoons or squirrels," I said. "They're difficult to remove."

"Not according to the home inspector, but he found plenty of other things to repair, which is why, while I like the idea of a book sale, **c'est impossible**. I'm way too busy. There are a gazillion things to do before we're ready for the open house. The place is falling down."

We heard another loud thud, and Eve and I looked at each other in alarm. Then a voice called out a long, "Halloo?" and we heard footsteps approach the kitchen. We turned to see our sheriff's head peeking around the corner. He had a big grin on his face. "Hello, ladies. Am I interrupting anything?"

"Good heavens, Mort, you gave us quite a start," I said.

"Sheriff Metzger, you're not to do that again," Eve said. "You must've taken ten—or maybe five—years off my life." She fanned her face with her hand.

"The front door was open," he said, coming into the room. "I've never been in here. Thought I'd take a look around before someone buys it. Pretty big, huh? My wife would love this kitchen, although I wouldn't love all the work it'll take to fix it up."

"It's reasonably priced," Eve said, recognizing a potential customer in Cabot Cove's top law enforcement officer. "If you're really interested, I'm sure we can work out a deal."

"Whoa! Slow down. I'm not in the market to move. I've already given up two weekends painting the bathroom at home. With a project this size, I'd never see another football game again."

"Well, if you change your mind, here's my card."

Mort tucked it in his pocket.

"Eve and I were just discussing what to do with Cliff Cooper's books," I said.

"Yeah? The guy must've been some brain. Did he really read all those books out there?" He gestured toward the hallway.

"I believe so," I said. "The trouble was he didn't know what to do with a book once he finished it."

"But I do," Eve said, making shoveling gestures.

A crackle of static and a tinny voice on a police radio reached our ears. "Come in, Sheriff Metzger. This is Deputy Chip. You got a ten-twenty-one B—that's a ten-twenty-one B. Do you copy?"

"Oops! Gotta go," Mort said.

"What's a ten-twenty-one B?" Eve asked.

"It's police radio code for 'call your home,'" I said.

"I hope it's not an emergency, Sheriff," Eve said.

"It'll be a ten-forty-five if I don't bring my wife the bottle of vinegar she asked me to pick up. She's practicing making an apple onion pie to enter in the Harvest Festival. See you, ladies."

"What's a ten-forty-five?" Eve whispered to me.

"A domestic dispute," I whispered back. "Send our best to Maureen," I called as he raced down the hall and out the door.

"He's such a nice man," Eve said.

"And a good sheriff," I added as he left the house.

Eve sighed. "Too bad there's no radio code for 'Who wants a book?' It will be impossible to stage the house for prospective buyers with all these dusty tomes cluttering up the place."

"Since there's so much on your calendar, why don't you wait a little before making a decision on the books?" I said. "I know a gentleman in New York who runs a secondhand bookstore. He might be interested in taking a look at what's here. He would know if Cliff had a gem buried among his odds and ends."

"That would be **absolument merveilleux**, Jessica," Eve said, clapping her hands. "I knew you would come up with a solution."

"I'm not promising anything. His shop's bookshelves are overflowing as it is. But even if he finds a prize or two, that doesn't solve your problem of getting rid of thousands of other books, most of them probably worthless. A book sale is really your best bet."

Eve pouted and cocked her head at me with a bright smile. "If you'd like to organize it, I'd split the profits with you, sixty-forty."

"I wasn't volunteering, Eve. I'm busy, too."

"I'll make it fifty-fifty."

"It's not the money," I said, laughing, "but I tell you what. If you agree to run a sale as a fund-raiser for the library, I'll help you make plans for it."

"These books have to go. I suppose it's better to make a little something on them than pay to have them hauled away."

"Make a little something for the library, you mean."

"You drive a hard bargain, Jessica Fletcher, but okay, I'll give the library my half, after I pay Herb to cart off whatever we don't sell."

"In that case, I recommend that you get in a cleaning service to dust first."

"They're coming tomorrow, along with the painters and the roofers. I'm thinking carpenters may be next."

"Who's going to pay for the work that's needed?" I asked.

"Fred Kramer said he'd allow me a small budget to fix up the place. He said he can do that as the lawyer for the estate. It's a nice idea, but it'll never be enough."

"It's ironic, isn't it?" I said. "Cliff must have done repair work on half the homes in Cabot Cove, but he didn't take the time to work on his own."

"It's like the shoemaker's children going barefoot," Eve said. "He told me the only place he did any carpentry in this house was in the basement. You'll never believe what's stored down there."

"I can guess. More books."

Eve sighed and nodded.

We paused at the entrance to the library and took a last look at the spacious room. The drapery had been pulled aside many years ago, and I suspected it might fall apart if anyone tried to close the panels now. The once-red oriental carpeting had darker patches where mounds of papers had kept it from fading. The few pieces of furniture included a well-worn leather recliner next to the fireplace, a round library table with stacks of books covering its surface, and two sturdy wooden chairs with frayed cushions.

Seeing that two books had fallen off the table, I crossed the room to pick them up.

"Oh, don't bother, Jessica. You can spend your life here picking things up."

"It's no trouble. I didn't notice them before." I leaned down to retrieve the first book, a paperback with a lurid cover showing a woman in the grip of a knife-wielding assailant. The title was **Betrayal!**

Meanwhile, Eve had picked up the other book. "I didn't realize Cliff went in for this sort of thing," she said, handing it to me so I could see the cover illustration.

"I guess he was a fan of noir mysteries." I grimaced at the picture of blood dripping down a shattered door over which black letters spelled out **Taking My Revenge**.

"Do you know the author?" she asked.

"Graham P. Hobart. No. His name is not familiar." I placed both books on the shortest stack on the table.

Eve shivered. "That's some imagination. I wouldn't want to meet Mr. Hobart in a dark alley," she said as we exited the room. "Do you really think anyone would want to buy books like that?"

"Cliff Cooper did. There are readers for all kind of books."

Eve opened the front door and drew a ring of keys from her pocket. "I'll drop you at home first, and you can call your friend about the books. If he's not interested, I guess we'll have to put on the book sale. Either way, the quicker we get rid of them, the happier I'll be."

As she pulled the door closed to lock it, I thought I heard another thud from inside the house. I cocked my head; the sound didn't repeat itself. I thought about the rumor that the Spencer Percy House was haunted. How silly, I thought as we walked to where she'd parked her car on the gravel driveway. I love a good ghost story as much as the next person, but that's what they are: stories—the inventions of fiction writers and people with vivid imaginations. I looked back at the imposing house, smiled, got in Eve's car, and she drove us toward town.

Chapter Three

"Arthur's Selected Works, secondhand but never second-class. May I help you?"

"Arthur? It's Jessica Fletcher. Am I getting you at a bad time?"

"Jessica Fletcher! How delightful to hear your voice again."

He yelled to someone in his shop, "Roger, put those Shirley Jacksons over in the horror section, and bring me the stepladder."

"I can call you back if you're too busy," I said.

"No! No! I may be up to my elbows in first editions, but I always have time for you, my dear. Just need to get off my feet so we can chat. There. That's better."

"Thank you, Arthur. It's been quite a while."

"Can't believe you abandoned the Big

Apple for the boondocks. How do you like it up there in the backwoods of Maine?"

"Actually, Cabot Cove is on the coast, and I like it just fine. Love it, in fact. How have you been?"

"Oh, toddling along. The city is being bought up by foreigners who don't read. The neighborhood streets are clogged with stroller pushers who won't touch a pre-owned Dr. Seuss unless it's guaranteed to have been sanitized. Do they think Barnes and Noble disinfects the children's section every night? Thank goodness for the tourists, who'll accept any souvenir so long as it has a 'New York' label. I've made up a thousand bookplates with the shop's name and added 'The favorite bookstore of knowing New Yorkers.' 'Knowing New Yorkers.' I like the subtle alliteration, don't you? They only get a bookplate if they buy a book."

"Clever marketing," I said. "Is it working?"

"Occasionally. I could make more money selling the bookplates, but unfortunately that's not my business. Well, you do what you have to do to survive." He called out to the other person with him. "Roger, the

Higgins Clark books go on the cozy shelf, not the hard-boiled. Yes, I know Clark is close to Chandler alphabetically, but that isn't the point." His sigh was exaggerated. "Sorry, Jessica. He's a new employee. Still there?"

"Yes, Arthur, but if you'd rather I call at another time—"

"This time is as good as any. The book business is never going to make me a millionaire. I can spare a few minutes out of the workday for an old friend. I tell you, Jessica, it gets worse every year. The landlord threatened to raise my rent again. He said his taxes are going up. Whose aren't? But when I told him I'd walk away and let him get rid of my inventory himself, he had a change of heart. Thank goodness for that."

"Yes, thank goodness. It would be a great loss to the city if you closed. And speaking of inventory," I said, hoping to stop Arthur's rant before he tired of talking or was pulled away.

"The books, you mean?"

"Yes, of course the books. That's why I'm calling."

"If you're looking for any first editions of your own work, Jessica, I'm sad to say I'm all out. Well, maybe 'sad' isn't the right word. Selling the books is what the shop is all about even if I'm loath to give up my old favorites."

"Oh, no, I have plenty of copies of my own books," I said. "I have boxes of them stored in the attic."

"You do know that if you ever want to sell any of them, you have only to call. We don't have to wait until you're at death's door. Brrrr. How did we get on this grim subject?"

"Thank you for the offer, Arthur, but I'm not ready to part with them just yet. Actually, I'm calling to ask you if you'd be interested in reviewing someone else's books—"

"Look out, Roger! That pile is about to teeter over!"

"Arthur?" I said. "Are you there?"

"Yes, unfortunately. You were saying?"

"That I've come across a collection of books—the owner passed away recently— and before we put them up—"

"No! No! No!"

"I understand if you're too busy to come up here. I just thought—"

"I wasn't talking to you, Jessica. Roger is going to be the death of me. I'm sorry to ring off, but we've got a near disaster here. So good talking with you, my dear. Let's do it again soon. **Ciao**."

Click!

I looked down at the phone and shook my head. I knew that it would be a long shot calling Arthur Bannister. After all, despite his complaints, there are many avid readers in New York City, and his shop was a mecca for them in four languages. Arthur was a linguist along with being a bookseller—he spoke Spanish, Italian, and French as well as English—and kept track of every New Yorker with an important book collection. By combing through the daily obituaries, he also knew when they died. That was how he'd built his inventory, helping bereaved families dispose of their dearly departeds' books. Not that Cliff Cooper's book collection was important, but I hadn't even gotten around to presenting my case. I decided to send Arthur a letter—old-fashioned, yes, but I knew if my message was on paper, it would get his attention.

I typed up my request on the computer, printed it out, and signed it, adding a handwritten P.S. that it had been nice speaking with him.

Cliff Cooper's book collection numbered in the thousands, between those on the shelves in his library, scattered throughout the house, and even more stashed away in the cellar at the Spencer Percy House. What were the chances that Arthur Bannister could find a valuable first edition among them? I didn't know. But I was hoping to coax him to bring his expertise to Cabot Cove, perhaps even to give a lecture at the library about collecting books. I was sure that his presence would stimulate a lot of interest in Cliff Cooper's books and would spur sales. It would also shine a light on the library.

As a member of the Friends of Cabot Cove Library, I was well aware of that institution's budget shortfalls, and I always contributed to the annual appeal. But now an opportunity had presented itself to do more, and if my hometown library needed my help, I wanted to be the first to raise my hand.

Where would we authors be without libraries?

I'd participated for many years in programs at libraries around the country to talk about writing and to promote my books. It was how many of my fans first came to know about the mysteries of J. B. Fletcher. Eve's casual comment about the library needing more staff had inspired my offer to help her with the book sale. It would benefit everyone. Book lovers could find bargains. Eve would clear the shelves at the Spencer Percy House. And the library would make money, maybe even enough to hire extra help.

I tucked my letter to Arthur in my shoulder bag, locked the house, and wheeled my trusty bicycle to the road. I intended to stop at the post office first and then visit the library. I hoped that Doris Ann, our librarian, would like the idea of a book sale. It wasn't as if the library hadn't held one before, but this time there would be a good many more books than usual. If Eve and I were to be successful in our quest to raise a substantial amount of money, we would need the cooperation of the library and its friends.

As usual, the post office was crowded. Charlene Sassi was juggling two cartons and trying to open the door when I arrived. I rushed forward. "Can I help you with those?"

She turned to me. "If you would take the top one, Jessica, I'd be eternally grateful. It keeps slipping to the side. I'm afraid it's going to slide off."

I picked up the top carton as a man exited the post office and held the door open for us. We found the last person in line and took our places behind him.

"Thanks, Jessica. You're a lifesaver. You can put the box back on top now."

"It's no trouble to hold it, Charlene." I lifted the box and sniffed it. "Sending some lucky person baked goods from Cabot Cove's best bakery?"

"Cabot Cove's only bakery, you mean." Charlene chuckled. She was being modest, though; her shop was one of the most popular spots in town. In addition to a variety of fresh breads and pastries,

Charlene served coffee, tea, and hot chocolate for those who simply couldn't wait to sample her goods. Many an evening's dessert was consumed in the morning at the picnic tables outside the bakery, resulting in duplicate sales with no one the wiser at home.

"I made cookies for my niece and nephew in Ohio, but if you can smell them, I didn't wrap them properly."

"It's probably just my imagination," I said. "Whenever I see you, the wonderful aromas in your shop reach my nose. But as long as I have your attention, may I run an idea by you?"

"Of course."

I told Charlene about the book sale that Eve and I were hoping to arrange, and asked if she'd be willing to hang a flyer in her store to help promote the event.

"I'll do better than that. I'll bring cookies to the sale and contribute the proceeds to the library."

"That's so generous. Thank you."

"No thanks needed, Jessica. This is a community event, and we're all part of the community. Once you set a date, I'll announce it at the Chamber of Commerce meeting. I'm sure every store in town will post your flyer and want to help out in any way they can."

By the time Charlene mailed off her cookies and it was my turn at the counter, we had worked out a plan for local merchants to sponsor a table of books in exchange for a sign at the event and a mention in the **Cabot Cove Gazette**. I stepped forward, pleased that arrangements for the book sale were already starting to take shape.

The postal clerk greeted me. "How can I help you today, Jessica?"

"I just need some stamps, Debbie. What have you got that's cheerful?"

Debbie pointed to a poster showing the post office's current offerings, including stamps celebrating the circus, the War of 1812, Harry Potter books, and the Battle of Lake Erie. I bought a panel of Forever stamps depicting American songbirds, and stepped aside so the next person could approach the counter. The colorful stamps were charming, and I was delighted to see that some visitors to my bird feeder were among them. I peeled off the evening grosbeak, affixed it to my envelope, and slipped my letter to Arthur Bannister into the mail slot.

"That reminds me—I need to buy birdseed," I murmured to myself.

"Well, you won't find that here," said a gentleman behind me, "but Cabot Cove Hardware is having a sale on suet and seed."

"Tim Purdy! Just the man I wanted to see," I said, delighted to encounter the town historian.

Tim held out his hands. "No bird food here."

"I can take care of the birds later, but right now I need to know everything you can tell me about the Spencer Percy House and how Cliff Cooper came to accumulate so many books. Do you have time? Are you finished with your business here?"

Tim patted his jacket pocket. "Just picked up my mail, Jessica, my major activity for the day. My time is yours."

"I'm on my way to the library. Walk with me?"

"Sounds perfect. The library has photos of the Spencer Percy House going back to the 1880s, maybe even earlier. Let's see what we can find."

Doris Ann, the library director, had the afternoon off, but Tim got the keys to the stacks from her assistant and ushered me into the Local History Room.

"I love this room," he said. "We've got all sorts of interesting things here, from high school yearbooks—even going back as far as mine—to old telephone directories, and loads of photographs." He took a gray box from one shelf and squinted at its label. "These are program books from the annual Moose Lodge banquet. Bet they're fun to read." He opened the box and pulled out a sheaf of papers stapled together. "These days they use a color copier for their programs, but this one dates back fifty years. Look at the advertising. It's just a page of business cards."

"Actually, I think they still do that," I said. "May I see?"

"Here you are. Just put it back in the box when you're done."

"Look, Tim, there's an ad for Knox on the

Docks. That was before Mara bought the property for her luncheonette from Elvin Knox. And here's one for Charles Department Store, and for Cliff Cooper and Son Carpentry."

Tim leaned over my shoulder to see the advertisement. "Must've been wishful thinking on his part, listing his son as his partner in the business. He would have been a kid at the time. Anyway, Cliff's son never had any interest in following his father into the business. He wanted to travel the world, and I hear Cliff's grandson is the same way. They had to track him down in Alaska to let him know about Cliff."

"Did you know Elliot's father?"

"Jerry Cooper? Not really. I was almost a decade ahead of him in school. You know teenagers. They never pay attention to anyone younger than they are. Did you ever have him in class when you were teaching?"

"I don't believe so. I think I would have remembered."

"Do you want me to hunt down his yearbook?"

"Sure," I said. "I'd love to see what he

looked like."

Tim pulled another box from the shelf and handed it to me. "Why don't you sift through this box of photos and see if any of them are of the Spencer Percy House while I check the yearbooks?"

I returned the banquet program to the preservation box, put it back on the shelf, and opened the photo box marked "Down East Historic Houses." Inside was an assortment of eight-by-ten photos, smaller ones with wavy white borders, and a few Polaroids from which the color was fading. There were also clippings from old newspapers in plastic sleeves.

"Find anything?" Tim asked.

"There's one picture of the house, but it doesn't indicate when it was taken. It doesn't look any different than it does today." I handed it to Tim.

"An imposing place, isn't it?" he commented.

"It certainly is large."

Tim handed the picture back to me. I was about to replace it in the box, when something caught my eye. "Look at this," I said.

"As I said, it's an imposing place."

"No," I said. **"This."** I pointed to one of the windows in the photo.

"What?"

"It looks like—well, it looks like a woman's face peering out."

"It does?" Tim said.

"Don't you see it? It's vague and not clearly defined, but see the ethereal figure in the window?"

Tim nodded. "I just see a white blur. Must be damage to the print or on the negative."

"It could be a woman in a white dress."

"You have a vivid imagination, Jessica."

"I suppose that's why I'm a writer," I said, returning the photo to the box.

"I found Jerry Cooper's yearbook," Tim said, "but his name is listed under the 'camera shy' section. I see he was in the Explorers' Club, but there's only a listing, no picture."

"Oh. Too bad."

"You're getting a firsthand glimpse into the tribulations of a historian. There are always gaps in the historical record."

"Do you know anything about Jerry's

wife?"

"Never met the lady. I understand Jerry married her right out of college. I heard they moved in with Cliff for a while. It was after Nanette died. Marina, that was her name, must have been very shy. I never saw her in town. The last I heard about them was that they left the baby with Cliff, and he raised Elliot."

"Cliff once told me that his son and daughter-in-law went to South America—Colombia, I think—to research the indigenous peoples," I said, "and that they were killed by the very tribe they were studying in the jungle. I was always curious whether he tried to recover their bodies to have them returned to Cabot Cove for burial."

"I wondered the same."

"Did you ever ask?"

Tim shrugged. "It was a touchy subject to raise, and he always deflected any questions, saying Elliot was safer in his care."

"Well, that much is true," I said. "If they'd taken him with them to South America, he would have been killed, too."

"Still want to look into the history of the

Spencer Percy House?"

"If you have the time," I said.

We spent the next two hours looking at papers about and photographs of the Spencer Percy House that the library had preserved on different devices.

"I think that's enough for one day," I said to Tim. "Thanks so much for taking the time with me."

"My pleasure, Jessica. Anytime you want to do it again, just give a holler."

I returned home and tended to a myriad of projects demanding my attention. But I kept thinking about the history of the Spencer Percy House, the young couple who disappeared, and the possible treasure trove of books that Cliff Cooper had collected over the course of his life. Filled with appreciation for the house and its long history in Cabot Cove, I eagerly looked forward to returning there to continue going through the books, no matter how dusty and dirty the task might be.

Chapter Four

"Somebody is definitely not resting in peace, **mes amis**," Eve Simpson said, looking around the table at Mara's Luncheonette. "I think it's Cliff Cooper."

Eve took a bite of her French fry and dropped the second half into the large canvas tote at her feet.

I leaned over and peered down into Eve's bag. Nestled next to a file folder holding a sheaf of papers was her Chihuahua, Cecil, working away at the fried potato with his few remaining teeth.

"If Mara catches you doing that, she's liable to call the cops," said Seth Hazlitt as he sliced into a short stack of blueberry pancakes for which Mara was famous.

"She doesn't have to call. I'm already here."

Eve batted her eyelashes at Mort Metzger. "Now, Sheriff, you won't tell on me, will you?"

"You're breaking the law bringing that dog in here, Ms. Simpson," Mort said, "but as it happens, you're in luck. I'm on my lunch hour."

"I knew I could count on you." Eve took another French fry from her plate and dropped it off the side of the table. "Anyway," she continued, "we have to do an exorcism or something, or I'll never get the Spencer Percy House sold."

"We?" I asked. "I don't know what **we** can do to help you."

"Why do you think it's a ghost?" Mort asked through a bite of lobster roll.

"The painters quit. They said they couldn't paint when the rooms were so cold. And they complained about hearing odd noises."

"I don't suppose it would hurt to turn on the heat," Seth said, adding a little extra maple syrup to his plate.

"I have limited funds for the renovation," Eve said. "Besides, they work with the windows open, and it's been positively balmy outside."

"It's been in the fifties," Seth said, "hardly a heat spell."

"You could try another painting company," Mort said.

"Painters are just the beginning," Eve said, waving around a French fry. "Two roofers got stranded up on the shingles when someone—or some**thing**—walked off with their ladder. And the janitorial service I hired said that not only were their cleaning ladies afraid to enter the bedrooms, but they wouldn't go anywhere near the basement."

"Did the previous owner ever indicate the house was haunted?"

"No, Sheriff, but Cliff Cooper always wore three sweaters even in July, so he wouldn't have noticed any ghostly chill. Plus, he was so preoccupied with his reading, he wouldn't have paid attention even if the walls fell down around him. I was hoping to find a prospective buyer before the funeral, but it doesn't look possible right now, even though Evelyn Phillips promised to put an article in the **Gazette**."

"Still can't believe he didn't make it," Seth said, spearing the last bit of pancake with his fork. "There was no reason why he couldn't have recovered." He scowled at the fork before finishing his meal.

"Tough to lose a patient, huh, Doc? What did you say he died from?" asked our sheriff.

"I wasn't there. Another doctor pronounced him. Attributed the death to respiratory failure due to pneumonia. 'Pneumonia,' my foot. It was just a bad case of bronchitis. I listened to his lungs."

"If you don't believe that's what he died from, why didn't you order an autopsy?"

"No point in doing an autopsy unless the grandson requests it. Funeral home has Cliff on ice till he arrives."

"You're the doctor. Seems to me that you should be the one to decide that."

"Does it now? Is that your medical opinion? Are you studying up to be a general practitioner, Sheriff?"

"Just common sense. Don't need a medical degree for that."

"Gentlemen, please," Eve said, "this conversation is so **inapproprié**." She spread her hands, indicating the surroundings.

"Sorry, Ms. Simpson. The doc and I have a few areas of disagreement."

"More than a few," Seth added in a low voice.

"Don't think I didn't hear that." Mort turned his back to Seth and addressed Eve. "Who owns your haunted house now?"

"The lawyer said it may take a little while to settle the estate, but it'll probably be Elliot Cooper until the house is sold. He's been living in Alaska, but he's coming home for the funeral."

"If he ever gets here," Seth put in. "I understand he's coming by motorcycle. Doesn't he know that airplanes fly to other places than the wilds of Alaska?"

"Are you sure Elliot won't change his mind and want to keep the house?" Mort asked.

"It's much too big for one person," Eve said.

"Only one person lived there for more than thirty years," I reminded her.

"True, but Cliff wanted the house sold. He made that point to both you and me,

Jessica. He even had you write it in his will. And he wanted **me** to have the listing. He said I was the perfect person to sell it. I happen to agree, although I think he was just flattering me. It's a veritable nightmare, that house, and he knew it. There's no way Elliot can manage a place that large. Frankly, I think he'll want to take the money and go back to Alaska as fast as he can."

"Isn't he the boy who had a crush on the Conrad twins' great-niece?" Seth asked.

"That's the one," I said.

Mort looked at me and squinted. "The Conrad twins, those elderly ladies who live in that little cottage across the way from Cliff Cooper's place?"

"Yes."

"I've seen them around town but don't think I ever met them. And I know I never met this Elliot guy."

"There's no reason why you'd have met Lettie and Lucy Conrad," Seth said, "unless they decided to become a live version of **Arsenic and Old Lace** and kill some-body."

"Elliot Cooper is Cliff's grandson," I said,

"but Cliff actually brought up the boy."

"What happened to Elliot's parents?" Mort asked.

Seth made a face. "No one knows anything for sure except that they abandoned their child."

"Well, that's not exactly true," I put in. "Cliff's son, Jerry, and Jerry's wife, Marina, were archaeologists studying ancient civilizations. Don't you remember, Seth?"

"So Cliff said. I rarely had any contact with Jerry. Wouldn't know him if I tripped over him in the street. Course, he'd be in his fifties by now." He looked at me. "Did you know him any better?"

"No, I didn't. I understand he met his wife in college. They had a child, and when they decided to pursue their studies in South America, they left Elliot in Cliff's care."

"And never came back," Seth added.

"Because they died there," I said.

"They were odd birds to begin with."

"Why do you say that, Doc?"

"Because they were all wrapped up in their own interests, had no friends, no desire to be proper parents, let their baby run naked until the neighbors complained. Tore off to some isolated part of the world. I felt sorry for the boy, but the child protective services couldn't do anything since he was being supervised by his grandfather."

"I'm sure the Conrad sisters were a civilizing influence," I said. "And Lucy told me what a nice young man Elliot turned out to be."

"Absolute miracle," Seth said.

"I hate to be a spoilsport," Mort said to Eve, "but why does this ghost of yours, if there is one, have to be the previous owner? Why couldn't it be Cooper Junior and his wife who died in the jungle, or some sea captain who built the place? Heck, it could be any number of other people who lived there a hundred years ago."

"I suppose it could be someone who lived there a long time ago," Eve said. "But one way or another, something has to be done. I spoke with one potential buyer who said the place gives her the creeps. She's convinced a ghost lives there, said others had mentioned it to her. I've heard that ridiculous rumor before, but I never saw anything to prove it. No, if the Spencer Percy House is haunted, I believe it's recent. Got to be Cliff. Maybe he left behind something unfinished in this world."

"Probably just never got around to finish reading all his books," Mort said.

"It really doesn't matter who the ghost is. The fact is I've got to get rid of it if I'm going to find a buyer."

"How old is this house?" Mort asked. "Maybe it simply needs a lot of work. Old houses tend to creak, you know. Or host critters in the attic. Doesn't mean there's anything woo-hoo going on."

"According to our town historian, the house dates back to the early 1800s," I said.

"It's certainly the oldest house in Cabot Cove," Eve added. "I could probably sell it as is if it had been designated a landmark. But someone in the last century pulled off half the molding and added an extension that wasn't approved. So now it's just a white elephant in need of repair."

I spooned up the last of my cup of clam chowder and sat back in my chair. It was

Friday afternoon, and Mara's lunchtime customers were hurrying out, anxious to finish the week's work or eager to get a start on the weekend. "If no one is willing to help fix the place, what are you going to do, Eve?"

"I don't know, Jessica. I was hoping you would help."

"What kind of help are you looking for?"

Eve was silent for a moment as she concentrated on cutting her hamburger into little pieces. "I've already taken some steps," she said at last. "I just hope that you'll keep an open mind."

"Oh, dear, Eve, what did you do?"

"I found a medium online and used your name to invite her." She rushed on, "She's such a big fan of yours, and she said she's heard how you're always so helpful to friends in need. And I'm very much in need right now, Jessica."

It took me a few moments to process what she'd said. I finally asked, "Just how did you use my name, Eve?"

"I sent her an e-mail telling her that you needed help getting rid of a ghost."

"Oh, Eve," I said, "how could you?"

Seth patted his mouth with a napkin and leaned forward. "Didn't this medium, or whoever she is, find it odd that Jessica didn't request the help herself?"

"Not at all," Eve said. "I think she thought I was your assistant."

"I don't have an assistant."

"Nevertheless, she agreed to come. And she said she was excited to be seeing you again."

"Again?" Seth and I said in unison.

"Yes. Her name is Arianna Olynski. She met you in Lewiston some years back. She was writing a book called **Our Supernatural Neighbors**, and she said you were very encouraging. Don't you remember?"

"The name doesn't sound familiar," I said, trying to remember the last time I'd been to Lewiston. "I did teach a summer course on creative writing at Bates College, but that was many years ago. Even so, I don't recall the name Arianna Olynski."

"Well, she certainly remembers you. She mentions you on her website in the section called 'Praise for My Work.' That's how I got the idea to invite her here."

"Seems she didn't make quite as deep an impression on you as you made on her," Seth said.

"If she's quoting me, I'd like to see what I said."

"You can look her up online like I did," Eve said, letting a few crumbs of chopped meat fall on Cecil's head.

"Better watch out," Seth said. "Here comes Mara."

Eve used her foot to nudge her tote bag under the table, and faked a cough to cover a little yelp from Cecil.

Bearing a pair of coffeepots, decaf in one hand, regular in the other, the proprietress of Mara's Luncheonette approached our table. "How was lunch, folks? Anyone here need a refill on coffee?"

"The soup was delicious," I told her.

"Pancakes were excellent as usual," Seth said, pushing his cup in her direction. "You can top me off."

Mara dipped to the side as she poured coffee into Seth's cup. "What about you, Sheriff?"

Mort waved a hand over his cup. "I'm

good."

She eyed the crumbled chopped meat on Eve's plate. "Having a bit of trouble with your teeth, Ms. Simpson?"

"**Moi?** Oh, no."

"I can recommend a good dentist."

"My teeth are just fine, thank you."

"Then do you want to take the rest of that home for your...**dog**?"

Eve gave her a bright smile. "That would be wonderful."

Mara rolled her eyes. "That beef is choice, you know. Shouldn't be wasted. We only use the best chopped meat for our customers."

"Cecil is such an admirer of your hamburgers," Eve said.

Mara grunted. "Don't think I've ever received a compliment like that. I'll be right back." She stopped at two more tables before depositing the coffeepots on their stands and bringing Eve a cardboard box for her leftovers. "Dessert, anyone?"

We declined more food, although Seth asked to hear a list of the available pies before deciding he'd had enough sugar for the day. Cabot Cove's favorite physician was accustomed to dispensing diet advice to his patients, but he found it difficult to follow his own orders.

"Need a lift home?" he asked as we left the luncheonette.

"No, thanks. I'm going to stop in at the library to see if Doris Ann signed up any volunteers to help me with the sale of Cliff's books."

"You should advertise it as a Halloween book sale," Seth said. "Trick the house up with cobwebs and broomsticks. That way if any ghosts should happen to show up for your event, you can say it's all part of the show."

"Seth! What a great idea."

"It is? I thought I was making a joke."

Chapter Five

"Where do you want me to put these, Mrs. Fletcher?"

Beth Conrad, the Conrad twins' great-niece, held up two volumes, **Birds of New England** and **Training Your Puppy.**

"There should be a carton of animal-related books on the table," I said, pointing across Cliff Cooper's library.

Beth and her great-aunt Leticia—called Lettie by all who knew her—were helping me sort Cliff's books into categories. It was a big project, and I was grateful for all the help I could get. We had plenty of boxes—generously donated by a local moving company—but volunteer sorters had been scarce after a story about the "haunted" Spencer Percy House surfaced in the **Cabot Cove Gazette**. The editor,

Evelyn Phillips, had jumped on the rumors when Eve had complained about the difficulty of getting good help to do the repair work. The newspaper had published a long article on the property and the recent strange goings-on, interviewing the roofers and one of the cleaning ladies, and ran a front-page photo of our favorite real estate agent standing next to the house.

The newspaper editor was delighted when that issue of the **Gazette** sold out. Eve had been ecstatic. "Isn't that the greatest publicity? And right after the article appeared, a handyman called me and said he wasn't afraid to work in the house. I hired him on the spot. He starts in a few days."

Nevertheless, the prospect of spending time in a haunted house was not as appealing to at least one member of the Friends of the Library. She actually offered to assist with the book sale only if she didn't have to cross the threshold. Others pleaded how busy they were. The end result was that we were short-staffed, and the responsibility rested on my shoulders. It occurred to me that if the weather didn't cooperate on the day of the book sale, we'd need a large tent to protect the books and the buyers, and that meant arranging for a rental from a local company. The sale was becoming a much bigger undertaking than I'd envisioned when I'd volunteered to take it on. Thank goodness I had at least two people helping me today.

I knew where the animal books were because earlier in the day I had discovered **Reptiles and Amphibians of the Amazon** by Richard D. Bartlett in the same box as **Cat and Mouse** by James Patterson. I removed the latter and added it to a carton marked "Thrillers." Cliff's literary interests were wide-ranging, and his collection would have been excellent competition for a bookstore, or even the Cabot Cove Library, had he shelved them in any order. But he hadn't. An Agatha Christie novel was just as likely to be found among the dictionaries as next to another mystery. I got the impression that once having finished a book, Cliff put it on any shelf where space was available.

"Should we keep the old encyclopedias, Jessica?" Lettie asked. "There's a full set of World Books."

"Doris Ann at the library said no one wants those anymore."

"I'll put it in the kitchen so it doesn't go into the sale by mistake," Lettie said. "Do you have another marker I can use to write on the box?"

"There's a package of them in my shoulder bag," I said. "I left it by the front door."

"It's not there now," Lettie said, carrying a box of books out of the library. She was tall and lean with steel gray hair cut short. Seth had described her as spry. I guessed that she must have been well over eighty, but she walked like a woman decades younger. "Comes from doing for yourself," she'd told me when I'd complimented her. "Who's going to chop wood for the fireplace if not me? My sister, Lucy, would be useless. I have to do more and more for her."

"I thought I saw your bag in the dining room, Mrs. Fletcher," Beth said. "I'll go get it for you."

"Thank you," I said, shaking my head and thinking, **I must be getting forgetful.**

I don't recall leaving my bag in the dining room.

"It was right next to the box of books on health and medicine," Lettie's great-niece said when she returned, holding aloft my tan leather satchel.

"You're a dear. I have half my life in that bag, not to mention my house keys." I took it from her and groped around inside for a new package of markers. "I'll bring one to Lettie. Do you need another marker, too?"

"No. Mine still has some ink left."

I dropped my shoulder bag next to the front door and walked down the hall to the kitchen.

The three of us had begun working that morning. Beth, a graphic designer for an architect, had made signs for the sale, which she brought to show us. In the library, I'd found a cabinet with some room—miracle of miracles—and stowed away Cliff's hollowed-out poetry book to save for his grandson. I'd previously put the money in an envelope and delivered it to the attorney, Fred Kramer.

By midafternoon we were knee-deep in boxes, and apart from four cartons of

"General Fiction," the only subgenre with more than three books was the box marked "Mystery: Hard-boiled and Noir," which held a dozen paperbacks, among them the two by Hobart that Eve and I had picked up from the floor.

"I'm making a cup of tea for myself," Lettie said when I brought her a new marker. "Would you like one?"

"That's a wonderful idea. Let me ask Beth if she'd like to take a break, too."

Beth joined us at the vintage table, which had a chipped enameled metal top and a drawer on one side. Lettie had put a kettle on the gas stove to heat. She pulled three spoons from the table's drawer and gave us each a paper towel. "Don't remember the last time Cliff bought napkins, if he ever did. Luckily he kept the tea and the sugar in tin canisters. They're fairly fresh." She opened a cabinet and took out three mugs, rinsing them with the boiling water before dropping in a tea bag and adding more water.

I helped her carry the mugs to the table and settled in my seat to wait for the tea to cool.

"It's too bad we didn't get more people to help with the sale," Beth said. "I can ask around at the office if you like. Most of my coworkers live south of here, so they probably don't read the **Gazette** and wouldn't be spooked by the idea of ghosts."

"Ought to be some other locals who can lend a hand," Lettie said. "Lot of foolish nonsense about this house being haunted. Cliff never complained, and I'd've known if he had. I'll have my sister call up her quilting cronies at the senior citizen center and see who she can scare up. 'Scare up'! Ha! I picked the right word, didn't I?" She chuckled.

The Conrad twins, Lettie and Lucy, were part of an old Cabot Cove family. I hadn't met their great-niece, Beth, before, but I knew that the young woman's father was a captain on a freighter and spent many months at sea. Lettie had told me that Beth had become a frequent visitor to the sisters' home after her father's new wife gave birth to twin boys, and she still was. She was a sweet young woman with the kind of fresh, youthful good looks that could be pegged at anywhere from eighteen to thirty-five, but I knew that she must be in her mid- to late twenties. It was nice that she'd come home to Cabot Cove after college. So many of our young people didn't.

Beth produced an unopened package of ginger cookies and held it up. "I figured you wouldn't find anything edible in Grandpa Cliff's kitchen, so I threw this in the car this morning," she said, tearing it open.

"Clever girl," Lettie said, plucking out a gingersnap. "I'll have Lucy bring over a pitcher of milk tomorrow morning. Miss Simpson said she was keeping the 'lectric on as long as we're here, so the fridge should work. Hope you can manage tea without milk today, Jessica."

"I'm just grateful for anything to soothe my parched throat."

"It's the dust does it to you. My hands are as dry as parchment. Don't know how Cliff lived comfortably in this atmosphere."

"Wait a moment," I said, backtracking to a point earlier in our conversation and addressing Beth. "You called him 'Grandpa Cliff.' Was he a relative?"

She smiled at Lettie before answering me. "He might've liked to be, but no, it's just an honorary term. That's what Elliot called him, and so I called him the same thing. I think Grandpa Cliff liked it. I know he liked having us around. We used to play all over the house. We found closets full of old clothing in the unused bedrooms, and we'd put on shows for him, parading around in feather boas and silver high heels. He would laugh." She smiled at the memory.

"So you know the house pretty well," I said.

"She practically grew up here until Cliff sent Elliot off to boarding school," Lettie put in.

"I used to know it very well before Elliot left," Beth said, fingering a string bracelet she wore on her wrist. "Except for the basement. Grandpa Cliff didn't want us to go into the basement. He said the stairs were rickety. He was going to fix them someday, but until he did, we might fall through and get hurt. I listened, but nothing fazed Elliot. He'd sneak downstairs when Grandpa Cliff wasn't home. Told me there was nothing there to be afraid of, but he got himself pretty banged up when, sure enough, one of the steps broke. I never saw Grandpa Cliff so angry. Yelled at him that he could've been killed. He sent him away to boarding school after that."

"He was a wild one, that motherless boy," Lettie said. "Hard to contain, but whip smart. Lucy and I, we tried to teach him manners, let him know how he was supposed to behave in polite company. But Cliff said he was on the road to becoming a delinquent."

"That was such an exaggeration," Beth said.

"Mebbe so, but Cliff insisted the school would teach him what he needed to know to get along in the world. And it did."

"Elliot hated it," Beth said, pulling a cookie from the container. "Tried to run away a couple of times, but he got caught. I told him not to bother, that Grandpa Cliff would just send him back. He stopped writing to me after that." She placed the cookie on her paper towel and pushed it away uneaten.

"That must've made you sad," I said.

"It did for a while," Lettie answered for Beth. "Cliff didn't want her to visit anymore without his grandson at home. He said she was a reminder, that he didn't want to see her 'cause he was missing Elliot something fierce."

"That's okay. I didn't want to be here without Elliot anyway."

"Did you ever hear from him again?"

She shrugged. "When he was in college, he had a short story published. He sent me the magazine it appeared in."

"How nice," I said. "Are you in touch with him now?"

"Not me, but he writes to Aunt Lettie and Aunt Lucy."

"Ayuh. Found himself in Alaska, he did. Got a job teaching writing and literature. Well, you wouldn't be surprised, seein' all these books here. Beth taught Lucy and me how to use Facebook, and one day, a message pops up from Elliot Cooper, wanting to be our friend." She stole a glance at Beth. "So, of course, we said yes."

"Are you friends with him on Facebook as well?" I looked at Beth.

"He never asked me," she replied. "Besides, he's engaged to some woman who runs a jewelry shop. She probably wouldn't appreciate him being friends with a girl from back home."

"Eve said that Elliot will be coming to Cabot Cove for the funeral. Maybe you'll get to see him then."

"I might not even recognize him. Aunt Lucy says he has a beard now."

Lettie waved a hand in front of her face. "Oh, you'll know him. Elliot hasn't changed that much."

We took our mugs to the sink, and while Beth washed and Lettie dried, I turned on the refrigerator to let it cool before we put milk or other food items inside. The ladies from Eve's cleaning service had washed down the interior, and except for the faint odor of bleach from the cleanser they'd used, it was as clean as a forty-year-old refrigerator could be.

"I think we should stop work for the day," I said. "It's going to be dark soon, and it's enough of a strain hauling books around. Let's not make it harder by trying to read titles in dim light."

"I walked here," said Lettie, "but Beth can give you a ride home. She has a brand-new truck. You can put your bike in the bed."

"I'm grateful for the offer, but I think I'll pass. I need to get some fresh air in my lungs, and I like the idea of getting exercise riding home. Thanks for all your help."

"You're welcome," Beth said. "Give me a call when you want me to come again." She looked around the kitchen. "It was nice to be back here. I have such good memories of this house."

After Lettie and Beth left, I checked that the stove wasn't on, shut off the overhead fixture in the kitchen, and walked down the hall, pausing to extinguish the lights in the library and to pull out the extra set of keys Eve had entrusted to me. As I reached for the knob on the front door, I was taken aback by a loud pounding. I flung the door open. A glaring light blinded me. I immediately stepped back and raised my arm to shade my eyes. "Turn that off, please," I shouted.

"In a moment," said a female voice. "Okay, Boris, I'm ready."

"Action," said a man's voice behind the light.

"I'm here with the celebrated mystery writer Jessica Fletcher, who has called upon my expertise to rid her home of a spectral visitor. New England is a hotbed of ghostly presences, and it's no surprise that even the rich and famous have to deal with supernatural manifestations."

"Now, just one minute," I said, blinking rapidly to rid my eyes of the temporary blindness the light had caused. "First of all, this is not my home. And second, I did not invite you here. And third, I certainly did not give you permission to film me or to use my name."

"Cut!"

The light was turned off, and as my eyes became accustomed to the dim light outside, I could make out a tiny woman with a pile of blond hair, holding a gold-topped cane.

"Well, your assistant wrote to me asking for my help in getting rid of a ghost for **you**." She knocked her cane against the door frame for emphasis.

"You must be Arianna Olynski."

She straightened and gave a brief nod. "I see you know who I am. You certainly called me in the nick of time, Jessica Fletcher."

"I'm sorry to disappoint you." I stepped outside, forcing her to move away from the door, which I quickly locked. I turned back to the diminutive medium and said, "Eve Simpson is not my assistant. I did not ask for you to come. I apologize for her if she gave you the wrong impression. Now that you know the truth, I would appreciate it if you would leave."

"But what about the ghost?"

"I don't know anything about a ghost, and if there is one, I have yet to encounter it."

"I think you're wrong, Mrs. Fletcher," she said, waving the cane at me. "I can feel it. I can feel it."

"Just what do you feel?"

"There's definitely an unhappy spirit here, a **very** unhappy spirit."

"I don't know anything about unhappy spirits. You'll have to excuse me. I'm in a bit of a hurry. The sun is going down, and I'm late getting home."

"Be that as it may, here's my business card," she said, stuffing it into my shoulder bag. "I'll still expect my fee. I get paid by the day."

"You'll have to talk with Eve Simpson about that."

I went down the path to where I'd parked my bicycle, leaving Arianna Olynski and her cameraman standing in front of the Spencer Percy House. I put my shoulder bag in the bike basket and glanced back. The cameraman's light was on again, his lens aimed at the little woman who had positioned herself in front of the closed door. As I pedaled away, I heard her voice addressing the camera: "As a professional medium, I'm trained to detect postdeath life forces...."

I only hoped that as a **predeath** life force, I would make it home before dark.

Chapter Six

Eve and I had had a heated conversation that evening.

"Jessica, think about what great publicity it would be—for both of us."

"It isn't that I don't appreciate your consideration in wanting to include me, but please leave me out of your publicity campaign. I'm not willing to appear in front of television cameras to help you sell Cliff's house."

"Why not? I thought any publicity was **good** publicity for a writer."

"Somehow, Eve, I don't see you doing this to support my writing career. The only reason I got involved was to help raise money for the library."

"But wouldn't Arianna Olynski's show be a great way to promote that?"

"I don't know anything about her show, except that it's not about books. Please, Eve, try to understand. I don't want to sound selfish or conceited, but I have a reputation to protect, and it is not one that would be enhanced by seeming to endorse someone who chases after ghosts and goblins in haunted houses."

"Well, it isn't as if it's a big network production, Jessica. It's probably not even seen by a lot of people. Besides, I have a reputation to protect, too, you know."

"My point exactly. Do you really want to be associated with a con artist?"

"You don't know that she's a con artist. Maybe she's providing a public service as someone with a special gift who only wants to help people connect with their departed loved ones."

"And who just happens to arrive with a television cameraman in tow. That's not exactly how I would expect a Good Samaritan to behave."

Eve had promised to make sure there would be no cameras present if I would accompany her to the house when the medium returned, rationalizing it by saying that she didn't want to be alone with the lady if a ghost actually materialized.

Reluctantly, I'd agreed.

Seth called the next morning.

"You requested an autopsy? I thought you'd decided to wait for Elliot."

"Well, the boy is taking his time in getting here, and I haven't slept, thinking about what I might have missed that caused Cliff's death."

I shifted the phone from one ear to the other while I sorted through items in my shoulder bag.

"Seth, you're an excellent physician. You said he wasn't helping in his own recovery. Cliff had convinced himself he was dying, and he'd given up trying to live. I'm sure you didn't 'miss' anything. And even if you did, it probably wouldn't have been caught by any other doctor either."

"I appreciate the vote of confidence from the esteemed Mrs. Fletcher, but I can't relax until I know the true cause of Cliff Cooper's death."

"Then I hope the results of the autopsy

will resolve those misgivings. When will it take place?"

I pulled out my wallet and placed it on the kitchen table along with my cell phone, a packet of tissues, address book, reading glasses, a retractable measuring tape, keys, and an unopened package of black markers.

"The medical examiner said he may not get to it today. Depends on when the funeral home sends the body back to the morgue."

"Can you do an autopsy after the body has already been embalmed?"

"It isn't the most favorable condition—I should have acted faster—but yes, it can be done. The embalming fluids replace bodily fluids, but the basic structures can still be seen."

"I hope you're not doing this because Mort Metzger goaded you into it."

"That know-it-all in a police uniform gets under my skin, it's true. In this case, however, I think he's right. Hate to say it—and I'll deny it if you tell him I said so. Truth is, I'm the proper one to order the autopsy, and I've pounded sand long enough."

"It's barely a week since Cliff died," I said, responding to Seth's use of a Maine term for wasting time.

"Mebbe so, but it's time the facts came out."

I felt around the bottom of my bag, my fingers connecting with a paper clip, nail file, and notebook, and three pens. I pulled out the skeleton key to my back porch door, which reminded me I'd been meaning to replace the lock. What I was looking for didn't seem to be there. I dropped the key back in my bag and said to Seth, "Will you let me know the results when you learn them?"

"Ayuh, if I haven't put my head in an oven."

"Oh, for heaven's sake, Seth," I said, stopping the forensic search of my bag, "I never knew you to be so insecure."

"I don't mind losing a patient to old age or disease if it's expected. Well, I do mind, but I don't take it personally. But if Cliff died of some stupidity on my part, I want to know."

"And if you accidentally missed some-thing, will you take to your bed and hide under the covers?"

"Doesn't sound like a bad idea."

"This isn't like you, Seth. Will you call me when you get the results?"

"Where are you off to now?"

"The medium has arrived, and Eve talked me into meeting with her at Cliff's house in an hour."

"You agreed to do that?" Seth asked, his tone incredulous. "Does Jessica Fletcher suddenly believe in ghosts?"

"Don't be silly," I replied. "I just want to placate Eve. If she thinks that this medium can put to rest the rumor that Cliff Cooper's house is haunted, then I'm willing to go along with it."

"I'll certainly want to hear the report on **that** visit."

"Then we're agreed. One exchange of information for another. I'll call you later."

"Take an umbrella. It's threatening to rain."

I hung up the phone and upended my pocketbook to let everything inside fall to the tabletop. **Aha! I knew it was in there.** I took the business card Arianna Olynski had dropped into my bag and went to my computer.

I still had time to peruse the medium's website before Eve was due to pick me up. I was also curious about what others might have posted about this "psychic sensation," as she described herself on her business card.

Her website was designed in varying shades of gray, lending a dramatic back-drop to glamorous photographs of a heavily made-up Arianna Olynski posing with people she called "celebrity endor-sers." Her beehive hairdo added almost a foot to her height and suggested a certain television cartoon character.

There were also pictures of the petite medium leaning on her cane in doorways of decrepit—and presumably haunted—mansions, as well as those of abandoned mental facilities and long-closed jails, along with a trailer for her television show, which turned out not to be on television at all but online as a series of YouTube videos. She also had a page of quotes supplied by "satisfied customers," includ-ing one from me that purported to be a review of her book, **Our Supernatural**

Neighbors. It read, "Vivid writing! Great work! Future bestseller!" I didn't recall the book but had a feeling I wasn't being quoted completely. In my past classes on creative writing, I urged my students to resist sprinkling their copy with exclamation marks. For that reason, I suspected that there might have been several words omitted before, after, and in between these shouts of praise.

I heard two toots of a horn and looked out the window to see Eve's car. I turned off the computer, hastily gathered up the items I'd dumped out of my shoulder bag, put them back, grabbed my umbrella, and joined her.

To my surprise, Arianna Olynski was perched in the passenger seat, so I climbed in the back, pushing aside several real estate binders and making certain not to jog a tan and red checked tote bag containing one small dog.

"Good morning, ladies. Miss Olynski, I thought we were meeting you at the house."

"Miss Olynski asked me to pick her up at the motel," Eve said. "Her truck wouldn't start this morning, and she had to have it towed to a garage."

Clearly, foretelling the future is not a skill possessed by the "psychic sensation," or she might have predicted that would happen, I thought uncharitably.

"I have accommodated your request for no cameras for my initial visit to the haunted location, Mrs. Fletcher, but I must tell you that my cameraman will be shooting there later today."

"I have no interest in preventing you from conducting your business, Miss Olynski. I simply don't care to be part of it."

"Your loss. My program will soon be being picked up by a national syndicate. You could have increased the public's awareness of your books in the eighteen to forty-nine key age demographic. Those people are the influentials, and I would expect you as a writer to be aware of your marketing audience and act accordingly. I certainly am."

I saw Eve nod in agreement, and I sighed inwardly. Rather than debate the promotional value of the medium's online program, I changed the subject. "I understand that we may have met in the past, Miss

Olynski. My apologies, but I don't recall the circumstances. When did we know each other?"

"I took your writing course, Mrs. Fletcher. Of course, I was a brunette then, and it was many years ago, so I'm not surprised that you don't remember me."

"Yes, it's true that we've both gotten older and my memory is not what it was. Still, I'm usually pretty good with names. Were you registered for the course as Arianna Olynski?"

"Oh, no. I was Agnes Pott then. But when I went into the medium trade as a psychic, I needed a more exotic name. Pott doesn't sound like a psychic expert."

"Ah, that's why I didn't recognize your name. Yes, Agnes Pott does sound familiar." I pictured an adult student, a bit older than I was, dark hair scraped back in a bun, wearing thick eyeglasses and a too-large purple sweater to class every day. "You were writing a book on vampires if I remember correctly."

"You do remember correctly. There's nothing wrong with your memory, Mrs. Fletcher."

"Thank you, and please call me Jessica."

"I'll be honored. You're welcome to call me Aggie. My friends still do. You, too, Eve."

"Aggie, it is," I said. "If you don't mind my asking, how did you get into the 'medium trade' as you call it?"

Aggie straightened and warmed to the subject. "It all started right about the time that Anne Rice's vampire books were being made into movies. I started writing about vampires, wanting to catch the popular wave as it were, but then more and more books were being written about vampires and no one wanted mine. A couple of years later, Charlaine Harris wrote about Sookie Stackhouse's boy-friend being a vampire. Well, it was too much. I didn't stand a chance against such big names. I figured that there was a glut in the vampire market, so I switched and made my book about ghosts—didn't even have to change the title—and discovered that I have the skill."

"And what skill is that?"

"I can connect. I can see them. I never did see a vampire, not that I looked very hard. Of course, vampires are back in the news now, but that's okay. Ghosts are all the rage, and there are far more of them, so my business is picking up."

"Do you actually see the ghosts?" Eve asked with a shudder.

"Not the way I see you, but I get visions. Sometimes it's in the form of a photograph or a locket or something else they possessed. Or I get a meaningful message that they send to my subconscious. I don't know how it gets there, but all of a sudden I'm thinking about Amato's pickles."

I stifled a smile. "Amato's pickles?" I said. "How is that a meaningful message?"

"Well, in this case, it was a message from a man whose family asked me to contact him. He died in front of the television, eating an Italian sandwich from Amato's, with sour pickles on the side. So that was proof that I communicated with the right man."

"Did he have anything to tell his family?" Eve asked.

"Not really. He said he was at peace. Wanted to know how the Red Sox were doing. I told him they lost the last game to the Yankees. He wasn't too pleased. Used language I'd rather not repeat."

"That was quite a conversation," I said.

"Yes." She sighed. "Some of them are like that."

"But you don't actually see a gauzy figure floating over the stairs, or shadows where they shouldn't be, anything like that?" Eve asked as she pulled into the driveway of the Spencer Percy House.

"I've seen those, too."

"You have?"

"Of course. It's part of my gift."

Eve pulled up to the door of the house, and the three of us trooped into the front hall of the home that Cliff Cooper once occupied. Eve put down her tote bag, and Cecil jumped out. He shook his little body and pranced into the library, nose sniffing the carpet.

"Let's not have any funny business in here," Eve said, following the tiny dog.

Aggie raised her head, seeming to listen for something. Then she hooked her gold-topped cane on the front doorknob and dusted off her hands. "Where do we start?"

"Don't you need that?" I asked, indicating

the cane.

"Not really. I carry it for effect. It's my signature piece—sets me apart from the competition."

"How did you happen to choose a cane as a signature piece?"

"I found it while browsing in a second-hand shop. It called to me. When I got it home and cleaned it up, I discovered that the top was gold. I considered it a good sign. Now it's my lucky charm. I don't go anywhere without it."

I started to say something, but Aggie put up a hand to stop me. She cocked her head, her gaze focused at the top of the stairs.

"Are you getting a message?" I asked.

"Not yet, but there's definitely something here. I'd like to sage the house first if you don't mind."

"Be my guest," I said. "What do you need?"

"Just a place to put down my things and get ready."

"Let's use the kitchen. It's the only room on this floor not chockablock with boxes of books."

Arianna Olynski, née Agnes Pott, followed me down the hall to Cliff's kitchen. "This is perfect," she said, going to the table and emptying the contents of her handbag, just as I had done earlier with mine. She pulled out a candle, a bundle of herbs wrapped in twine, a feather, what looked like an abalone shell, and a small glass jar with a metal lid that she unscrewed before putting it down. "Sand," she said. She looped the strap of her now-empty bag over the back of a chair and turned to me. "Do you have a match?" she asked.

I peered into my shoulder bag and shook my head. "It's probably the only thing I don't have in here," I said. "I don't smoke."

"No matter. You have a gas stove here. Does it work?"

"Yes. Would you like a cup of tea before you begin?"

"Maybe later. Right now I need to light the sage. Would you please ask Miss Simpson if she would like to join us?"

I found Eve in the library, lecturing Cecil about his manners, and escorted them both back to the kitchen, Cecil's nails making a **tip-tap** sound on the wood floor of the hall as he followed his mistress.

Aggie was standing behind the kitchen table, facing us as if about to give a cooking demonstration. "Are we ready?"

"What are we doing?" Eve asked.

"We are going to sage the house," said Aggie. She picked up the bundle of herbs. "This is a smudge stick made of sage and lavender. Sometimes sageing is called smudging. They're the same thing. Sageing is an ancient Native American ritual for cleansing ourselves and our homes of any lingering negative energy and harmful influences."

"Harmful influences?" Eve scooped up Cecil and hugged him to her chest. "Is it dangerous? Do we have to do it right now?"

"Now is as good a time as any," Aggie said. "Do you have an objection?"

"No, but you haven't even seen the rest of the house."

"You're going to show me the house as we go room to room with our smudge stick."

"Will you be able to tell where the negative energy is or…um…where the spirits are?"

"Eve, is something the matter?" I asked.

"It was your idea to bring in a medium to exorcise the ghosts."

"Exorcise?" Aggie shrieked as though Eve had used an offensive four-letter word. "Oh, no! I don't do exorcisms. No, ma'am. That's a specialty practice. I've been brought here under false pretenses." Aggie rapidly replaced all the materials she had removed from her bag. "I don't deal with those kinds of spirits. You didn't tell me about them. That's not what you asked for."

"Wait! Don't leave," Eve said. "Jessica must have misspoken. She didn't mean anything bad, did you, Jessica?"

Aggie paused in her repacking and looked at me expectantly.

"What kinds of spirits don't you deal with?" I asked.

"Demons! I don't touch those. Too many ramifications."

I wasn't sure if I wanted to know what those ramifications were, but I also didn't want Eve to have wasted her money.

"I don't think we have any demons here, do we Eve?" I said, successfully keeping mirth from my voice.

Eve shook her head vigorously.

"Perhaps just mischievous spirits who move things," I said, thinking of my wandering shoulder bag and some errant books falling to the floor when no one was around.

"Those would be poltergeists," Aggie said. "They're pranksters who make noises or throw things across the room. They're actually fairly low-level spirits, in the sixth class, third order. Not very impressive."

"Do you deal with poltergeists?" I asked.

Aggie snapped her fingers. "Easy peasy."

"And other spirits, too, like those of the recently departed?" Eve put in.

"No problem, assuming that they **want** to come through. Some of them don't."

"I'm sure Cliff Cooper will want to come through," Eve said. "He was a nice man. Please, go ahead with your sageing. Did I use the right word?"

Aggie pulled herself up, as if attempting to become taller. She gave us each a stern look. "If we are all in agreement, I will sage now."

She unpacked her materials and had begun her instructional spiel again when we were interrupted by a loud pounding on the back door.

Now what? I thought, following the clamor into a short hall, which had access to the garden behind the house. I unlocked the door. Mort Metzger pushed a disheveled young man in front of him into the kitchen.

"Here's your ghost, Mrs. F.," Mort said. "Found him skulking around the house."

Chapter Seven

"That's no ghost—that's my cameraman," Aggie said, disgusted.

"Yeah? What's he doing sneaking around outside, peeking in windows?" Mort asked. "I caught him with his foot up on the sill."

"I was just trying to get the right angle," the cameraman said.

I glanced at Eve and raised an eyebrow at Aggie. "Miss Olynski, you promised me there would be no cameras while I was here."

"He was just exploring the location for later," she said, giving me an innocent smile. "Isn't that right, Davy?"

"I thought his name was Boris," I said.

"That's my stage name. It's how I appear in the credits," the young cameraman said. He turned to Miss Olynski. "Actually,

I already got a few good shots, Aunt Aggie, just like you told me. I found an open window."

"Where's your camera?" I asked him.

"I left it behind in the bushes when the sheriff grabbed me."

"You mean you didn't want me catching you red-handed peeping through windows and taking pictures," Mort said. "You ever hear of 'Peeping Toms'? In this state it's a felony to trespass on private property for the purposes of peeping in on others. You're facing a fine and maybe a little jail time."

"No way! Look, I gotta return the camera day after tomorrow or I owe 'em more dough. Tell him, Aunt Aggie. I was just shooting for your video program."

"We'd better get his camera in case it rains," I said. I turned to Mort. "I'll see if I can find it while you question your—your captive."

"Sure, Mrs. F." Mort pulled over a chair for Boris, also known as Davy. "Have a seat, son," he said. He turned to Eve and Aggie. "So, ladies, what's going on here?"

I walked out the back door and scouted

the perimeter of the house until I found the video camera lying on its side in a thicket of bushes on a jacket I presumed belonged to Davy. Several sets of footprints caused a pattern in the damp earth beneath the window where Mort had nabbed him. The window was open as Davy had claimed, and an apple crate sat on the ground below it. I stepped up on the crate to see which room the window looked into. It was the library. I held up Davy's camera and opened the viewfinder. If he had angled his camera just right, he could also have seen into the front hall when we'd come in. So much for the promises of the "psychic sensation" not to film that morning while I was there.

I stepped off the crate, still holding Davy's camera. **But how did he get here? I don't see any truck.**

I retraced my steps to the back door, holding the camera and jacket. The property had a large barn where Cliff had maintained his workshop, and I wondered if Davy had parked behind it, or maybe inside. Aggie had told Eve her truck wouldn't start, but maybe she'd given it to Davy with instructions to park it out of sight.

When I returned to the kitchen, Aggie was explaining the details of using a sage stick to Eve and Mort.

"Hey, Mrs. F.," Mort said, "Miss Olynski here said I can watch while she—what was it again?"

"While I sage the house," Aggie supplied.

"That okay with you?"

"Why would I have any objections, Mort? But what about your prisoner here?" I handed Davy his jacket and camera.

"Miss Olynski explained it was all a big mistake. She has an online television show, or I guess you'd call it a video show. Right?" Mort looked to Aggie for confirmation. "She said I could be in it. That'd be fun. You think Maureen would like to see me ghostbusting on YouTube?"

"I'm sure your wife would enjoy it very much," I said, "but I'm not so sure the Cabot Cove Council would appreciate its chief uniformed police officer chasing after ghosts while on duty."

Mort nodded, clearly disappointed. "Yeah, you're right," he said. "Sorry, Davy, but no shooting while I'm on the premises."

He looked at his watch. "I'm due for a break anyway. I can watch this thing called sage-ing before I get back to the office. Go ahead, Miss Olynski. I'm looking forward to this."

"You must be quiet while I go about my business," our medium warned.

"Can I ask a question now and then?" Mort asked.

"Only if you must, but you must keep your voices low, or the spirits will gather around you instead of me."

Aggie handed me the jar of sand. "You carry that, Jessica, and have it available if I need it." She turned on a burner on Cliff's stove, lit the end of her smudge stick, and waited until the stick emitted a steady stream of smoke. Then, waving it in front of her body, she used the feather to guide the smoke toward herself, starting with her feet and ending with her head. "I have to cleanse myself first," she explained.

"Do we all have to be cleansed, too?" Eve asked.

"Shh! No questions now."

Aggie laid the stick in the shell and picked up her feather, waving it above the smok-ing stick. "We are standing in the heart of this home, the kitchen." She traced the outlines of the windows and doors, and directed the smoke toward the ceiling and corners of the room. "Negative energy tends to gather in corners," she explained as she took up a position in the center of the room. "Watch the smoke. If it moves sideways, the negative influences have not been cleared. It should go straight up."

The stream of smoke wavered for a moment and then wafted toward the ceiling.

"And we proceed," Aggie said.

"Cool, huh, Mrs. F?" Mort said, following the medium from the room.

We left the kitchen in single file, Aggie waving her feather over the smoldering smudge stick, Mort right behind, me carrying the jar of sand, Eve hugging Cecil, and Davy bringing up the rear. I wondered briefly if our little parade would set off smoke alarms, if there were any. I hesitated to ask and break Aggie's concentration. The sooner this was over, the better.

We marched in a circle on the main floor. In each room, Aggie studied the movement of the smoke, muttered some incantations, and waved her feather. "I cleanse this room of its negative energy." **Swish, swish**. "I invite in only positive forces to support whoever lives here."

Eve began to relax; she even looked amused. "Do Cecil and I have to worry about secondhand smoke?" She giggled at her own remark, but quickly stifled it after Aggie scowled at her and sent a puff of smoke her way.

At the base of the stairs Aggie paused and looked down at the half-consumed smudge stick.

"Is something wrong?" Eve asked.

"I hope I brought enough sage," Aggie replied. She shrugged her shoulders. "If not, I can always come back tomorrow."

I looked at Eve, who raised her eyebrows and rolled her eyes at me, and I had the distinct impression that she was beginning to question her invitation to Arianna Olynski. I also wondered if it had occurred to her, as it had to me, that the medium might have purposely neglected to bring enough materials so that she'd need to return to finish the job, a clever way for the psychic to increase her fee.

The five of us climbed the stairs to the next floor, the smoke trailing behind despite Aggie's efforts to wave it ahead. "There must be a window open in one of these rooms," she said.

I felt my eyes stinging from the smoky air and was glad to reach the landing. Aggie seemed to be debating which direction to take when Cecil made the decision for her. He raced down the hallway, barking, and stopped in front of a closed door, where he scratched the wood with his claws.

We followed Cecil, and when Eve opened the door, a gust of wind grabbed it, blowing it back against the wall with a loud bang.

"Well, now we're getting somewhere," Aggie said, stepping across the threshold and waving the smudge stick overhead. "Spirits, reveal yourselves or be forever gone."

Cecil yelped, whined, and backed away from the open door, then chased down the hall the way he'd come, his tail tucked tight. He paused at the top of the stairs, looking toward Eve, his tiny body shaking.

"Cecil, sweetie. It's okay. Momma's here. Come back, sweetie." Eve walked toward him with her arms out and made kissing noises.

"I think I might've stepped on his tail," Mort said as we followed Aggie into the room while Davy hung out, just outside the door, the camera dangling from his hand.

The room was one of the abandoned bedrooms. It had an acrid odor, which struck me as peculiar since the casement window was ajar and the lacy curtain, which had blown through the opening, was fluttering outside like a large gray bird.

While Aggie saged the room, calling out to its otherworldly residents—if they were present—I looked around. The mattress, instead of being folded over as I'd seen in another bedroom, was flat on the iron bedstead with a rumpled sheet on top as if someone had used it recently. But I knew this wasn't Cliff's bedroom. An overturned cardboard carton sat next to the bed. Someone had placed a lamp with a crooked shade on the box; the weight of the lamp indented the top. I put my hand under the shade to feel the bulb. It was warm. Perhaps the handyman had started earlier than expected and was camping in the house.

I saw a book on the floor and picked it up. It was a noir mystery by Graham P. Hobart. The title was **Buried Sins**, and the cover, a bloody head rising from a grave, made me shiver. I slipped the book in my pocket, intending to add it to the box of noir books downstairs.

Mort looked out the window. "It's going to rain any minute. We'd better wrap this up."

Eve peeked around the doorjamb on the opposite side from Davy. She held a trembling Cecil in her arms. "Are the spirits gone yet?"

"Not yet," Aggie said. "I'm working on it."

"If you don't mind, I think I'll wait in the car with Cecil."

"Go ahead. I'm almost out of sage anyway," Aggie told her. "Jessica, you still have my container of sand?"

"Yes," I said, holding up the jar.

Aggie took the jar, buried what was left of the smudge stick in the sand, and waved the last bits of smoke toward the ceiling. "That's all we can do today," she announced. "I do hope Cabot Cove has a place to buy smudge sticks. Otherwise, you're in big trouble."

"Oh?" I said, wondering what her next proclamation would be.

"This place is riddled with negative energy. Did you see the way the smoke wavered?"

I thought the open window might have been a factor in keeping the smoke from rising straight up, but I didn't say anything.

While Aggie and Davy retreated down the hall, whispering to each other, Mort and I gave the room another once-over.

"With a storm coming, we should close this window," I said. "Eve doesn't need water damage adding to her problems." I pulled the curtain inside and turned the crank until the casement window shut with a thud. The room became eerily quiet except for the sound of Mort's opening and closing drawers in the bureau.

"Find anything interesting in there?" I asked.

"Mostly ladies' stuff," he said, holding up a blue and green striped scarf. "And there're some green scrubs."

"Scrubs? You mean what doctors and

nurses wear."

"Yeah. Did Mrs. Cooper ever work in the hospital?"

"Not that I'm aware of, but I'll ask Lettie Conrad. She'd know."

"You know, Mrs. F., that kid was trying to take pictures with his camera while we were walking around."

"I didn't notice."

"Yeah, he pretended just to be carrying the camera, but I saw him pushing its buttons. I know you didn't want to be videotaped, so I tried to block his view every chance I got."

"That was thoughtful of you, Mort, but you didn't have to do that."

"No? You mean you wouldn't mind being on Miss Olynski's show?"

"I definitely don't want to be on her show, but I think Davy will be surprised when he examines the camera later."

"Why's that?"

I reached into my pocket and held up a black square. "Because I took out the recording disk before I gave him back the camera."

Chapter Eight

"Let's see. Cliff and Nanette bought the house from the Ballards. They were from away and only lived in the mansion for twenty years. The Ballards had purchased the house as a vacation property from a family by the name of DeSelle, who owned it for two generations. Before them were the Robichauds, who settled there right after World War One. They bought the house from Emil Charles of Charles Department Store fame."

Tim Purdy had undertaken a history of the Spencer Percy House, and Elsie Frickert, the president of the Friends of Cabot Cove Library, had invited him to read from his notes at the organization's meeting.

"It gets a little murky in the nineteenth

century. There was a fire in the clerk's office and a lot of the records were lost, but I found an old newspaper article that reports a wedding reception in the grand parlor of the Spencer Percy House generously hosted by its owner, Abner Nessier. Nessier was a lumber baron who added all the elaborate molding around the doors and windows that somebody has stripped off over the years. The only remnant of Nessier's work—or I should say the work of his carpenters—is the intricate wood carving on the newel posts and balusters of the staircase, and of course, the library bookcases. I guess we have to be grateful those still survive. That's all I have."

Tim gazed out over his half glasses at the gathering in the library's meeting room and smiled at the smattering of applause from his audience.

"But you didn't learn whether anyone had died in the house?" asked Elsie.

Tim shook his head. "That doesn't mean it didn't happen. I just couldn't find a citation for it."

"Do ghosts inhabit a house where

someone hasn't died?"

Tim lowered his glasses to peer at her over the frames. "And do you believe in ghosts, Elsie?"

"I have a wait-and-see attitude, Tim. Since I'm getting up there, I figure I'll find out pretty soon. But the **Gazette** quoted a woman who said she saw a figure in a white gown floating at the top of the stairs. That was why the cleaning ladies refused to go up to the bedrooms."

"They just didn't want to tackle the junk Cliff had been collecting for thirty-some years. I'd be afraid to go in them rooms, too." The speaker was Barnaby Long-shoot, who wasn't really a member of the Friends. He liked to spend time in the library playing games on one of its computers, but showed up at any of the many meetings the library hosted when he found one to his interest.

"Well, I heard that Eve had a ghost-buster there this morning to exorcise any beings from the underworld," Elsie said, laughing, "so I guess we're all safe for now."

Considering her distressed reaction to

that term, I was glad Arianna Olynski wasn't present to hear that her sageing was considered an exorcism.

"Tim and I will be helping Jessica tomorrow," Elsie announced. "If any of the other members of the Friends would like to join us, you're welcome. We could use some extra hands."

Barnaby raised his. "What about non-members?"

"You're welcome to come along, but I remind everyone that we're there to help Jessica pack up Cliff's books. Tim will point out any noteworthy historical elements, and if there's time, we'll tour the house."

"Thanks for your help with the book sale," I put in. "Eve Simpson has promised that customers who purchase a book will be able to choose another at the end of the sale from among those leftover."

"Are there any cookbooks, Jessica?" Lucy Conrad asked.

"There's definitely one box of cookbooks, Lucy, maybe more. I'm sure I saw a **Joy of Cooking** and a couple of Betty Crockers. Isn't that right, Lettie?"

"Yes, and a **Maine Coastal Cooking** and a Fannie Farmer, but you don't do the cooking anyway, Lucy."

"I like to read them, though," she responded.

Elsie looked around the room. "If there aren't any more questions, we'll adjourn. Thanks to Tim Purdy for his presentation. Those coming to help sort books will meet tomorrow morning at nine at the Spencer Percy House. Wear your oilskins if you have them. The MPBN forecast is for rain and more rain."

Tim folded his notes. "Jessica, a word, please."

"Yes, Tim?" I said as I slipped on my jacket.

"Got a present for you."

"You do?"

"Ayuh. Here it is." He handed me an envelope.

"What is it?"

"It's a copy of the only picture I could find of Jerry Cooper. It's a group photo of the Explorers' Club from the year before he graduated high school. I marked which one he is."

"Thank you, Tim." I opened the envelope and unfolded the copy paper. The picture was clear, but even so, I didn't recognize the face Tim had circled.

"Look familiar?"

"No, I'm afraid not," I said, and tucked the envelope in my shoulder bag. "But thank you anyway."

He grinned. "I'm pretty proud of myself if I do say so. Persistence. That's what you need to be a historian."

The radio station's forecast had been accurate. The storm had come onshore late in the evening, and a northeast wind had picked up more moisture from the bay, resulting in a good soaking. Tim had kindly picked me up in his gray sedan at a quarter to nine the next morning. I had on the yellow slicker that I often wear when I go fishing with friends, and a pair of rubber boots from L.L.Bean, as did Tim. Our Bean boots were caked with mud by the time we walked from the side of the house where he'd parked to the front door.

Elsie was already there, huddling under the umbrella she shared with Barnaby.

Lettie had said that she might join us later —Lucy had forgotten altogether that we would be here—but other members of the Friends had probably decided to forgo helping until a drier day.

I unlocked the front door, and the four of us crowded into the dark hall. The wind pushed at the door as we struggled to shut it behind us, and another door, somewhere upstairs, slammed shut. Barnaby warily looked up the main staircase.

"There should be a roll of paper towels in the kitchen," I said. "I don't want to make muddy footprints down the hall."

"I'll get it," Elsie said.

If it hadn't been raining, we would have left our boots outside the front door, but the inclement weather had forced us indoors, still shod. Elsie slipped off her raincoat and boots, and padded down the hall in her stocking feet. Barnaby shrugged out of his slicker and draped it over a newel post. He sat on the bottom stair and pulled off his shoes, revealing a large hole in one sock where his great toe poked through. After removing our muddy boots, Tim and I hung everyone's coats in the hall closet in the hope that they would dry by the time we were ready to leave.

"Is there any newspaper here we can put under our boots, Jessica?" Tim asked.

"I think Eve has gotten rid of all the newspapers, but there are a few empty boxes here. We can put our wet footwear in one." I reached into my shoulder bag and withdrew a pair of soft slippers that I'd packed in anticipation of the nasty weather, slipped them on, entered the library, and turned on the lights. I looked for a box that we hadn't already used for books, and, finding one, brought it into the hall. "This should do."

Elsie came from the kitchen empty-handed. "I can't find any paper towels," she said.

"That's funny. I used a roll there just the other day."

"I could've missed it. My eyesight isn't what it used to be."

Tim entered the library and took in the scene. "I see you've already emptied the top shelves of each of these bookcases, Jessica. Would you like us to start on the next ones down?"

"Good idea."

Elsie and Barnaby wandered in, peering at the rows of labeled boxes covering the floor.

"What's 'hard-boiled' and 'noir' mean?" Barnaby asked, pronouncing it **noyer.** "Sounds like an order of eggs."

"Those are detective stories with a cynical point of view and perhaps more graphic violence than you'd find in other books," I said. "**Noir** is the French word for 'black.' Those mysteries are darker."

"Would I like them?"

"I don't know, Barnaby. What do you usually like to read?"

"Whatever anyone leaves behind at Mara's Luncheonette. I guess I'm sort of a magazine or newspaper kind of guy."

"You don't want to read noir," Elsie told him. "It'll scare the pants off you. If you want to read a good book, start with one of Jessica's." She turned to me. "You do have a box here, don't you, Jessica?"

"Yes, I do. It's over here." I pointed out a carton that held books I'd either given Cliff as gifts over the years, or that he'd purchased himself.

Barnaby lumbered over. "Which d'ya think I'd like?"

"Work first, sir," Tim said, scowling at Barnaby. "There'll be time to choose a book later." He winked at me while sliding the library ladder over to the first book-case. "You'll notice, ladies and gentle-man," he said as he climbed up the steps, "that the bookcases in this library are in the late Regency style, popular in this country in the first third of the nineteenth century. Six shelves on the upper two-thirds, and a cabinet on the lower third." He slid his glasses up to his forehead and squinted at the upright between two cases. "These are made of birch, I believe, native to Maine, probably built by the carpenters employed by Nessier, the lum-ber baron I told you about yesterday, and stained to resemble rosewood, which was popular in England at the time."

Elsie gave Tim an arch look. "Work first; lecture later," she said. "Hand me down some of them books. I'll call out what category I think they should be in and, Barnaby, you find the right box."

"I can't thank you enough for your help,"

I said.

"We'll be fine," she said. "Go do whatever it is you have to do."

"I brought lunch for everyone, so the first thing I have to do is put our sandwiches in the refrigerator. Then I'll start on the books downstairs." I picked up an empty box. "If you need me, the door to the cellar is off the kitchen. Just give a shout."

Tim handed Elsie a thick volume.

"**Roget's Thesaurus,**" she called out. "Barnaby, find the box that says 'Reference Books.'"

"You sure it's here?"

"We gotta start one if it isn't," Elsie said.

" 'Reference and Language Arts.' Got it."

I smiled as I walked out of the library and down the hall to the back of the house.

In the kitchen, the roll of paper towels was nowhere in sight, but a mug and spent tea bag stood in the sink. **Eve must have been here again,** I thought. **Or perhaps the Conrad twins**. A loud hum reminded me that we'd already turned on the refrigerator. I opened the door. A quart bottle of milk, half-empty, stood on the top shelf, alongside something wrapped in foil. I didn't investigate. The sisters had said they would come to help later. Perhaps they'd left something to share. I made room for my sack of sandwiches and placed two cans of Moxie on the shelf in case anyone wanted a soft drink.

I tucked my cell phone into a pocket of the old blue jeans I wore and looked down at my feet. The jeans were my go-to clothes for painting or other dirty work, but the pair of folding slippers I'd brought had a soft sole—not much protection if I dropped a book on my foot or bumped into debris that might have been left on the basement floor. I parked my shoulder bag on one of the chairs around the kitchen table and headed for the door leading to the basement, hoping that Cliff had gotten around to fixing the broken step that had precipitated the departure of his grandson, Elliot.

The door to the lower level was in the same hall off the kitchen that led to the back door. A skeleton key had been left in the lock. I put down the carton and used both hands to simultaneously turn the key and the doorknob. A current of musty air greeted me as I swung open the door to a black void.

I squinted into the dark in search of light switches. I patted the wall on either side of the doorway with my hands in the hope of feeling what I couldn't see. My hand connected with a raw wood railing on the right side, but nothing else. I left the cardboard box on the floor outside the door and used the flashlight on my cell phone to shine a beam of light down the stairs. **There must be a pull cord for a lightbulb somewhere. I can't believe Cliff would have no lights at all in the basement.** Gripping the railing with one hand and holding the cell phone aloft with the other, I cautiously placed my foot on the top step, then slowly descended. The stairs creaked under my weight, but even though one or two felt bouncy, they didn't break. I was so focused on my feet that I was startled when a string brushed my cheek. I grabbed it with my right hand and gave it a tug, trusting that it was not attached to some overhead panel that would swing down on my head. I was rewarded with light from a bare bulb in a socket. The bulb was the kind used in a night-light, putting out seven watts at the most, but it was enough for me to get my bearings and see a few feet into the dim space.

An electrical cord dangled from an outlet above the bulb and ran to the back of a nearby piece of metal equipment. It was fortunate that I'd turned on the light first, or I could easily have gotten tangled in it. I stepped down the last stair and stood on the cold concrete floor. I felt the damp coming up through the soles of my slippers. When a loud clanking sounded, I nearly jumped out of them.

"What on earth," I said, my heart pounding in my ears.

I turned toward the racket to discover a large, old metal dehumidifier that Cliff must have installed to protect his books. The clanking indicated to me that the motor was in desperate need of repair. If it had come on when the painting service was here, it was no surprise that the men reported hearing strange noises.

But if the dehumidifier was for the books, where were they?

I turned to my left, holding up the cell phone again to add to the bulb's weak light. Along the wall was a series of bookcases, not as elegant as the ones in the library, but neither were they rough-hewn. Cliff must have built them himself. They were perhaps six feet high with six shelves each. He'd painted them black, making them harder to see in this subterranean room, but probably sealing the wood to keep it from warping in the damp air.

"Good heavens!" I muttered to myself. "Clearing these books out may take another week. They all have to be hauled upstairs."

I went to the first bookcase, shining my light on the floor as I walked to be sure there wasn't anything to trip over. I didn't want to use up my cell phone battery, but I had to see what books were so important that Cliff had built shelves for them in the basement. Phone books! And legal-size banker's boxes bulging with papers. I tipped up the cover of one to see old school papers, photographs, and a child's drawings. Next to the box were textbooks that I recognized from my days of teaching high school English.

One case held row upon row of the yellow spines of **National Geographic** magazines. How many hours had Elliot's father spent poring over the stories and photographs of exotic places before taking off for parts unknown and disappearing forever with his wife?

As I moved down the line of bookcases, I noted medical tomes, perhaps consulted when Nanette had been diagnosed with cancer, and stacks of woodworking magazines. It seemed the more personal reading material in Cliff's collection had been stored belowground. On one shelf, a paperback lay on its side in front of a row of books. It was another Graham P. Hobart, entitled **Hidden Grave**. Cliff certainly was a Hobart fan. I pocketed the book to add to the ones upstairs.

I'm not certain what inspired me to aim my cell phone's flashlight along the top of the shelves, but as the beam moved across the wall above the bookcases, I noticed a change in the paint color. **Oh, dear, is Eve facing a major leak?** Repairs to this house were getting more expensive by the day. I stepped back, trying to get a better angle. As I stood on my tiptoes, holding the light higher, I took another step back and lost my balance. I started to fall, but an arm reached around my body and righted me. I gasped and dropped my cell phone, which skittered along the floor. I smelled sweat and tobacco and heard the rasp of a man's heavy breathing.

"You don't belong here," he growled into my ear.

Then I saw what he held in his left hand—a hammer.

Chapter Nine

"Who are you? What are you doing here? You'd better tell me or I'll use this." He raised the hammer threateningly.

I tried to wrestle free. He wore a rubber coat, the sleeve of which was wet. "Let go of me!"

I contemplated screaming, but the clanking of the dehumidifier would make it difficult for anyone upstairs to hear me, which was why I hadn't been aware of someone sneaking up behind me.

The arm loosened. I pushed it away, stepped forward, and whirled around. I couldn't see his face in the dim light, but the shape of him was tall and broad shouldered, perhaps magnified by the voluminous coat he wore and the hammer he wielded overhead.

"I'm a friend of Eve Simpson's," I said quickly. "I'm helping her clear out the books for a sale to benefit the library. There are other people upstairs. They know I'm down here."

"There's nothing here anyone would be interested in buying. Just junk." He had a gravelly voice that sounded as if he smoked too much. He took a few steps toward me, backing me into one of the bookcases. He still held the hammer, though no longer overhead, but I wasn't certain what he intended to do with it.

"Your turn," I said. "Who are you?"

"No one you need to know." He squatted down and ran his right hand along the floor before standing again. "Here," he said.

"What is it?"

"Your phone. It's not broken."

"Thank goodness for that," I said. I'd been trying to see his eyes, but his features were too shadowed. "You still haven't told me who you are."

"Why do you need to know?"

I pressed the button on my cell phone and was glad to see the black screen come to life, although the battery icon indicated the power was getting low. I put my finger over the emergency button. "I want to know because if you don't belong here, I plan to call the police."

He snorted and scratched the back of his head with the hammer before letting his arm swing down.

My eyes followed his every move, and I was ready to shout as loud as I could if he took a more-threatening action. It was all I would be capable of. I knew I'd never make it past him and up the stairs if he wanted to stop me.

"You're pretty brave for someone alone in a dark basement with a stranger, especially one holding a hammer." He raised it so I could see, and made hammering motions in my direction before letting his arm fall.

"I told you who I am. Now answer my question, please."

He waited a long time before mumbling something.

"What?"

"I'm the handyman. See?" He raised the hammer again. "Ms. Simpson hired me."

"And what are you doing for Ms.

Simpson?"

"Repair work, obviously. She didn't tell me there would be other people working here."

"Well, there are." I let out the breath I'd been holding. "Nice to meet you, Mr. Handyman. Do you have a name?"

He nodded slowly, his eyes avoiding mine. "Geraldo Tonelero." He pronounced his first name the Spanish way as if it were spelled Heraldo, but he didn't speak with a Spanish accent.

"Thank you, Mr. Tonelero."

"Call me Tony," he said gruffly. "Mr. Tonelero was my father." He sniggered as if he'd made a joke.

"Then thank you, Tony." I slipped my phone into my side pocket.

"So you know my name, but you didn't bother to tell me yours. You just said you were a friend of Ms. Simpson's."

"I'm Jessica Fletcher."

"Okay, Ms. Fletcher, you can leave now."

"I have no intention of leaving," I said. "I have work to do. Do you happen to know if there's another light down here?"

"Doubt it."

"That's going to make my job difficult," I
said.

"What job is that?"

"I told you. I'm here to pack up the
books. I left a box at the top of the stairs."

He mumbled again.

"Speak up, please. I can't understand
you."

"I thought you were a thief," he said,
raising his voice, "only I thought you
weren't a very smart one. I don't see
anything here worth stealing."

"I don't see how you see anything at
all," I said, thinking that this was one of
the strangest conversations I'd had in a
very long time. I brushed past him and
grabbed hold of the staircase's handrail.

"All right. All right. Don't get mad." He
turned in a circle. "I probably can rig up a
light for you in a day or so."

"Not sooner?"

"Can't do it now. It's raining." He waved
at me to go up the stairs.

"What difference does the weather
make?" I said over my shoulder, glad my
shaking legs held me up as I climbed.

"I'd rather not go to the hardware store

on my motorcycle."

"Good point. I'll appreciate anything you can rig up when you can get to it."

"Thank **you**."

I thought I detected a note of irony in his thanks, but I said, "You're welcome." I reached the top of the stairs, picked up the box I'd left in the hall, and gave Tony a good once-over now that I could see him.

He wasn't quite as tall and menacing as he'd seemed in the dark, but he was a muscular man. His shaggy hair was streaked with gray, the same color as his eyes, and the nose above his bushy mustache appeared to have been broken sometime in his life. As I followed him into the kitchen, he turned his head toward the voices coming from the library.

"Would you like to meet the others?" I asked.

"No. I'm going to have my lunch." He opened the refrigerator and took out the package wrapped in foil and the half bottle of milk, dropped them both in the pocket of his yellow slicker, and went out the back door. I watched as he pulled up his hood and sprinted across the yard to the barn. **He must be using the tools in Cliff's workshop,** I thought. I wondered what projects Eve had asked him to undertake, and when he had started to work. **I must remember to ask her about him. And now that she has someone working on the house, is she going to invite the medium to come back?**

The phone in my pocket vibrated. I pulled it out and looked at the screen. A message warned me the battery was in need of charging. I quickly dialed Seth Hazlitt. We hadn't spoken since he'd told me he was requesting an autopsy on Cliff Cooper, and I'd promised to report on the meeting with the medium. I put the phone to my ear and waited to hear the call connect. But my phone chose that moment to die.

Chapter Ten

"It was such a scary noise, Jessica. I nearly jumped out of my skin," Elsie said as we sat at Cliff's kitchen table having our lunch.

"It's just an old humidifier, Elsie. It needs a new motor," I said.

"Barnaby was halfway out the door when he heard it," Tim said, chuckling.

"I wasn't scared. It just startled me a tad," Barnaby said.

"The only thing that kept you inside was the pouring rain," Elsie said.

"A practical decision," I said, smiling at Barnaby.

He tugged at his collar. "People do say there's a ghost in this house, Mrs. Fletcher. I just don't wanna meet him."

"Who says that, Barnaby?" I asked.

"I heard it down at Mara's. They say it must be Cliff Cooper's spirit come back to haunt the place 'cause he lived here so long."

"Then who's the figure of a woman the cleaning people supposedly saw?" Elsie said. "You forgot to mention her."

"You mean there's more than one?" Barnaby looked decidedly uncomfortable. "Are we almost done here?"

"Nothing to worry about, Barnaby," Tim said. "Jessica will protect you."

"Tim's only teasing you, Barnaby. There are no ghosts here. It's just an old house with lots of noises. Oh, and Eve hired a handyman to help fix up the place. So if anyone heard footsteps, it was probably him."

Tony had never returned to be introduced to my friends. I didn't know whether he'd left or had decided to stay in the barn until the rain subsided. I told everyone about meeting him, although I didn't describe the circumstances.

"Tony Tonelero, huh? Have to say, the name is not familiar," Tim said.

"I've never heard of him, and I thought I

knew all our local handymen," Elsie said.

"Probably from away," added Barnaby.

"But why would Eve Simpson hire someone from out of town when there's local men aplenty could use the work?"

"They're scared o' ghosts is why, Elsie," Barnaby said.

"But you know there's no such thing, don't you, Barnaby?" I said.

"It was in the **Gazette**. Ms. Phillips wouldn't put it in the newspaper if it wasn't so."

Elsie snorted. "Maybe not, but she's not past exaggerating some if it'll help sell more papers. I heard that issue disappeared from the shelves. Couldn't even find a copy in the post office, and there's always piles of them there."

"In that case, the three of you have my undying gratitude for risking life and limb to work in a haunted house," I said, unable to keep the whimsy out of my voice.

"Speaking of work," Tim said, "this is the only day I can spare, so let's try to finish up as much as we can."

I'd decided to leave the materials on the basement shelves for another time when, I hoped, Eve's handyman would be able to supply me with enough light to illuminate the task. I spent the rest of the afternoon sorting books with Tim, Elsie, and Barnaby. We continued to work until we ran out of boxes and the piles of books on the floor became a hazard to movement. I debated asking to borrow one of their cell phones but decided that the call to Seth could wait until I had some privacy.

It was late afternoon when Tim dropped me off at home, the rain still pelting down. I brought in the mail and left it on the kitchen table while I hung up my yellow slicker on the back porch where it could drip onto the same rubber tray on which I set down my Bean boots. I plugged in my cell phone next to my desk and checked the answering machine for messages.

I don't give out my cell phone number to many people. Seth had it, of course, as did Mort Metzger, but I preferred to carry a cellular phone more as an emergency apparatus than one with which to occupy my time. I didn't need to be immediately available to everyone who took a notion to call me. It distresses me to see so many young people—and some older ones, as well—with their eyes riveted on their palms while life takes place around them. Even though I was happy to use my computer to exchange e-mail with people who live far away, I'd determined that the telephone in my house would be my chief device for non-face-to-face communication, and left my old answering machine plugged in to record messages while I was away, or when I was concentrating on work and didn't wish to respond to calls immediately.

Seth had left me a message, and I was certain that once my cell phone was charged, there would be voice mail awaiting me there as well. He was usually persistent in his efforts to contact me.

"Jessica, Seth here. If you're going to march around with one of those new-fangled fruit phones, at least have the courtesy to keep the thing charged up. I hate talking to machines. We need to chat. Call me when you get home. Please!"

That last part was said in an aggravated tone, and I decided that I needed a nice warm cup of tea in my hands before returning the call. While I waited for the water in the kettle to boil, I flipped through the envelopes I'd retrieved from my mailbox. They looked to be mostly solicitations for credit cards, or letters from competing television or computer companies urging me to change my service. There were a few bills, which I set aside to pay later that evening.

One envelope had a stamp that had been canceled in New York City, and I opened it first. Inside was the letter I'd sent to Arthur Bannister at his bookstore. On the top of the page he'd written in pencil, "Just ran out of stationery. Sorry. Happy to help. Just tell me where and when and where I can stay. Always on the lookout for first editions, so if you see some, please set them aside."

I shook my head and smiled. Much as I was eager for Arthur to lend his expertise to our book sale, there was no way I was going to check the copyright page of every book in Cliff's collection to cull the first editions for my old friend. I debated the wisdom of telling him that before he made the trip, and I decided not to. I didn't want to give him any excuses to turn me down. I knew that once Arthur was faced with a sea of books, he would be as happy as a clam in mud, diving into his favorite preoccupation, discovering hidden treasures.

At the bottom of the page where I'd added my handwritten postscript to him, Arthur had scrawled, "It doesn't snow in Cabot Cove in October, does it? If it does, I won't be able to make it."

The kettle whistled at the same time that the phone rang. I picked up the receiver and turned off the flame.

"Well, you certainly took your sweet time getting back to me."

"Seth, I just walked in. You've barely given me time to hang up my coat and look at my mail." I poured the boiling water over a bag of decaf English breakfast tea and took my mug to the table. "Tim, Elsie, Barnaby, and I worked all afternoon sorting the books, and I think I'm finally beginning to see good progress, although —can you believe it?—there's another set of bookcases in the basement to deal with. By the way, I met Eve's handyman, too, a disheveled sort who retreated into Cliff's barn without waiting to be introduced to the others."

"I hope he's not planning to take off with all Cliff's carpentry equipment."

"That's doubtful since he said he came by motorcycle."

I heard Seth grunt. "Who **is** this guy? Did Eve ever work with him before?"

"Good questions. I'll have to ask her. She must have trusted him with the key since he made himself at home. He was using the back door and had left his lunch in the refrigerator."

"Maybe he can explain all this haunted house nonsense."

I laughed. "You have to admit that it adds a certain drama to the old Spencer Percy House."

"If anybody believes in ghosts," he said. "I don't."

"By the way, I'm a little concerned about Lucy Conrad," I told him. "She seems so withdrawn these days."

"Death is a difficult ordeal to get through. You of all people should know that."

"I do, but I'm afraid it's more than that. Lettie hinted that she's not as sharp as she used to be."

"Happens to the best of us."

I changed the subject. "Sorry that I didn't get back to you sooner," I said. "The cell phone is charging as we speak. I assume you called me for the same reason I tried to reach you. Did the autopsy take place?"

"It did and it was no easy task. The medical examiner was mighty piqued at me for waiting so long, but the funeral home finally sent back the body and we did the postmortem together."

"And did it set your mind at ease?"

"Not exactly, although I was right in my analysis of how Cliff Cooper died. He did not die of 'respiratory failure' due to pneumonia. His diagnosis was chronic obstructive pulmonary disease, COPD. It was right there on his chart. He had chronic bronchitis, typical for such patients. Sometimes it becomes pneumonia, but in this case, it didn't."

"He did have a terrible cough."

"Ayuh, that he did, and the damn fool

kept resisting the medicine that would ease his symptoms. Even so, he showed no signs of being in the end stage of life. He was alert, read your book in one night. No mental confusion. He made sense when he talked to you, didn't he?"

"Very much so. He was insistent about what he wanted when he dictated his will to me."

"Exactly. He had a good appetite, enough that he complained about the hospital food the day before he died. It just didn't add up."

"So what does that mean? What was his cause of death?"

"He died of asphyxiation. He died of no oxygen. He couldn't breathe."

"Isn't that respiratory failure? Did his lungs fill up with fluid?"

"I suppose you can call it that in a generic sense. But no! His airway was completely closed off."

"How?"

"Possibly with a pillow."

"Good heavens, Seth! Are you saying that someone **killed** Cliff Cooper?"

"That's what it looks like to me."

"Are you certain?"

"There were hemorrhages in his eyes that could have been the result of the coughing. I'll give you that. But there was a cut inside his lip, made by his own teeth. And we detected a little bruising around his nose and mouth. That could only happen if someone pressed something over his face and maybe pinched his nostrils closed."

"When I was there, he used a pillow to muffle his own cough. Couldn't he have made those bruises himself?"

"That's what I wondered, too. But we found fibers in his nose, mouth, and in his trachea."

"From the pillow?"

"No. We looked at them under the microscope, and the fibers were green. The hospital doesn't have green pillowcases. I checked."

"So it's homicide," I said. "Have you notified the sheriff?"

"Ayuh. Called him before I called you. He said it was okay to share the results with you, but the four of us—you, me, the sheriff, and the medical examiner—have to keep this information under wraps until Mort can contact Cliff's next of kin."

"That would be his grandson, Elliot."

"And that young man is somewhere between Anchorage, Alaska, and Cabot Cove, Maine, but no one knows exactly where."

"That gives Mort some time to look into Cliff's death before Elliot gets here and the news becomes public knowledge."

"I thought you might see it that way. He said he trusted you to keep the information confidential until his office was ready to make the announcement."

"You know I will."

"That's what I told him. He's coming to the hospital tomorrow afternoon to view the body."

"Do you mind if I tag along?"

"I don't. That's why I mentioned it. Can't speak for the sheriff."

"I'll call and ask to accompany you. What time will you be there?"

"Around four, if I can finish up my office hours on time. I'll meet you in the waiting room of the rehab wing."

"Oh, Seth. I still can't believe it. Who

would want to kill Cliff Cooper? He was such a nice man. I can't imagine he had any enemies."

"Well, he had one—the person who smothered him to death."

Chapter Eleven

Eve picked up a square pillow and draped a length of turquoise and orange patterned material across it. "What do you think about this for the living room sofa, Jessica?"

"I don't know if I'm the right person to give you decorating tips, Eve. You know more about this than I do." We were standing in front of a bin of pillows in the home furnishings section of Charles Department Store.

"It's not really decorating. That would require more time and money than I have for this project. We're **staging**, adding just a few right touches to make it more interesting. The living room furniture is so dark. This would bring in nice contrasting colors against the burgundy velvet sofa.

Don't you think?"

"If you're asking my opinion, I think it looks more Miami Beach than Cabot Cove," I said. "Sorry."

"Quel dommage," she said, folding the fabric and tucking it under her arm. "What about that one?" She pointed to a round pillow covered in pleated white silk with tiny red flowers on it.

"Eve, I didn't meet you here to talk about pillows."

"You wanted to know about Tony Tonelero."

"Yes. Where did you meet him? What do you know about him? Did he give you the names of other people he's worked for?"

"Honestly, Jessica. Meeting him was an absolute blessing. It was right after Evelyn ran that article in the **Gazette** about the house being haunted and my repair people refusing to work there. It was an incredible stroke of luck. He came to me after those other people walked out. He was like a knight in shining armor riding to my rescue. And he's not bad on the eyes, is he? I've always been attracted to a man with a mustache."

"A bushy mustache is not a recommendation for a handyman. How do you know he can do the work? Did he give you any references? Show you photographs of work he's done before? Where is he from anyway?"

"You think his mustache is bushy? I kind of thought he looked like that actor Tom Selleck."

"Looking like a television star is not a guarantee he can fix what needs to be fixed. Did you pay him in advance? Did you say he could stay on the premises?"

"Well, he said he needed money to buy the wood for fixing the window sashes and paint for the trim. And there was no point in his traveling down the coast and back every day. He said he'd be fine in the barn. He said there's a storage room he can use."

"And how will he transport that wood to the house? He told me he had to wait for the rain to stop before he could get to the hardware store on his motorcycle."

"He doesn't have a truck?"

"Did you see one?" I asked.

"Then I assume he'll have the material he

needs delivered."

"How much money did you give him? Don't answer that. It's none of my business. I just don't want you to get taken in by a handsome face. Cliff left valuable tools in his workshop. You don't want this person selling them off when you're not looking."

"Oh, dear, I hadn't thought of that."

"I'm not saying Tony is a thief, just that you need to know a little more about him before you give him the keys to Cliff's house."

"It would be awkward to ask for them back at this point, don't you think?"

"No doubt. But I'd like us to protect Elliot's assets as much as possible. I'm concerned so many people have access to that house, myself included. How many sets of keys did you have made?"

"Me? Only four or five. The Conrad twins already had a set of Cliff's keys. He gave them to Lucy and Lettie."

"And what did you do with the sets of keys that you had made?"

She began counting on her fingers. "I have one. You have one. I gave one to Tony." She winced at me. "He couldn't very well fix the windows without going inside, now could he?"

"I hope that's all he's doing."

"The painters and the roofers never had keys. I let them in."

"That's good."

"I got back the set I gave to the cleaning service."

"Okay."

"But I gave them to Aggie, only temporarily of course."

"Aggie! For heaven's sake, Eve, why would you trust her with a set of keys to Cliff's house? She's a stranger. She has no business being there."

"She said she needs a location to shoot her Internet show. She's thinks it won't take more than a day or two, Jessica."

"And if it does?"

"We made a deal. She even paid me a location fee. Well, she said she wouldn't charge me for the sageing. She's going to come back and finish the job and make sure all—now, what did she call them?—all 'nefarious spirits' are rousted. Then we can sell the house guaranteed ghost-free."

"But, Eve, the house isn't yours to rent out. Did you check with the lawyer?"

"Not exactly. But if you think I should, I will. I'm only trying to get this real estate nightmare off the ground, Jessica. You don't know how difficult it is to sell an old house needing so much work."

"You could ask less for the house and tell prospective buyers that they'll need to do most of the repairs themselves."

"You're the one who talked about protecting Elliot's assets, Jessica. Lowering the price might save me some headaches, but it will net him a lot less in the end."

And a lot less for you in commission, I thought. Instead I asked, "What happens when Elliot comes home and so many people have the keys to his house?"

"I can get them back, of course. But if I do, how will you finish packing up the books? And how will Tony do the repairs?"

"And how will Aggie do her show?" I asked.

"Oh, I know you don't cotton to her, Jessica, but we haven't had any trouble with a ghost since she came."

"And you didn't have trouble with a

ghost **before** she arrived."

Eve pouted. "You don't know that. All kinds of strange things were going on there."

"I think you were the victim of a lot of overactive imaginations on the part of the cleaning and repair people," I said. "And Evelyn Phillips didn't help your cause with that fanciful article in the **Gazette**."

"Or your cause either," Eve added, "since it kept away volunteers for the book sale."

"Perhaps. But we're still responsible for protecting Elliot's inheritance. I don't see how allowing Aggie to film her show in the house is helpful to Elliot."

"**Peut-être**. But this way we're double-insured in case you're wrong and there is a ghost in the house."

A saleswoman approached us. "Hello, ladies. Do you need assistance with these pillows?"

"Not really," Eve said. "Oh, wait! We could use your opinion on something."

"Certainly. I'm happy to help."

"What do you think of this fabric?" Eve spread the turquoise and orange pat-terned cloth over the square pillow again and cocked her head.

The woman looked from Eve to me and back at the fabric. "Well," she said, trying to be diplomatic, "it's bright and colorful, isn't it? It reminds me a bit of those decorator houses they show on the home channel on TV."

Eve raised her eyebrows at me and smiled.

"You know the ones I mean," the salesclerk continued, "the beach houses in Miami, Florida."

Eve's face fell.

"I have another appointment," I said, looking at my watch. "Eve, please ask Tony for some references. It's not too late to do that. And I'd call Fred Kramer, if I were you, just to be on the safe side."

"I'll get to it as soon as I can, Jessica." She turned to the saleslady, plucking a pillow from the pile in the bin. "How do you think this would look against a burgundy sofa?"

Chapter Twelve

Cabot Cove Hospital had recently gone through a series of expansions to better reflect its growing status as more of a regional hospital, serving a wider range of patients than only those from our community. There was a time when I knew almost everyone who worked there, and they knew me. But with a series of wings built on, and an influx of additional medical staff, that was no longer the case. And, of course, security had been beefed up considerably.

Seth's view of the expansion was two-sided. On the one hand, he appreciated the increasingly cutting-edge technology that accompanied the growth, but he also confided to me many times how he missed the small-town feel of the facility.

But no matter how large the hospital became, Seth was still considered one of its best diagnosticians, the physician to consult on the most difficult cases.

In the afternoon, Seth was meeting Mort Metzger at the hospital where Cliff Cooper's body was being held in the morgue, and I'd invited myself along. I wasn't certain whether Mort wanted me there, but since he hadn't voiced an objection when I'd asked to come, I proceeded to make arrangements. I'd called a cab to pick me up and drive me out to the campus where the hospital and other medical buildings were located. As was my usual practice, I left myself plenty of time to get there. As it turned out, I was glad that I had. There was a lot of traffic leading out of town, and at one point cars were stopped altogether. I could see the buildings a half mile ahead, but only one lane of the two-lane road was usable.

"Sorry for the delay, Mrs. Fletcher. Looks like we got a work crew inspectin' the road bed," my driver, Dimitri, informed me. "They're fixin' all the breaches in the blacktop to get ahead of the job before the winter weather starts to come in. Want me to turn around and try another route?"

I looked at my watch. "That's not necessary, Dimitri. I have plenty of time before my appointment. I'm sure they'll let us pass soon."

Up ahead, officers waved through northbound traffic, while those of us in the southbound lane waited our turn, all except a helmeted man on a motorcycle—at least I assumed it was a man—who threaded in and out of the stopped cars, sometimes riding along the shoulder, gunning his engine as he passed the stranded motorists to warn them of his presence.

"Don't you hate guys like that?" my driver said. "No one else's time is as important as theirs."

"He'd better hope no one swings open a car door and steps out to get a better view of what's ahead," I said.

"That'd knock him off his perch, that's for sure," Dimitri said, chuckling, "He'd probably get to the hospital a lot faster that way, only he'd ride in the back of an ambulance instead of on his fancy wheels."

Luckily for the motorcyclist, the drivers stayed in their seats, although several rolled down their windows to express their disapproval of the selfish individual who put his own needs ahead of others on the road.

Eventually there were no more on-coming cars, and our lane began to move, inching forward at first, and then going slightly faster as flagmen waved us around the tie-up and back into our proper lane. A little cheer went up from the driver's seat, and I saw that one of Mort's deputies had pulled over the motorcyclist and gone back to directing traffic, making the scofflaw wait to get his ticket until all of the south-bounders had passed.

"I gotta remember to give Deputy Chip a pat on the back next time I see him," Dimitri said, grinning as we sailed on down the road. He was still smiling as we pulled into the circular driveway, then drove past the front entrance of the hospital and around to the new rehabilitation wing.

"Sometimes it's the little victories that make it a good day," I said.

"You said it! Will you need me to pick you

up later, Mrs. Fletcher?"

"No, thank you, Dimitri. I think I'll be able to catch a ride back with Dr. Hazlitt."

The rehabilitation wing where Cliff had been a patient had a separate parking lot and public entrance in addition to the connection from inside the hospital. I pressed the automatic door button, and the heavy glass doors slid open. A stream of warm air poured down from above, serving as a curtain to keep the weather outdoors from chilling the vestibule. I walked through another set of doors. To my right, there was a waiting room where Seth had said he'd meet me—although our appointment was not for another half hour—and a glass enclosure where the admitting staff worked.

Every time I'd come to visit Cliff, I'd abided by the rules, stopping at the security desk, signing the guest book, and receiving a visitor's pass. I thought of the motorcyclist who'd declined to follow the rules and who was now about to pay a fine for his self-centered behavior.

But what about the person who had come to the hospital with the intention of taking Cliff's life? Would that person have signed in as required? Unlikely. Chances were that he or she would have found a way inside without alerting anyone to their presence.

How easy would it be to enter the hospital without the required visitor's pass? And without one, would a person be able to get around without someone in authority asking to see it? If I could make it into the hospital unchallenged, how long would it be before someone questioned my reason for being there? Or could I sneak in, explore the territory, and escape undetected, as the killer apparently had?

Because there was time before I was to meet Seth and Mort, I decided to put it to the test. Since no one was sitting at the security desk, I waited until the staff in the glass enclosure was occupied and not looking my way, and used the opportunity to walk down the hall without stopping for a pass. Had anyone questioned me, I would have told them truthfully that I was looking for a nurse on the afternoon shift named Carolyn, or an aide called Theresa. Those were the names written on the whiteboard hanging in Cliff's room when I'd visited him.

I hadn't met Theresa, but I assumed that the woman who'd threatened to chase me out of Cliff's room should he become upset was his nurse, Carolyn.

I didn't see her at the nurses' station, but she could have been in a patient's room. The department secretary, the only staff member in street clothes, was typing on her computer when I approached. A badge on her shoulder identified her as Ursula.

"Good afternoon, Ursula," I said when she looked up momentarily from her work. "Is Carolyn here today?"

"She has Tuesdays off," she said, her fingers resuming a rat-a-tat on the keyboard.

"What about Theresa?" I asked. "The aide?"

She glanced up at the clock on the wall. "She's here, but she took an early break."

"Oh, good. Do you know where she takes her break?"

She shrugged. "Where everyone does, I assume, the cafeteria. Unless she's a smoker. If you didn't see her outside on the far end of the parking lot, she's probably in the cafeteria."

I thanked Ursula and walked down the hall toward the connection to the hospital. Although I'd recognize Carolyn if I saw her again, I had no idea what Theresa looked like. Asking the department secretary would likely have raised alarm bells, and she might have demanded to know why I wanted to see her and perhaps checked for my visitor's pass. But I hadn't asked, and she hadn't noticed my lack of credentials. So far so good.

I've always found that the best way to make your way around someplace where you don't belong is to look as if you do. As a consequence, I walked swiftly down the hall, keeping my eyes in front of me and nodding with a smile at anyone I passed.

Once inside the hospital proper, I went to the nearest elevator bay and pressed the down button. The cafeteria was on the ground floor and was used by both staff and visitors, although those wearing a staff badge paid lower prices for the food. What I wasn't certain of was how long Theresa's break would last, and whether it would be over before I found her.

The elevator came, and I stepped into it in front of a group of white-coated staff. When the doors opened on the ground floor, I exited and pretended to read the directory on the wall to allow them to get ahead of me. They followed the arrow indicating the location of the cafeteria, and I followed closely, hoping anyone in authority would think I was part of their group.

At the entrance to the cafeteria, my luck ran out. A hand grabbed my elbow.

"Madam, where's your visitor's pass?" The tall guard in a blue uniform looked at me sternly.

"Oh, my goodness, isn't it here?" I said innocently, patting my shoulder and looking around as if my pass might have fallen off. "Wait! Let me see if I stuck it in my bag." I made a big show of digging through my shoulder bag, checking both the inside and outside pockets. "I must have left it in his room," I said. "I just came down to get him a cup of tea."

"They have tea on the floors. Why would you need to come to the cafeteria for tea?"

"And a slice of chocolate cake. They don't have cake on his floor. And he has such a sweet tooth. The doctor said it was all right if I brought him up a slice of cake. Just this time. He promised he wouldn't ask again." I flapped my hands in distress. "He hasn't had any appetite at all, but he said he would try some cake."

"All right. Calm down, lady. I'll let you get your husband some cake. But make sure you find that visitor's pass and wear it so I can see it."

"Thank you so much, Officer."

"I'm not an officer. Go on inside. Make it fast."

I stepped into the cafeteria and took a tray from the pile inside the door. I slid it along the metal counter of the hot foods buffet, walking behind a doctor in blue scrubs. I tapped him on the shoulder. "Excuse me, Doctor, but would you happen to know an aide named Theresa? She works in the new rehabilitation unit."

He shook his head. "Sorry. I'm in the OR today. Don't know any of the rehab staff."

Two nurses debated items from the dessert section. "That custard looks good," one said.

"Excuse me," I said. "Do any of you know a rehab aide named Theresa? She would be on her break now."

"Sorry, no," they answered.

I glanced behind me to see the security guard leaning through the door, his eyes scanning the cafeteria. I picked up a plate with a big piece of vanilla cake with chocolate frosting, grabbed a cup of water and tea bag from the coffee and tea station, and got in line to pay.

"Do you happen to know a nurse's aide named Theresa? She works in the new rehabilitation unit," I asked the cashier.

"Honey, I don't know where any of these people work. I only know the kitchen staff."

"Oh." "Listen," she said, ringing me up, "if you go around the corner, there's always a loud table of ladies. If anyone knows, they will."

I gave her my best smile and a nice tip, and carried my tray into the dining area, hoping the security guard hadn't spotted the direction I'd taken.

Around the corner were two long tables at which a group of nurses in white slacks and multicolored tops chatted with one another. A loud whoop went up from one table, and the group dissolved in laughter. Smiling, I slid my tray onto the table next to the last nurse and sat down. She gave me a quick look, shrugged, and turned back to her companions.

"Excuse me," I said. "I hope you don't mind my barging in. The cashier said you know everyone in the hospital, and I'm hoping you can help me find someone."

"I don't know everyone," the nurse next to me said, "but Margery probably does. Who are you looking for?"

"An aide named Theresa who works in the new rehabilitation wing. She was working with Carolyn the last time I was here."

"Hey, Marge, do you know an aide named Theresa?"

"You mean Theresa up in ICU?"

"No, an aide. In the new rehab unit? She works with—" She turned to me. "Who'd you say she works with?"

"Carolyn," I replied. "Carolyn's a nurse."

"Oh, yeah. I know Carolyn. The aide who works with Carolyn Helmer in rehab? Name's Theresa?"

"You mean her?" Marge said, pointing to a dark-haired woman two tables removed.

"That her?" the nurse next to me asked.

I nodded, hoping it was the Theresa I was looking for, thanked them, and asked, "Would anyone like my piece of cake?"

"Give it here. It won't last long at this table."

I left my cake and the cup of tea and walked to the table where Theresa sat reading a book. When I got closer, I saw that the book in her hands was one of mine.

"I believe I gave that book to Cliff Cooper," I said, taking the chair across the table from her. "Are you enjoying it?"

She smiled. "He gave it to me."

"I'm delighted he gave it to someone else to read. Do you like it?"

"So far."

"Oh, good. I wrote that book."

"You did?"

I nodded. "Cliff and I were old friends. I often gave him copies of my books when they came out."

"He was a nice man. I was sorry when he died."

"Yes, I was, too. I wonder if you wouldn't mind answering a few questions for me?"

She closed the book and looked at her watch. "I really don't have time to talk, Mrs.—"

"Fletcher. J. B. Fletcher." I pointed to the book.

"Oh, right. Mrs. Fletcher. I'm afraid I have to get back from my break."

"I promise I won't take up much of your time. Why don't we talk while we walk back to your unit?"

"Okay."

"I really appreciate your help. You see, Cliff's grandson is coming home soon. He hadn't seen him in some time, and I'd like to be able to tell him a little about how his grandfather spent his final days."

Theresa stood and tucked my book under her arm.

I glanced toward the cafeteria entrance. "Is there another exit closer to the rehab unit?" I asked.

"Actually, I usually use that one. Follow me." She led me through the eating area to a door on the far side, which enabled me to avoid the security guard.

"What would you like to know?" she asked when we reached the corridor and walked toward the rehabilitation unit.

"I was just wondering if you happened to notice who came to visit Cliff while he was a patient here. I know he turned away most people."

She gave me an odd look but thought about my question. "When I was there, he only had three visitors that I saw, except for Dr. Hazlitt and other doctors. Do you know Dr. Hazlitt?"

"Seth? Not only do I know him, but I'm due to meet him in a few minutes. I hate to be late and hope he'll forgive me if I am." I couldn't quicken my pace because Theresa took her time strolling down the hall. I matched my steps to hers, wishing she would move a little faster. "I'm sorry," I said. "You were saying Cliff had three visitors."

"No. I said I only **knew** about three visitors. I work one of the three shifts, evenings. I mean, if someone visited him in the morning, I wouldn't know about that person."

"Of course," I said, smiling. "I like your precision. You'd make an excellent witness."

"A witness?"

"Just thinking about trials I've attended. Judges and juries like witnesses to be precise. Please tell me a little about the three visitors you did notice. What were they like?"

"There was an old lady." She looked at me. "Older than you. Not that you're an old lady."

"I'm happy to hear that," I said.

"I guess she was about eighty or so. Tall, short gray hair. She walked very fast. That's what I noticed about her. I mean you don't think about old people walking that way. The ones I see here can barely walk at all. This lady, she just marched around like she owned the place."

"I think I know who that may be," I said, thinking her description fit Lettie Conrad. "Did she visit more than once?"

"I don't know. Maybe."

"Who else visited Cliff?"

"There was a guy who drove a motorbike."

"How did you know that?"

"He was carrying a helmet."

"Do you happen to recall the color of the helmet?"

"Black, I think."

"What was the man like?"

"Average height, I guess. I only saw him once, and Mr. Cooper didn't like seeing him. I could tell right away. His cough became worse. I didn't hear their conversation, but when I came in to take his vitals later—you know, his temperature and his pulse and his blood pressure—his blood pressure was way up. They must have had an argument, because Carolyn told me she had to ask him to leave."

"He came just once?"

"That's the only time I saw him."

"And who else?"

"Well, there was a young woman."

"How young?"

"My age, I'm guessing."

"And how old are you, if you don't mind my asking?"

"Twenty-eight last September. I'm a Virgo. We tend to be organized and analytical. Lots of nurses are Virgos."

"I didn't know that."

"What sign are you?"

"Um, I'm a Pisces, but I don't see..."

"You must be very imaginative."

"Well, I **am** a writer."

"And intuitive. Pisces is a very creative sign."

"Thank you, but we were talking about the people who visited Cliff Cooper. You mentioned a young woman. Can you describe her?"

"Not really."

"Why not?"

"Well, she was wearing sunglasses and a hat, kind of like the ones women wear who lose their hair from chemo. I don't know if that was the case, but her head was completely covered, so I couldn't tell you what color her hair was, if she had any."

"Then how did you know she was your age?"

"From her bracelet—it was a friendship bracelet like the kind I wore in high school. That pattern was very popular ten years ago."

"Would you recognize her if you saw her

again?"

She shook her head. "Only if she was wearing the same things. I don't pay attention to our patients' visitors as a rule."

"You've done very well, it seems to me."

We took the elevator up one level and walked down the hall toward the rehabilitation wing.

"One last question," I said as we entered the unit. "Were you on duty the day Cliff Cooper died?"

"Uh-huh. I work evenings, three to eleven. It's the busiest time, but that makes the shift go faster. Carolyn was the one who discovered that he had died. She was late getting to his room, and he was gone when she finally got there."

"Why was she late?"

"Someone had tripped over a medication cart and it fell over. It was pandemonium until we cleaned up all the pills fell on the floor, and then we had to refill all the prescriptions. Security had to block off the hallway, and visitors were upset. It was a mess. By the time Carolyn got to his room with his meds, he was gone."

"I understand," I said. "Do you recall if any of those visitors were here the day Cliff died?"

"I'm pretty sure that's when I saw the one wearing the hat." She shrugged. "Can't really say about the others."

"There you are," Seth called out. He and our sheriff stood next to the nurses' station. "I thought you hadn't gotten here yet. You didn't sign the book."

Chapter Thirteen

"I don't suppose there would be any fingerprints or other evidence left by his visitors," I said to Seth and Mort after I'd told them about my conversation with Theresa.

"No one understood that his room was the scene of a crime," Seth said. "It was disinfected and readied for another patient within hours. That's hospital policy. They wash down everything, blinds included."

"Well, let's see the crime scene anyway," Mort said. "Which room was he in?"

Seth pointed to a closed door. "That one, but…"

Mort opened the door and walked in before Seth was able to finish his sentence. Six startled faces looked up from a feast's worth of food arrayed in dishes that had been spread around the new patient occupying Cliff's former bed.

"Sorry," Mort said, tipping his hat to the family as he backed out of the room. He turned to Seth. "They're practically running a restaurant in there."

"Beats hospital food," Seth said. "I was about to tell you that there was another patient in Cliff's room."

"Well, if we can't see his room, what can we see here?" Mort said.

"We can ask to take a look at the visitors' book," I said, "although I'm pretty sure Cliff's assailant didn't sign in."

"No record of any visitors that day," Mort said. "I checked that first thing."

"But someone was in his room," I said. "It seems to me that whoever tipped over the medication cart might have wanted to create a diversion to keep the staff occupied while the murder took place, or maybe after."

"But he had no visitors. Are you suggesting someone on staff wanted him dead?" Seth asked.

"Not at all. I'm afraid that the lack of a visitor name doesn't mean very much. The hospital's security is far from efficient."

Mort looked at me sideways. "How do you know that, Mrs. F?"

"I tested it today and easily skipped the security procedures when the guard wasn't there. I walked around the hospital, and only one person demanded to see my pass, and even he let me go after some playacting on my part."

"I don't suppose anyone expected that a patient would be in danger while in a hospital room being monitored by doctors, nurses, aides, physical therapists, dietary workers, and the cleaning staff," Seth said.

"Okay, so the killer got in undetected. Did the deed," Mort said. "How did he get out without anyone seeing him?"

Seth said, "He might just as easily have waltzed down the hallway and gone outside after the medications were cleaned up and the staff was still distracted."

"Or he—or she—could have escaped into the hospital itself and gone out any convenient door," I said. "It's unlikely a security guard would challenge someone leaving and ask to see their visitor's pass."

Mort insisted I sign Security's book and clip on my visitor's badge this time. He stayed to talk with the guard while Seth and I continued down the hall.

"I was hoping hospital security would be tightened in the wake of this incident," I said.

"I'm sure it will be when we're able to discuss the situation openly," Seth said. "I called the administration's executive vice president to alert him to the need for stricter rules."

"Was he receptive?" I asked.

"Had to dance around the reason for my call until I'm cleared to tell him the truth. Kind of like shutting the barn door after the horse has run out, but what can you do?"

"Couldn't you tell him the reason, in confidence of course?"

"Our sheriff there said no, and I happen to agree. There's no such thing as 'in confidence' in a hospital. News spreads faster here than in Mara's Luncheonette. You didn't say anything to the aide, did you?"

"No! Of course not, and I don't think she

suspected why I was questioning her. I just told her I wanted to know about Cliff's last days so I could tell his grandson. Speaking of Elliot," I said when Mort had rejoined us, "does anyone have any idea when he's due?"

Seth shook his head. "For all I know, the boy's motorcycle broke down and he's hitchhiking here. Wouldn't surprise me. That family had the strangest ways. Don't know as I ever met his mother. Rumor was, his father, Jerry, kept her locked up because he was jealous of other men. Some said that's why he hauled her off to the jungle, where he could keep her all to himself."

"Wasn't Elliot born in Cabot Cove Hospital?" Mort asked.

"Heck, no. Don't even know if he was born in this country. Jerry and his wife showed up one day with their baby. Dropped him into Cliff's lap and took off again."

"And never came back?"

"If they did, I never saw them."

"You would think Cliff would look for them when they were gone such a long time," I said.

Seth shrugged. "I think by the time he learned that they were gone for good, their trail was cold. Frankly, I don't think he was that upset. He wanted to keep that boy—spoiled him rotten, that is, until the day he decided not to."

"When he sent Elliot off to boarding school."

"So I understand."

"What a difficult childhood for Elliot, never knowing if his parents were going to come back, both yearning for it and dreading it in equal measure."

"That's a sensitive analysis, Jessica, but we don't know if those thoughts ever crossed his mind. He was a wild child. That's what I remember."

We'd been talking as we walked through the hospital and down a set of stairs to the ground floor. We eventually reached a pair of metal doors quite a distance from the cafeteria. Seth held up his badge to a reader on the wall. A buzzer sounded, and we pulled open the doors and entered the morgue. A technician in a white uniform sat behind a high wall overlooking a small vestibule. The three of us signed our names in the logbook with the date and time.

The morgue had recently been renovated, and I looked around, curious to see what changes had been made. To the left, through a glass wall, was the new viewing room for families. It had low lighting and chairs and a small sofa upholstered in gray mohair. A square table between the sofa and chairs held a box of tissues. The glass wall was fitted with curtains that, open now, could be drawn to provide privacy for the family during a viewing.

"Will anybody be touching the body, Dr. Hazlitt?" the technician asked.

"I may."

"In that case, we'll want all of you gowned and gloved."

The technician unlatched the door to his area, and we were led past the viewing room, down a short corridor, and through another secured door into the autopsy room. It occurred to me that the hospital's security was tighter for the deceased than for the living patients in the rooms upstairs.

Seth, Mort, and I were each given blue paper gowns that tied in the back and a pair of latex gloves. The drawers holding the bodies could be opened from both ends. One end could be slid out into the viewing room for the purpose of family identifying the individual; the other end of the drawer could be pulled the full length of the body into the autopsy room where we stood. The morgue technician slid open the drawer holding Cliff's body.

Seth pulled back the sheet covering the body. "Proving homicidal asphyxiation is very difficult," he said. "I want to caution you that the courts could challenge our findings. But I'm convinced that these markings on the corpse indicate foul play." He pointed out the red dots on both the outside and inside of Cliff's eyelids, the bruising around the nostrils and lips, and the line where his lower teeth had cut into the soft tissue inside his mouth.

I've seen many bodies over the years, but it's not something you ever get used to—at least I don't. While the body may be thought of as simply the husk that held the organs, bones, and blood vessels, I am always acutely aware that this was once a living, breathing person with thoughts and feelings, someone loved or loving—if he or she was fortunate. And those who come to the morgue to view the body, or observe it lying in a coffin at a funeral home, don't consider what they see as simply a shell either. Instead, they invest the body with all the emotions and sentiments evoked when the person was alive.

Seth looked at Mort. "I'm planning to send the body back to the funeral home unless you need the morgue to hold it longer for some reason."

"Did you take photos of the bruising?" Mort asked.

"We documented all our findings, both by photograph and X-ray, followed a comprehensive checklist as required in a forensic postmortem," Seth said in clipped tones. "Apart from the delay in examination, we adhered to the model protocol meticulously."

I knew Seth was beating himself up about not calling for an immediate autopsy following Cliff's death, but he couldn't take offense at Mort's questions, much as he'd probably have liked to.

"Were there any defensive wounds?"

Seth shook his head. "The only thing we found were a few fibers caught in his fingernails. We sent the samples off for analysis."

"Were they the same color as the fibers that you found in his throat?" I asked.

"Yes. They were green."

"Do you have any idea where they came from?" Mort asked.

"I'm afraid I do."

"What's that?"

Seth covered Cliff's face and slid the drawer closed. "My best guess is that they came from a hospital uniform."

Chapter Fourteen

There is nothing more jarring and confusing than a phone ringing next to your bed at five a.m. The first few rings sounded distant to me, as though they came from another place, another house. But by the third ring there was no mistaking the origin—on my nightstand within a few feet of my ears.

"Hello?" I managed.

"Mrs. Fletcher?" a man's voice said.

"Who else would—yes, this is Jessica Fletcher."

"It's Barnaby, Mrs. Fletcher."

"Barnaby? Barnaby Longshoot?"

"Yes, ma'am, it's me, Barnaby. Hope I didn't wake you."

"As a matter of fact you did, Barnaby." I looked at the clock next to the phone. Five oh five. The dim light through my window confirmed that the sun still hadn't made an appearance.

"Didn't mean to, Mrs. Fletcher. I've been up for an hour—was planning to go fishin'. Best time for fishin' is right around sunup."

I pushed myself into a sitting position in the bed and rubbed my eyes with my free hand. "Do you mind if I ask why you're calling me at such an early hour, Barnaby?"

"Well, I wouldn't have, 'cept I thought you'd want to know."

"Know **what**?"

"That somebody's broken into the Spencer Percy House."

Now fully awake, I turned on the lamp on the nightstand. "Broken into the house, you say?"

"Yes, ma'am. Like I said, I was about to go fishin' and was walkin' past the Spencer Percy House when I saw it."

"You saw someone break in?"

"Not exactly, but somebody sure is in there, playin' music real loud, you know, that rock-and-roll kind of music. Plenty of lights on, too."

"Have you called the police?"

"No, ma'am. I thought that since you've been sort of in charge of getting the house ready for Miss Simpson to sell and all, and going through everything, that you were the one to call."

I started to say something in response, but he added, "Besides, Mrs. Fletcher, everybody knows that you know a lot about such things."

"I do?"

"You know, crimes and such."

"Oh. Yes. Well, Barnaby, as much as I appreciate your thinking of me, the next call you make should be to the police."

"Wouldn't want to get involved with the police, Mrs. Fletcher. The sheriff, he's got a short fuse as everybody knows and—"

"All right," I said, eager to end the conversation, "I'll call the sheriff's office."

"That'd be great, Mrs. Fletcher. Sorry I woke you. I figured you were always up early writing your books and all."

"That's all right, Barnaby. Have a good day."

I got up, slipped on my bathrobe and slippers, and padded to the kitchen, where

I turned on the lights and took a few seconds to finish clearing my thoughts. Once I had, I used the phone to call police headquarters, where the deputy on duty answered. I explained who I was and told him about a break-in having been reported at the Spencer Percy House. I was quick to add that there probably was a logical explanation for it but thought I should report it.

"You're down around that house at this hour, Mrs. Fletcher?" the deputy asked.

"No. Barnaby Longshoot called to tell me about what he saw, loud music and lights on, and—"

The deputy laughed. "Good ol' Barnaby," he said. "He sure is some character."

"Yes, well—"

"I'll send somebody over there to take a look," he said. "May be just some kids having themselves a party."

"You're probably right," I said. "Thank you."

It occurred to me after hanging up that Eve Simpson should be notified in the event someone was in the house and possibly causing damage. But it was too early to call her at home, and her office wouldn't open for another three hours. Now wide awake, I made myself a cup of coffee, shook cereal into a bowl, added sliced banana, poured in some two-percent milk, and enjoyed a very early breakfast before showering and getting dressed.

The sun was now over the horizon, providing light as I climbed on my bicycle and pedaled in the direction of the sea-coast where the Spencer Percy House cast a long shadow over the bluff above the beach. I thought of the rumors about the house being haunted, and had to smile as I envisioned the ghost—if there was one—playing loud rock-and-roll music as Barnaby had reported. Either that or who-ever was playing the music had probably driven any ghosts far from the premises.

A Cabot Cove patrol car was parked in the driveway when I arrived, but there was no sign of the officer who'd driven it. I leaned my bike against a tree and looked at the house's imposing front façade. Barnaby had been right. Rock-and-roll music was coming through open windows, and I heard male voices but couldn't make out the substance of their conversation.

You really have no business being here, I told myself. But since I was, I decided to make my presence known. As I passed the patrol car, I noticed a large red motorcycle parked to the side. It was a lethal-looking machine resting on its kickstand with a red and yellow helmet hanging from one of the handlebars. Even though I had the key to the front door in my shoulder bag, I knocked. From inside I heard the same voices, louder this time, and the sound of footsteps. The door opened, and I was face-to-face with one of Sheriff Metzger's veteran deputies, an old friend.

"Hello, Mrs. Fletcher," he said. "Surprised to see you here at this hour."

"Good morning, Henry. I was the one who called in the report about someone being here," I said. "Since I was already awake, I—"

"Come on in."

He stepped aside to allow me to enter. Inside, the music was considerably louder. It came from upstairs.

"Who's playing that music?" I asked, raising my voice to be heard.

"Elliot Cooper," the deputy shouted back, "old Cliff Cooper's grandson."

"He's here?"

"He surely is. At first I figured it to be some teenagers having a party, but turns out it's just him."

"How did he get in?" I asked.

"I asked him the same question, Mrs. Fletcher. He showed me a window around the side that he said he used to go in and out of when he lived here as a kid. No question about who he is—got lots of ID. He rode all the way here from Alaska on that hog out front."

"Hog?"

"Motorcycle."

"Right. I saw it when I arrived. I'd like to meet him."

"Be my guest. I'm just leaving."

"I'm sorry to have gotten you out for no reason."

"No problem. Turned out to be a wild-goose chase, but better safe than sorry, I always say. You have yourself a good day, Mrs. Fletcher."

The deputy left, and I stood at the foot of the staircase leading to the upper floors. It dawned on me that seeing a strange woman suddenly appear might unnerve Elliot Cooper, and I considered yelling before ascending the stairs. But I wasn't sure whether my voice would be heard over the raucous music, so I went up, reached the landing, and found the bedroom where a young man was playing a guitar in sync with the recorded music—except there was no guitar. What was it called when someone pretended to hold a guitar? Air guitar. Yes, that was it. He was playing an "air guitar."

"Excuse me," I called out. I wasn't sure if he heard me. I waited in the doorway until his gyrations caused him to turn in my direction. I waved with both hands.

He stopped twisting and turning and smiled.

"Hello," I shouted.

"Hi," he said.

"Could you turn down that music, please?"

"What?"

"The music. Could you turn it down or

off?"

He nodded and, still bouncing up and down, reached out to turn a dial on the portable CD player. Now, there was silence.

I entered the room and extended my hand. "Good morning. I'm Jessica Fletcher," I said, "and you're Elliot Cooper. I was a friend of your grandfather."

"You were? He had a lot of friends, I guess."

"Yes, he was well liked. You've come all the way from Alaska."

He grinned. "Finally got here."

"Welcome home," I said, even though I wasn't sure that he still considered Cabot Cove his home.

"That was always the great thing about this house," he said.

"What was?"

"You could play your music as loud as you wanted and there were no neighbors close enough to complain. That's how it used to be anyway. Did I disturb you?"

"Me? Oh, no, I don't live nearby. I can't speak for the Conrad sisters, though."

"They never minded my music. Or so they told me. Of course, by now, they're probably a bit hard of hearing." That prompted another smile, wider this time.

I took the opportunity to take him in more closely. He was a handsome young man, slightly more than six feet tall, and with a full head of thick black hair, its color matching his scraggly beard. He wore jeans, a tee shirt with a psychedelic swirl of red and yellow, and what appeared to be tall military boots laced all the way up, probably handy footwear when riding a large motorcycle.

He seemed amused by my perusal. "Do I pass?" he asked.

"I beg your pardon?"

"Do I pass your inspection?"

I smiled. "You do. But I recommend you get used to it. People in town haven't seen you since you were a young teenager, and they're likely to search your face for the boy they once knew."

"Yeah. I figured that might happen."

"How was your trip here?"

"It was great as long as the weather was okay. And a sticky clutch held me up for a while. Had to get it replaced."

"I can't imagine coming such a distance

on a motorcycle."

"Piece o' cake," he said.

"Especially from such a cold place as Alaska," I added.

"It's not that cold this time of year unless you're up in the mountains."

"Do you like living there?"

"Sure. I live in Sitka. It's a seaside town not unlike Cabot Cove. Funny, I never thought of that until now. But it's also different in that there's lots of room to stretch out once you get beyond the shops. Lots of hiking and camping. You can be very happy by yourself. If Grandpa Cliff hadn't died, I'd still be there."

"You never thought about a trip home to see him?"

"I invited him to come visit me."

"Did he ever go?" I asked, but I knew the answer.

"He said he would think about it, but I knew what that meant. It meant he didn't want to turn me down outright, so he pretended a visit was under consideration. But I saw right through him."

"Mind if I sit down?" I asked.

"Oh, sure." He pointed to a small

upholstered chair, which I took. He remained standing.

I wasn't sure where to take the conversation and decided to talk with him about the house. "It must seem strange coming back to this house where you grew up, Elliot."

"Yeah, it is a little, only I didn't really grow up here. I mean, I was a baby when my folks left. Grandpa Cliff brought me up until—well, until he lost patience with me, I guess." He chuckled. "He got annoyed with something I did and sent me off to boarding school to get straightened out, as he put it." He paused as though gathering his thoughts about having been sent away. "I was pretty angry when Grandpa Cliff did that," he said, "but I got over it. I liked being on my own and still do. He meant well, thought it would be best for me. It actually turned out pretty good, got me reading a lot of good books. I'm even writing a novel."

"That's wonderful," I said. "I'm a writer, too."

"Yeah. I thought your name was familiar. Some friends back in Alaska have all your books."

"I'm happy to hear that."

He pulled up a faded red leather hassock and sat. "Listen. I have to ask you a question."

"Shoot."

"Is it true that somebody killed Grandpa Cliff?" he asked.

"I, ah—well, it appears that someone did. Who told you?"

"The attorney, Mr. Kramer. I contacted him yesterday to let him know I'd be arriving. He said he had something important to discuss with me when we met. I never was very good at waiting for anything. I'm not very patient. I nagged him until he told me the news." He fixed his large gray eyes on me. "I hope they catch whoever did it."

"I'm sure they will," I said, though I didn't know if I was answering honestly.

We talked for another fifteen minutes before I said, "Well, I'd better be going. It was nice meeting you, Elliot. I'm sure we'll get a chance to spend more time together while you're here."

"That'd be nice," he said.

I asked while we headed downstairs, "Will you be staying here at the house?"

"That's my plan," he said.

"It is, after all, your house now. Your grandfather left it to you."

"Not quite," he said. "He left a will instructing that the house be sold and that I get the money from it."

I almost mentioned that I'd been the one who'd helped his grandfather draft the crude will, but I didn't. Instead, I told him about the plans to sell his grandfather's books to benefit the library.

He laughed. "You know, I think he probably would have loved that idea. He never knew what to do with a book when he finished it. I hope you don't mind if I move the boxes out of the kitchen. It's getting a little crowded in there."

"The kitchen?" I said. "I don't recall leaving boxes in the kitchen."

"Well, they're there now. Nearly killed myself trying to get to the refrigerator."

"May I see?" I said, hurrying to the kitchen to find boxes scattered around the floor and piled up against one wall.

"I'll stack them up. I hope that's okay."

"Of course," I said. "But I never left these here." I opened the flap of one of the boxes and peered inside. It contained a stack of woodworking magazines. Another was filled with medical volumes. "These were on the bookshelves in the basement," I said. "The handyman must have packed them up."

"Well, that was nice of him. Saved you some work."

"Have you met him yet?"

"The handyman?" He shook his head. "Haven't seen him around. What's his name?"

"Tony Tonelero," I said.

"Haven't even met Miss Simpson," he said, "but Mr. Kramer said he'd bring her by soon."

"You know, or perhaps you don't, there's a rumor going around that the house is haunted."

Elliot laughed. "When I was little, I used to think my mother came and read me bedtime stories."

"What a lovely memory."

"It was, for a while. Stupidly, I told Grandpa Cliff about the lady who visited me at night and who I thought she was. He said my mother was dead and I should forget about her."

"That wasn't very sensitive of him, was it?"

Elliot shook his head. "What can I say? He did the best he could for an old man stuck with raising a little kid. Must've been tough bringing up yet another rambunctious Cooper and this time without the help of Grandma Nanette. I don't carry any grudges." He was quiet for a moment. "But you know, she never came back after he said that."

"Who's that?"

"My mother, the ghost."

We said good-bye and I left, aware that he was watching me from the doorway as I climbed onto my bike and pedaled down the driveway. My thoughts at that moment were that despite being abandoned as an infant by his parents, being brought up by his grandfather, and then being shipped off to a boarding school, he seemed like a very put-together young man.

I also decided that he should know more

about his parents and their disappearance in the jungles of South America. And so should I. Perhaps that information would provide a clue as to who wanted to see Cliff dead. Surely there were people in Cabot Cove who'd been around long enough to know something of this mysterious couple whose son I'd just met. The town historian, Tim Purdy, had shared what he knew. But I was betting that Lucy and Lettie Conrad possessed a lot more information about Elliot's parents than was common knowledge.

Chapter Fifteen

Beth Conrad answered the door when I rang the bell at her great-aunts' home across the road from Cliff Cooper's place.

Tim Purdy had speculated that the Conrad twins' cottage might have been the gatehouse for the Spencer Percy House at one point. It had been built in the nineteenth century, but it was of a later vintage, probably sometime after the Civil War, possibly when Abner Nessier, the lumber baron, had occupied the larger building. The road between the two structures had been paved in the twentieth century when a developer bought the adjacent parcel on one side of the historic house, intending to put up several smaller houses for veterans returning home after World War II. He never got the financing, and the land remained vacant. The few houses on Cliff's side of the street had a view of the ocean, although they had only part-time access to the water when the tide washed against the rocky shore many feet below the bluff. The houses on the same side of the street as the Conrads' house lacked a clear view but had the benefit of less wind off the ocean, although not a lot less. I'd been buffeted by the currents of air the whole time I'd pedaled my bicycle down the peninsula to the Spencer Percy House.

"Hi, Mrs. Fletcher. We weren't expecting you. Aunt Lettie and Aunt Lucy went into town this morning," Beth said. "I'm not sure how long they'll be. It could be quite some time."

"I should have called before I disturbed you," I said, sighing. "I'm thinking I may need to replace my bike seat with one that has a little more padding if I'm going to continue taking these long trips. Do you mind if I sit with you and rest a little before I ride back?"

She glanced behind her. "No. Of course not. Come in."

I wondered if she knew that Elliot had arrived, but I hesitated to be the one to tell her.

"I hope I'm not interrupting anything important," I said.

"Not at all." She swung the door wide and invited me to enter. "How is the book sorting going? I'm sorry I haven't had time to help you out again."

"It's going reasonably well," I said, looking around the cozy living room. A Christmas tree quilt was folded on a chair. There was a crocheted afghan bunched up on one side of the chintz sofa, as if Beth had kicked it off to answer my ring. A pamphlet was open facedown on the cushion. I angled my head to see what it was she'd been reading, but Beth scooped it up, closed it, and slid it under a magazine on the coffee table.

"Please excuse the mess here." She smoothed the afghan and laid it across the arm of the sofa.

"Nothing to excuse. I'm the one who barged in uninvited." I sank down on the cushion and unbuttoned my jacket. I chuckled. "It feels good to be seated on something soft."

"Would you like some tea or coffee?"

"No need to fuss for me. Come sit with me and tell me how everything is going."

"It's no fuss," she said, hurrying toward the kitchen. "Aunt Lucy made cookies the other day. I'll put some on a plate." I heard her open and close a cupboard.

I leaned forward and pushed the magazine to the side. "Are your aunts well?" I called out. The cover of the brochure had a color photograph of snowcapped mountains beyond a village on the edge of a bay. Across the top in script was the banner **Visiting Sitka.** "I was expecting to see them at Cliff's house the other day, but the weather was terrible. I certainly understand if they didn't want to venture out in that rain." I slid the magazine over the brochure again as Beth carried in the cookies.

"Actually, Aunt Lucy has a little cold."

"I'm sorry to hear it."

"It might be contagious, you know," she said, looping a finger into her bracelet and twisting the string. "Are you sure you want to stay?"

"I'm not going to be here long. I'm surprised Lettie didn't insist that Lucy remain at home."

Beth placed the plate on top of the magazine and laid a folded napkin next to it. "Oh, she tried, but Aunt Lucy wanted to go. She gets restless if she stays in the house too long, and she needed to get out a little." She shifted her weight from one foot to the other.

"Aren't you going to sit down?"

"Oh, sure." She grabbed a sugar cookie off the plate and sat at the edge of a wing chair.

"I wanted to thank you again for the signs you made for the book sale," I said, taking a cookie.

"Oh, no thanks are needed. It's a worthwhile cause, and I'm happy to help."

"I really stopped by to see Lettie and Lucy, but while I have you here, do you mind if I ask you a question?"

"Me? Sure. I guess. What do you need to know?"

"I'm not sure how to ask this," I said.

"'Straight ahead' is what Aunt Lettie always says."

"And she's right, so I'll be direct. Cliff Cooper didn't allow many people to visit him when he was in the hospital, but I understand that he did see you."

"Oh, no, you're wrong, Mrs. Fletcher. I never went to see Grandpa Cliff. Aunt Lucy told me not to."

"That's funny," I said. "One of the nurse's aides identified you."

"How could she possibly...I mean, I wasn't there."

"You mean, how did she know it was you wearing a hat and big sunglasses?"

Beth curled her shoulders in, seeming to collapse in on herself.

I pointed to her string bracelet. "She said there was a woman wearing a friendship bracelet just like yours."

Beth twisted her finger around the string again. "I shouldn't still be wearing this. It doesn't mean anything anymore."

I thought that it still meant a great deal to her, but I didn't contradict her statement.

She gave a big sigh. "Please don't say anything, Mrs. Fletcher. I wasn't supposed to go. I mean, I don't think Grandpa Cliff even knew I was there. I thought if I could catch him when he was awake, I could talk to him about allowing Aunt Lucy to see him. She was so upset that he shut her out. Before he got sick, he was talking about their getting married."

"I didn't realize they were still considering marriage."

"He wanted to move in here. Of course, Aunt Lettie wasn't happy about that. She said if he wanted to marry Lucy, he could bring her to his own house. But you've seen what that place looks like. Aunt Lucy would never have lived in that mess."

"So you're saying Cliff Cooper didn't know you'd come to see him?"

"I was in his room less than a minute. He was sleeping, and I was afraid to wake him. Then I had second thoughts about being there at all. When I left, I thought I saw Aunt Lettie coming in."

"Was it Lettie?"

"It was just a fleeting glance. I can't be sure. I got spooked and hid in the ladies' room down the hall. I waited awhile and sneaked out when no one was looking. There was a big commotion over something that fell down. I didn't think anyone saw me."

We heard voices coming up the path, then a key in the lock of the front door and laughter.

Beth looked at the door in alarm. "Please don't say anything, Mrs. Fletcher," she said, her eyes pleading with me.

"You have my word," I said. "For now."

The door swung open, and Lettie and Lucy spilled into the house, their arms entwined with Elliot's.

"Look who we found walking on the road," Lettie called out.

"Doesn't he look handsome?" Lucy said, giggling. She touched her hair as if she were a young girl preening for him.

"We went to the pharmacy as you requested, but it wasn't open yet," Lettie said.

I looked at Beth. The blood had drained from her face. It occurred to me that she might have been hoping to have a private reunion with Elliot. She must have heard him playing his loud music. The cottage was just across the road from his house, and he'd had the windows thrown open. Perhaps that was his signal to her that he was home.

"Hello, Beth. You've certainly grown up since the last time I saw you."

"I wouldn't have recognized you with a beard if Aunt Lucy hadn't shown me your picture on Facebook."

Elliot smoothed a hand over his scruffy beard. "I guess a beard's not as popular in Cabot Cove as it is in Sitka. You think I should shave?"

"I? I don't have any opinion on whether or not you should shave. What does your fiancée think about it?"

Elliot chuckled. "So you heard about her?"

Lucy suddenly noticed my presence. "Jessica! What are you doing here? I was so captivated by Elliot, I didn't even see you sitting there."

"I just stopped by for a moment," I said, "and Beth was entertaining me."

"Let me introduce you to our beautiful boy. This is Elliot"—she hesitated—"Cooper."

"Hardly a boy, Aunt Lucy. And probably not very beautiful right now. But Mrs. Fletcher has beaten your time. I've already met her this morning. She came by to tell me how wonderful my music is." He winked at me.

"We're already old friends," I said, stealing a glance at Beth, who looked ill.

"Are you feeling all right, Beth?" Lettie asked. "I didn't think you really needed that medicine, but now I'm not so sure."

"I'm—I'm just fine," Beth said.

"Well, I could use a cup of tea," I said. "I've been up since five o'clock."

"What on earth got you up so early?" Lettie asked.

"If you make me some tea, I'll tell you my tale of woe," I said, herding the sisters ahead of me into their own kitchen.

I heard Elliot in the living room speaking to Beth: "Wow! You're still wearing our friendship bracelet?"

"Let go of my arm, please."

"Sorry."

"What happened to yours?"

"When I first got to Alaska, I got work in a logging camp and the foreman made me get rid of it."

"Oh? You had it that long?"

"He was afraid it would catch in the

machinery and take off my hand."

"How awful."

"I hated to cut it off, but I still have what's left of it. I carry it in my wallet."

The front door closed behind the young couple as they went outside. I sat at the kitchen table with the twins. I'd been asked not to talk about Cliff's death. But we could talk about the past. I was hoping, with Cliff gone, that they'd be willing to disclose some of the family skeletons kept closeted all these years.

Chapter Sixteen

"So Barnaby heard Elliot's music and was sure someone had broken in," I said, summing up the story of my early-morning telephone call and bicycle ride to the Spencer Percy House.

"I hope he doesn't play alarm clock for you again," Lettie said.

"I hope so, too."

I'd promised Beth that I wouldn't tell the sisters that she'd been to see Cliff at the hospital, and while I wanted to ask Lettie about her visit, I thought I'd wait for a time when I could speak with her privately.

"Beth must've known what it meant the second she heard the music," Lettie said.

"They make a nice couple, don't they?" Lucy said, an approving smile on her face. "We always wanted them to be together."

She filled my cup from the teapot on the table.

"Let's not forget he's engaged to someone else," Lettie said. "He's very charming like his grandfather, but I don't want Beth to get hurt." She sat ramrod straight in a chair, her hands folded on her lap and a stern expression on her face.

"It's too bad that Elliot had to come all the way to Cabot Cove because of Cliff's unfortunate death," I said.

"Those things happen," Lettie said matter-of-factly.

"I'm sorry that Cliff isn't alive to see the fine young man that Elliot has become." Lucy's eyes filled with tears. "I'm so sorry."

"Nothing to do about that. When it's your time, it's your time," Lettie said.

"Just like Amos," Lucy said, wiping her eyes.

"Who's Amos?" I asked.

"Our cat," Lucy replied. "He had arthritis and a terrible limp."

"Jessica isn't interested in our cat, Lucy."

"Oh, sorry."

"What happened to the cat?" I asked.

"We had to put him down. He was

suffering. Animals shouldn't suffer," Lucy said.

"That was very kind of you both," I said. "It must have been difficult."

"Often doing the right thing is difficult."

"Speaking of the right thing, how long had it been since Elliot came to visit Cliff?" I asked.

"Too long," Lettie said. "That young man owed Cliff for having raised him the way he did. It wouldn't have hurt if he'd come home now and then to see his grandfather. Going off to Alaska was a slap in Cliff's face."

"Oh, no," Lucy said. "Cliff understood. You know how he was. He believed that every young man should strike out on his own."

The noise her sister made almost sounded like a snort.

"Did he encourage Elliot's father to travel, too?" I asked, happy to have the opportunity to introduce the topic.

"He might have," Lucy said. "I don't remember."

"Probably did," Lettie inserted. "Cliff's son, Jerry, was a brooder, never had a smile, stayed in the house instead of out playing with the other boys. Cliff's wife, Nanette, always worried about him."

"He was very studious," Lucy countered. "And I think he was crushed when his mother died. It's hard for a boy to lose his mother. I don't think Cliff understood how much her death affected him."

"He didn't have a lot of patience with Jerry, it's true," Lettie said. "I think Cliff was relieved when his son went off to college."

"What did Jerry study in college?" I asked.

"Anthro...anthro ...," Lucy said, "What was it?"

"Anthropology. Only he never completed his degree," Lettie said scornfully. "A waste of Cliff's money."

"What about Jerry's wife? Wasn't she interested in anthropology, too?"

"That was a strange pair if there ever was one," said Lettie.

"Now, Lettie, she wasn't that bad." Lucy poured more tea into my cup.

Lettie ignored her sister's comment and continued. "When Jerry came back from college with **her** on his arm, I thought Cliff would drop dead on the spot."

"Her?" I said.

"Marina," Lettie said. "She'd hooked Jerry around her little finger with her big sad eyes and pouty mouth. Poor Cliff. It was bad enough that his son had taken up with Marina, but the fact that they'd gotten married on the sly by some justice of the peace was the final stake in Cliff's heart."

"More tea, Jessica?" Lucy asked.

"Thank you, no," I said. "Where did they live?"

"With Cliff, of course," Lucy said, "in his house."

"Did Jerry work?" I asked.

"For the short time he and Marina were living there," Lettie said. "Cliff always said that Jerry had the makings of a good carpenter and wanted him to go into business with him."

"Did they?" I asked. "Go into business together?"

"Jerry wasn't very good at talking to people," Lucy said. "Isn't that right, Lettie?"

"Yes."

"He stayed home and did some of the woodworking in the workshop behind the house."

"They must have had groceries delivered and ordered things from catalogues," Lettie added. "The only time I saw Jerry was when he'd be walking from the house to the barn in back, and Marina almost never left the house as I recall."

"What did she do all day?" I asked.

"Ha!" Lettie said. "She did nothing. Word had it that she spent her days reading about exotic, faraway places and dreaming about going to them. She got Jerry all excited about it, too. They never would have gone to South America if it weren't for her hold on him."

"Elliot's birth must have put a crimp into those plans," I offered.

Lettie and Lucy looked at each other as though trying to decide who should answer, and what to say. It was Lucy who finally spoke. "No one knew that Marina was pregnant."

"No one? Not even you two, who lived so close?"

"No one!" Lettie confirmed emphatically.

"They never went out together, never went to a restaurant or for a walk through town."

Lucy nodded. "They were like a—well, like a—"

"A mystery couple?" I said.

"Yes, a mystery couple," she said, smiling. "Like in the books you write."

"All we knew was that they'd gone away," Lettie put in. "I asked Cliff about it, and he said that they were taking a little vacation, but he didn't say where they'd gone. Then, they arrived back with little Elliot."

"So Cliff knew that Marina was pregnant," I said.

"He had to know," Lettie said. "I'm sure that's why Jerry married her in the first place."

The front door opened, and Elliot and Beth crowded into the kitchen, interrupting my questioning of the sisters.

"Have a nice walk?" Lucy asked them.

"Yeah, it's so warm down here in the lower forty-eight," Elliot said, yawning. "Makes me sleepy."

"Does the town seem the same as when you left it?" I asked.

"Haven't had time to see the whole town. Around here nothing's really changed, I guess," Elliot said. "Looks pretty much the same, especially you lovely ladies. You haven't aged a day."

"Oh, my goodness, what a charmer." Lucy waved a hand in front of her face.

Elliot grinned. "Now, Beth here. She's changed a lot."

"I just grew up, same as you."

"You grew up prettier than me, though."

Beth's face grew flushed. "And you're more of a flirt than you ever were."

"I'm getting in a lot of practice. Used to be twice as many men in Alaska as women, but these days it's a lot more even. You need to sharpen your skills to attract the opposite sex."

"What about your fiancée?" Lettie asked. "Does she like your flirting with the opposite sex?"

"She's pretty good at flirting, too. Found herself another man she likes even better than me. So it's okay if I flirt with the lovely Miss Conrad here. Right, Beth?"

Beth stared down at her shoes. Elliot must have told her that he wasn't engaged anymore.

"Just remember, he lives in Alaska," Lettie said to Beth.

Beth rolled her eyes. "Aunt Lettie, we're just talking. We have a lot of years to catch up on."

He looked at his watch. "And you'll have to excuse me now. I have to get into town and meet with the lawyer before I fall asleep on my feet. Good seeing everyone again. Bye."

"I'll walk you out," Beth said, probably eager to escape an interrogation from her great-aunts.

Lucy waited until she heard the door close. "He certainly has grown into a fine young man. Did I already say that?"

"Don't get your hopes up about Elliot and Beth," her sister said. "For sure, he's going back to Alaska after the funeral. Wanderlust runs in that family."

"Is that why Jerry and Marina left? Wanderlust?" I asked.

"Well, they insisted that they were scientists, but you couldn't tell it by me," Lettie said.

"When did Elliot's parents leave Cabot

Cove for South America?"

Lucy answered, "Actually, we didn't know that they'd left until after the fact. Right, Lettie?"

"Right. I spoke with Cliff one day, and he told me that they were gone and had left their child with him to be raised." She put her hand on Lucy's when she said to me, "Cliff didn't seem to resent being left with the baby, but we could tell that deep down it distressed him plenty."

"We tried to help," Lucy said, tearing up again, "but a toddler was more than we could handle."

"We did the right thing," Lettie told her. "We weren't related to him or the child. It wasn't our place to help raise Elliot." She turned her gaze to me. "Cliff hired a couple of nursing students to take care of Elliot, two shifts, day and night. Must have cost him a fortune. And one of them got very attached to the baby, began ordering Cliff around and making noises about how she should be Elliot's mother." She looked at her sister. "You know, she was pursuing him again in the hospital."

"Who was?" I asked.

"That little nurse who took care of Elliot when he was a baby. Always did have her hopes pinned on Cliff. He only had eyes for Lucy, of course."

"Did he keep her on?" I asked.

"No. By that time he could manage without them. Got rid of the nurses and took over Elliot's upbringing himself."

"And did very well with our help," Lucy put in.

"And a few teenage babysitters," Lettie added.

"Did Cliff have any idea when Jerry and Marina left that they would never return?" I asked.

Lucy picked up the teapot, then put it down. "Did you know, they kind of sneaked off without telling him?"

"He didn't drive them to the airport himself?" I asked.

Lucy shook her head. "Cliff said they left him a note saying where they were going and that they'd be in touch. He was sure that they'd be returning, but then—"

I waited for her to finish.

"Then the word got back that they'd been killed by a band of savages in South

America," Lettie put in. "There was a short piece about it in the newspaper at the time."

Lucy dabbed at her eyes with a tissue. "I remember reading it and asking Cliff about it. Naturally, I waited a decent amount of time until I broached it with him. He was broken up, of course, but Cliff was made of steel. I was so proud of him. He said that what was important was that he and Elliot move ahead with their lives."

Lettie displayed her first smile of the morning. "Yes," she said, "that was Cliff all right. They don't make men like him anymore."

Chapter Seventeen

I thanked the Conrad twins for giving me their time, left the house, and rode my bike into town, where I stopped in at Tim Purdy's office. When not acting as the town's historian, Tim managed farmland in other states from his room on the top floor of a three-story office building.

"Hello, Tim," I said, knocking on the frame of his open door. "Can you spare a minute?"

"For you, Jessica, more than a minute." He saved the document he was working on and swiveled in his chair to face me. "Please have a seat." He waved at an extra chair next to his desk. "What can I do for you?"

"I thought you'd like to know that Elliot Cooper has arrived."

"Wonderful! Now the funeral can go forward, I assume."

"Yes. I'm hoping for that, too."

"Was that all you wanted to tell me?"

"No," I said. "Remember when we were talking about Cliff Cooper's son, Jerry, and his wife?"

"Yes, and I finally found a photo of the young man for you. Did you misplace it?"

"No, I have it right here," I said, patting my shoulder bag. "I know it's many years ago, but I understand there was a report in the paper announcing the young couple's deaths at the hands of a tribe they were supposed to be studying. Do you remember that?"

"As I told you, it was the prevailing story, but I'm still a bit skeptical."

"Why would you doubt the story?"

"I don't know if you recall what the **Gazette** used to be like. It wasn't a full-fledged newspaper at all, simply an attempt on the publisher's part to come up with local news, more scandal sheet than information. She printed whatever anyone gave her, verbatim, misspellings and all."

"And you think Cliff gave her the story?"

"In all likelihood."

"And you weren't sure it was true?"

"It wasn't just me. But I have to say, even though Cliff didn't ask, I took it upon myself to scan the national newspapers." He leaned back in his chair.

"And?"

"And I never saw any reference to scientists or even plain Americans being murdered in South America. Don't you think that would have been a newsworthy event?"

"I do, but why would Cliff have lied about such a thing?"

"I don't know that he did. Might be that Jerry trumped up a story so that he and his wife wouldn't have to come back, do some real work, raise their own child. They may be dead anyway for all I know. All kinds of contagion in those places."

"Lucy Conrad said Cliff had no idea that they were planning to go to South America. He found a note they left for him. What I'm trying to figure out is how they got away without his knowing."

"Probably the same way you get around town."

"By bicycle?"

Tim chuckled. "No, I meant by cab. It would have been a long trip to the airport on a bicycle with two people and their luggage. Makes quite a picture, doesn't it?"

"By cab, of course. They could have arranged to be picked up at the end of the driveway, and if they left in the middle of the night, Cliff might never have known they'd slipped out until the baby woke him in the morning."

"You have to admire the man. Cliff Cooper simply took up the responsibility of caring for his grandson and went about his business. Not an easy task. Pardon me if I sound sexist, but it must've been especially difficult without a woman to help."

"Men can be just as nurturing as women." My reply was automatic, but my mind was already skating ahead to where I could find out if Jerry and Marina used a taxi in their escape from Cabot Cove. My usual driver, Dimitri, was too young to have had a driver's license that many years ago. But the business had been founded by his father, an old friend of mine in both senses of the word "old."

I thanked Tim for his time and trotted down the three flights of stairs. My bicycle was leaning against the side of his building, but I'd had enough of pedaling for the day. I would pick it up later. I dialed the taxi service, and Dimitri arrived in short order. He was surprised when I asked to be taken to his father's house.

Dimitri Cassis Sr. was the paternalistic head of a family that had emigrated from Greece to the United States many years ago. They'd initially settled in New York City, where the elder Dimitri found work driving a taxi on the chaotic streets of Manhattan. But one summer, the Cassis clan, which included Dimitri, his wife, Eva, and their two children, took a week's vacation to escape the city's hot, muggy weather. They drove to Maine, where they spent five days in Cabot Cove.

Dimitri fell in love with the town—he saw parallels between it and the Greek coastal city they'd left—and by that fall, he and his family had packed up their apartment in the Astoria section of the New York City borough of Queens, and bought a small house in a development that had sprung up on the outskirts of town. Not without ambition or imagination, Dimitri saw an opportunity to provide Cabot Cove with something it didn't have, a cab company, which also provided a way to support his family.

Dimitri's Taxi Service was born. And it grew. Dimitri expanded to launch a shuttle service to Boston's Logan Airport, and he established a driving school that flourished under a contract with the local school district. Everyone in the family pitched in. They not only helped run the business; they became active in a variety of civic affairs.

For me, Dimitri and his taxi company were particularly important. I don't drive a car and never have, and I've depended for many years upon Dimitri and his friendly drivers, including his cousin, Nick, and his son, Dimitri Jr., to take me places beyond the capabilities of my trusty bicycle.

The elder Dimitri was retired—although he could always be counted on to don his chauffeur's hat in a pinch—and enjoyed his days of relative leisure, playing golf, fishing from his twenty-two-foot Aquasport boat, and cooking Greek delicacies. He was in the midst of making his signature dish, spinach pie in phyllo pastry, when I knocked on his door that afternoon.

"Ah, Mrs. Fletcher, my best and favorite customer. My wife will be distressed that she missed you. Come in, come in. Sit down. A glass of Metaxa? Coffee? Tea?"

"Nothing, thank you, Dimitri. I won't be staying long."

"Stay as long as you wish, provided you don't mind my keeping an eye on the oven. I don't want to burn the spanakopita."

"I won't mind at all," I said as I sat at his kitchen table and breathed in the wonderful aroma of the dish he was lovingly creating.

"So," he said, "I hope that you didn't come with a complaint about the service. Sometimes Dimitri runs a little late, and I have been lecturing him about it. He is a good son, but, you know, today's young people sometimes do things differently than the older generation."

I laughed. "No, no complaints, Dimitri.

Actually I'm here to test your memory."

"My memory? Ah, it is not as good as it once was."

"That makes two of us."

"I remember the past, yes, but not what I had for breakfast yesterday."

"Then we're both in luck," I said, "because what I need is a little history from you."

He sat across from me and grinned. He was a stocky fellow with a broad, square face, a full head of hair the color and texture of steel wool, and a ready laugh. He was the sort of man you immediately felt comfortable with.

"Dimitri, you've been driving people in Cabot Cove for many years."

"Too many, maybe. After so many years behind the wheel, my back finally protested. I tell Dimitri Junior to be sure and use the backrests in the cabs I provide for all my drivers or he will end up the same."

"And I'm sure he listens to his father."

"Sometimes. But since I'm grateful you have only good rides with him, I won't scold him. Tell me how I can help with your history lesson."

"Dimitri, do you remember a young couple that lived in the Spencer Percy House?"

His face creased in thought. "Yes," he said, "I remember them, but I didn't know them. They were, as we say in Greek, **idiómorfos**. Peculiar. I believe that carpenter, Mr. Cooper, lived with them."

"You're right," I said. "Cliff Cooper was the young man's father. Cliff recently died, you know."

"Yes. I was sorry to read that in the newspaper."

"His son, Jerry, was married to a woman named Marina. They had a little boy named Elliot and—"

Dimitri waved his hand over the table as though to banish what I'd said. He grunted. "It was terrible what happened to them, terrible what they did, leaving the baby with the grandfather and going off for their own pleasures."

"To South America," I said, following up on what he'd said, "where they were killed, as I understand it."

He simply nodded, got up, checked his spanakopita, and returned to the table.

"I was wondering, Dimitri, whether you or one of your drivers took them to the airport the day they left for South America."

"I did," he said flatly and without hesitation. "It was the only time I ever met the carpenter's son."

I was surprised at how quickly he remembered having driven them.

"And I suppose that it was the only time that you met her," I said.

He shook his head. "No. I didn't meet her."

"But—"

"When I went to the house to pick them up, only the man was waiting for me outside the door."

"Without Marina?"

"Only him. I remember he told me that his wife had already left and that he was meeting her wherever it was they were going in South America."

"I'm impressed that you remember it so clearly," I said.

"I remember because I didn't like him." He slapped his palm down on the table. "There was something about him, something in his eyes. After he told me about his wife, we drove to Boston without another word between us. I was relieved when I dropped him off."

"Did he say how his wife got to the airport?"

"No. Maybe he drove her himself. I only know that I did not drive her, nor did anyone who drove for me back then."

"Did he mention the baby, Elliot?"

"He said nothing, Mrs. Fletcher, nothing. I am ashamed to admit it, but when I heard that he and his wife had been killed in the jungle, I was not sad. I know that isn't a nice way to feel—and I wasn't **happy** that he'd been killed—but I felt no sorrow."

"You really didn't know the man, Dimitri."

"I am sad when anyone dies, Mrs. Fletcher. I felt sorry for Mr. Cooper, who had a small child to care for and raise. **Him** I felt sadness for."

I understood, and I appreciated his candor.

Dimitri opened the oven door and used two pot holders to pull out the pan of spanakopita and set it on the stovetop. The pastry was browned and flaky. "You'll stay for dinner?" he said. "My wife will be back soon and—"

"I appreciate the invitation, Dimitri, but I'm afraid I have other plans."

"All right, but you are not to go until I have given you a portion of my wonderful dish. My wife always says, 'Good food tastes better if it's shared.'"

Dimitri cut a large square from his spinach pie and wrapped it in foil for me. Then he called his son to pick me up.

"Thank you for the spanakopita, and thank you for spending this time with me," I said. "Please give my best to your family."

He walked me out to the waiting cab.

"What happened to the baby?" he asked.

"He grew up into a fine young man," I said. "He's returned to Cabot Cove for his grandfather's funeral."

"Please send him my best, and condolences on the loss of his grandfather."

"I'll be happy to do that."

Dimitri's son drove me back to Tim's office to pick up my bicycle, and he dropped me and the bike off at home. The whole time my mind was in overdrive.

The lives of Jerry and Marina Cooper had always been shrouded in mystery, but what Dimitri Cassis had told me only added to the enigma. Why had Marina traveled ahead of her husband instead of accompanying him? What was it about Jerry Cooper that had engendered such negative feelings in Dimitri Cassis? Who had reported to Cliff that Elliot's parents had been murdered in South America?

The answers to those questions, and more, were locked away in the Spencer Percy House, along with, as Arianna Olynski would say, the negative energy of unhappy spirits.

Chapter Eighteen

Cecil was sniffing around a paperback that had been placed on the bottom step when I arrived the next morning and brought in an empty carton that Lettie had left outside the front door. The Chihuahua's mistress was pacing in the hallway, yelling at someone on her cell phone. "What do you mean you need a few days off? We have work to do. I already gave you money to buy materials."

I slipped out of my Bean boots and tip-toed past Eve into the library, where Elliot was perusing the books that remained on the shelves. He waved a greeting.

"Grandpa Cliff used to have a volume of poetry by Henry Wadsworth Longfellow," he said, his hand running over the spines of the books. "Have you seen it? I couldn't find it in any of the boxes."

"Are you short of cash?" I asked.

He turned to face me. "Boy, nothing gets past you, does it, Mrs. Fletcher?"

"Your grandfather wanted me to pay the lawyer." I opened a cabinet door and retrieved the hollowed-out book of poems Cliff had used for what he called his "stash," and handed it to Elliot. "I paid Fred Kramer and gave him the rest of the money in the book for safekeeping. Perhaps he can provide you with funds the next time you see him."

Elliot snorted. "Wish I had known that yesterday when I had an appointment with him." He opened the book and ran a finger around the rectangular hole in the center of its pages. "I used to sneak a dollar or two when I was short, figuring Grandpa Cliff would never notice. I figured wrong, of course. He'd confront me the next day and threaten to dock my allowance. He never did, though. Instead, I'd find a ten-dollar bill in the pocket of my jeans that I knew I never put there." He closed the book, a wistful expression on his face. "Makes a nice souvenir, doesn't it."

"Yes, it does."

"**Sacré bleu**, Jessica! This will never do." Eve stood in the doorway of the library, fists on her hips. "There's barely room for Cecil to walk in here, much less my client, who's a very big man. We'll have to get rid of these boxes."

"That's the whole idea behind the book sale, Eve, getting rid of the books in the boxes," I said.

"Well, when is this momentous event going to take place? I think I've been very patient, but it would be just as easy— probably a lot easier—to have Herb, the junk man, come and haul them away."

"Eve Simpson, you are not going to renege on the promised fund-raiser for the Cabot Cove Library," I said, barely resisting the urge to stamp my foot. "And furthermore, don't complain to me about how long this is taking when your pledge to help organize it seems to have evaporated into thin air."

"Tell me how I'm supposed to show the house when it's chock-full of boxes," Eve said, her voice rising. "I can't even **think** about attacking the bedrooms when I can't navigate the first floor."

"Where's your knight-in-shining-armor handyman?" I asked. "Why not have him move the boxes to the barn?"

"I'm not sure where he is. He called to say he was taking a few days off. Can't I count on **anyone**?"

"Moving the boxes somewhere else would work for me," said Arianna Olynski, coming into the room. "The kitchen will never do as a set."

I knew that the medium, the former Agnes Pott, had returned to town with her cameraman and nephew, Davy, known professionally as Boris, but I hadn't realized they were already at the house.

"I didn't see your truck when I arrived," I said.

"We parked it behind the barn, like before," Davy said. "Aunt Aggie doesn't want a truck in the opening shot. Spoils the mysterious atmosphere."

I'd guessed that Davy had hidden the truck behind the barn the last time they were here, when Mort had caught him filming through an open window. Aggie had told Eve her truck wouldn't start and had requested a ride to the house. I didn't know if Aggie realized that Davy had exposed her lie, but I decided not to challenge her. It was enough to have my suspicion confirmed.

"If you empty the room," she said to me, "we could use the library to shoot our next episode. Does that work for you, Elliot?"

"I'm easy."

"What is Elliot doing in your show?" I asked.

"He's going to tell a story about how his mother's spirit found its way from the jungles of South America to Cabot Cove in order to read bedtime stories to her little boy. It's so touching."

"Elliot, are you sure you want to do this?" I asked.

"Sounds like fun. Maybe if I talk about her again, she'll reappear. I haven't seen her ghost since I was ten."

"Oh, but she's watching out for you," Aggie said, waving her gold-topped cane in the air. "I'm certain of it. I can feel her spirit."

"Which reminds me," Eve said, pointing at Elliot, "you cannot just take up residence in one of the bedrooms while I'm trying to get the house in order. You'll have to move somewhere else."

"Me? Where am I supposed to go? This is still my home, you know."

"Only until I can sell it," Eve said with forced cheer.

I had the impression that she was trying to tamp down her temper before she alienated everyone in the room.

"You want the money, don't you, Elliot?" Eve continued. "Think what you can do in Alaska with all those wonderful greenbacks to spread around. You'll be the toast of—where is it you live?"

"Sitka. It's a nice little city situated on Baranof Island—"

"You'll be the toast of Sitka. Women will be flocking to your door. You could buy a home or open a business or simply put your feet up for a year or two and read. Take some of these books with you. Or you could skip Alaska altogether and travel the world. Where would you like to go?"

That last question was posed through Eve's clenched teeth.

"Right now I'd like to go upstairs. I'm a little tired from traveling by motorcycle so many days. I could use a little rest, if that's all right with you."

"Rest all you want, but not in this house, please. I can't sell this monstrosity with so many boxes around, especially if people keep adding to the clutter rather than taking it away. Find somewhere else to go. Like Blueberry Hill Inn or some other bed-and-breakfast. And make sure you take that motorcycle with you. We can't have prospective buyers thinking this is a biker hangout."

"I can't afford a hotel until you sell the house and give me the money," Elliot said. "You'll just have to deal with my clutter for a day or two. I don't know that many people who would be willing to put me up, especially when they know there're eight empty bedrooms upstairs."

If Eve hadn't just paid for a wash and blow-dry at Loretta's Beauty Shop, I was certain she would have pulled out her hair with both fists. I was feeling her frustration myself. Every time I'd proposed a date for the book sale, it conflicted with another event on the calendar of the Friends of Cabot Cove Library. We'd finally settled on the thirty-first of October, which was a Saturday and, not incidentally, Halloween. It was the date that Seth Hazlitt had lightheartedly recommended, but I wasn't certain I could count on people to help out with the sale when there would be other events taking place around town, not least of which was the library's Halloween Parade for children. And would Charlene Sassi still offer to provide cookies when she had so many bakery orders for holiday parties at that time of year? At least we had most of the books off the shelves and boxed by category. Only the bottom two shelves remained to be sorted, and maybe I could get Elliot to help me finish up before he starred in Aggie's YouTube program.

"I'm leaving," Eve announced. "Come along, Cecil."

Cecil gave a sharp bark, trotted over to Eve's tote bag, and jumped in.

"Boris and I are going to shoot some establishing shots on the grounds," the medium said, following Eve out the door.

"If the books have to stay, perhaps we can find another location to film."

"Suit yourself," Eve called over her shoulder. "I have to find another handyman."

Elliot looked at me and shook his head, chuckling. "I don't even have a key to this place," he said. "I've been coming in and out through a window."

"Eve didn't give you a key?"

"No, ma'am, but don't worry about me. I'm going to ask Aunt Lucy if I can use their spare room. That'll get me out of Ms. Simpson's hair. Fortunately, I don't have a lot to pack." He covered a yawn. "Can't seem to get used to this time zone," he said, shaking his head like a dog shaking off water.

"It's very nice of you to accommodate Eve," I said. "She doesn't deserve your cooperation after her temper tantrum today, but she'll be grateful, I know."

"I seem to remember that selling a house is considered a major life crisis that causes people a lot of unhappiness and strain."

"It does," I said, "as do death, divorce, job loss, and illness, among others."

"Thanks to Grandpa, I don't have to do the selling," he said, stifling another yawn.

"I'm not surprised that you're tired," I said. "You've experienced a lot of turmoil in your life recently—the death of your grandfather, and having to leave your job and home to travel across two countries to help settle his estate. Not to mention the breakup of your engagement. All those upheavals take their toll."

Elliot put his hands up as if I were pointing a gun in his direction. "Not to forget that Grandpa Cliff's death is suspicious. No wonder I can barely keep my eyes open. But that last part you listed, Mrs. Fletcher, the breakup of my engagement. That's frankly a great relief. I knew it the instant I saw Beth again. Oh, it stung my ego, no doubt about that, but I'm really glad I'm free to get to know my childhood friend again. I only hope she's as glad to see me as I am to see her. We were really close once, and I wasn't very nice to her when she tried to help me."

"That was a long time ago, and I'm sure she's forgiven you," I said, noting the bags under his eyes. "Why don't you go upstairs and take a nap?"

"You wouldn't be offended?"

"Not at all. Do you mind if I stay? I have more work to do, and I'm curious about a few things I've found."

"The house is yours to explore. You can ask me about anything later. I'll tell you whatever I know, or what I can remember."

While Elliot climbed the stairs to the second floor, I looked around the room wearily. Seth has often accused me of assuming projects without weighing the consequences. Sorting the contents of Cliff Cooper's library for a book sale to benefit Cabot Cove Library had become a massive undertaking, and I was feeling overwhelmed. There was so much left to organize in the remaining days until the sale. I'd never been able to gather the help I'd expected to materialize. Was Eve right? Should I have let her hire Herb to cart away all the books and not have devoted all my efforts toward selling them? After all, realistically, how much money could be raised to support the library? Very likely not enough to expand the staff. Maybe only enough to get part-time help with a project. Was it a worthwhile endeavor?

Meanwhile, if Seth's analysis of the autopsy was correct—and I had to assume it was—Cliff Cooper had been murdered, and the discovery of who might have wanted him dead had taken a backseat to investigating his family history. What good was that going to do? A son and daughter-in-law sacrificing their lives on what was most likely a fool's errand in South America. A grandson who moved across the United States and Canada right after college. What was it about Cliff that drove his family members as far away from him as they could get?

All I knew about the day Cliff Cooper died was that no visitors had signed the book, but that Beth, possibly Lettie, and someone who sounded suspiciously like Elliot could have been there. Elliot had shown up in the Spencer House almost ten days after his grandfather's death. He couldn't have been hiding in Cabot Cove all along, could he? He seemed such a nice young man. Was it possible I'd misjudged him so completely? If so, it wouldn't have been the first time I'd been taken in by a handsome face and a pleasant manner.

I picked up the book that had been left on the bottom step, carried it into the library, and deposited it in the box marked "Mystery: Hard-boiled and Noir." **Another Hobart,** I thought, sighing. This one, entitled **Masquerade!**, had a picture of a figure in a green cape, face hidden behind a black mask.

Green, I thought. "Green," I whispered. "Of course." Seth had said he'd found green fibers in Cliff's throat, but there were no green pillowcases in the hospital. Then in the morgue, he'd speculated that they might have come from a hospital uniform. And when Aggie had saged the house, Mort had found green scrubs in an upstairs dresser drawer. "Scrubs" was a term used to describe a medical uniform. I'd forgotten that I'd meant to ask the Conrads if Cliff's wife, Nanette, had ever worked in the hospital. Or could they have been left behind by the nursing students who'd helped care for Elliot as a baby?

I went to the base of the stairs and looked up. Elliot's room was on the opposite side of the house from the bedroom with the dresser. If I walked carefully, I wouldn't wake him. Still in my stocking feet—my boots were next to the front door—I climbed the stairs, wincing at every creak. At the top, I tiptoed down the hall, hoping he wouldn't hear the squeak of the boards as I peeked into each room until I found the one Aggie had saged. The bedroom still bore a trace of the scent of lavender smoke in the air. The bedding appeared to be as it was when I'd last seen it. I'd taken the book I'd found downstairs. There was nothing on the top of the overturned box except the lamp that had been there before. Out of habit, I checked the bulb, but this time it was cool.

There were two half drawers at the top of the dresser and four full drawers below them. Slowly, I opened one of the half drawers. The wood had swollen, and it was a tight fit. Inside was an old jewelry box, the top missing. In the felt-lined compartment I found one earring and a silver bracelet with a broken clasp. The other half drawer held socks, some of them unpaired. I found the blue and green striped scarf Mort had pulled out in the first full drawer, but no green scrubs. I closed the drawer, careful not to slam it shut, and checked the next drawer down. It contained a few half-slips and a fur collar. The next one was empty and so was the bottom drawer. What had happened to the scrubs? I started at the first full drawer again, this time pushing aside the scarf and running my hand along the back of the drawer in case the fabric had gotten caught. I pulled out the bottom drawer altogether to see if the uniform had fallen between the back of the drawers and the rear wall of the dresser.

"What are you doing?" said a hoarse voice behind me.

"Oh, goodness. You startled me." I stood up, forcing the drawer closed as I did. "I was trying not to wake you. I'm looking for a pair of scr—"

Elliot's form filled the doorway. He was taller than I'd realized. He raised his left hand to scratch the back of his head. He was wearing the green scrubs.

"Good heavens!" I said. "Take those off immediately."

Chapter Nineteen

To say that Elliott was surprised and confused when I demanded that he take off the scrubs was an understatement. "Surely you can find something else to sleep in," I said.

"I guess, but why?" he asked. "No one's using these."

"Dr. Hazlitt needs them."

"These in particular? Can't he get a pair of scrubs for himself? They must have others at the hospital."

"Those in particular. You took them from this drawer, am I correct?"

He nodded.

"And were you the one who put them there?"

"Now, how could I have done that? I only got back yesterday."

"Just checking," I said.

"You know, Mrs. Fletcher, the whole idea when you go cross-country by motorcycle is to travel fast and light. I didn't bring anything to sleep in. I barely have two days' change of clothes."

"Nevertheless, I need those scrubs, and I need them now."

"Can I go put something else on first?"

"Yes, but hurry, please."

"All right, but it doesn't make any sense to me."

"I'll make sure that it does eventually. Go! Change!"

He left the room and returned a minute later wearing a tee shirt and sweatpants. "Okay?" he asked as he handed me the scrubs, a puzzled expression still on his face.

"Yes. Thank you." I heaved a sigh and looked around for a plastic bag to put them in.

"Can't you tell me why you need these specific scrubs?"

I hesitated before saying anything. I really didn't want to go into detail. For one thing, I could be completely wrong; this uniform could have had nothing to do with Cliff Cooper's death. But leaving the scrubs in the drawer, or letting Elliot wear them as pajamas, wasn't an option, even though I didn't know how useful they might be. Any evidence left on the fabric was likely to be contaminated. At least four people had handled them: whoever put them in the drawer, Mort, Elliot, and now me. But I couldn't afford to leave them behind. "I think that Dr. Hazlitt might want to examine these," I said.

"Why?"

"I really can't go into it right now, Elliot. You'll just have to trust me."

"I trust you," he said, shaking his head, "but I know I'll never get back to sleep, wondering what the heck you're up to."

"I'm sorry if I disturbed your rest. I'll leave now. If you find you can't sleep, why don't you go downstairs and wash the clothing you've brought with you?"

I'd been spending a lot of time at the Spencer Percy House, wading through Cliff Cooper's chaotic book collection, not to mention his convoluted family history, and had let chores pile up at home. I was glad to abandon the book sale/fund-raising project for a time and return to the relative orderliness of my home and the promise of a much-needed cup of tea. On my arrival, I immediately went to the kitchen and put the kettle on to boil. I had found a box of green garbage bags in Cliff's kitchen, and one of them now held the scrubs, protected from further contamination.

The flashing light on my telephone answering machine indicated that I'd received a half-dozen calls while I was out. I made notes as I listened to the messages, deciding which ones to answer first. Seth Hazlitt was at the top of the list. Other calls were from Evelyn Phillips, editor of the **Cabot Cove Gazette**, who sounded her usual breathless self; Sheriff Mort Metzger, who asked that I call him at the office; and a few others who could wait.

"Where were you off to so early this morning, Jessica?" Seth asked when he picked up.

"I've already been to the Spencer Percy House and back," I replied.

"Anyone giving you a hand with the

project?"

"Not really. Eve Simpson was there briefly with Cecil. Arianna Olynski, the medium, and Boris, the cameraman, who's really her nephew, Davy. And oh, yes, Elliot Cooper. Did you know that Elliot is finally back in Cabot Cove for his grandfather's funeral?"

"And about time, too. Of course I know. Every patient I've seen had something to tell me, including that the young man rode here on his motorcycle from Alaska. Darn fool! They ought to ban those machines. And another thing—"

"Seth," I said, hoping to stave off a rant on the dangers of motorcycles, "I have something I want to give you."

"Why? It isn't my birthday."

"It's not a gift. It's a set of green hospital scrubs."

"And why would I need hospital scrubs, Jessica?"

"They were in a dresser drawer in the Spencer Percy House. Mort saw them when he was there, but we didn't think anything about them at the time. But now that your autopsy indicated that Cliff

Cooper had the remnants of green fibers in his throat, I thought you'd like to have them for analysis."

"You sound like you're writing a scene in one of your mystery novels."

"Far from it," I said. "If you're not interested in having them, I can—"

"Seems to me, if they have any value at all, they ought to go to our esteemed sheriff."

He was right, of course.

"I'll see that Mort gets them as soon as possible."

Seth grunted.

"Is there anything wrong?"

"No, just that the autopsy results that you, me, the medical examiner, and Mort were supposed to keep secret are apparently common knowledge all over town. Every patient I saw today made a point about Elliot having returned and his grandfather not having died of natural causes."

"It's the Cabot Cove rumor mill run amok," I said.

"My question is, which one of our little quartet spilled the beans?"

"Don't look at me," I said. "I've been a

model of discretion. Oh, but it could have been Fred Kramer, the attorney. Mort must have told him. I know Fred told Elliot, and he may have told someone else, too. Or maybe Elliot unintentionally spread the news. He didn't hesitate to mention it to me."

"Cooper's grandson knows that his grandpa was murdered?"

"Yes. He said that he wormed the information out of Fred. So Mort must have taken Fred into his confidence to prepare Elliot for some upsetting news."

"I suppose it doesn't matter who let the cat out of the bag. The whole town knows the truth now."

"Is Mort aware that your autopsy results are no longer secret?" I asked.

"Can't imagine that it hasn't gotten back to him. I haven't spoken with him."

"He left a message on my answering machine. I'll call him next. I hope he doesn't think I'm the guilty party."

"You'll probably get a call from Evelyn Phillips at the **Gazette**, too."

"She's on the list of calls I have to return."

"She left a message with my nurse, but I

don't intend to call back and get into a hassle with her. I have enough to worry about without dealing with the press."

I didn't necessarily agree with Seth but knew better than to debate the issue with him. We chatted for a few more minutes before ending the conversation, leaving me free to return Mort Metzger's call, which I did with some trepidation.

"Thanks for getting back to me, Mrs. F. I suppose you've heard that Cliff Cooper's murder is now public knowledge."

"I just got off the phone with Seth. He told me."

"What do you think?"

"Pardon?"

"What's **your** take on the murder?"

"The murder? I'm sorry to say I haven't given it a lot of thought."

"Now, Mrs. F., that's not like you. My deputies and I have been running our tails off interviewing people. I thought for sure that you'd have something to contribute."

"I **do** have something for you," I said, realizing that a murder was hard to keep secret when the police had launched an investigation. "Remember when Seth said the autopsy turned up green fibers in Cliff Cooper's throat and airways?"

"Sure I do."

"And do you remember finding green hospital scrubs in a dresser drawer at the Spencer Percy House?"

"Of course, and don't think that I forgot them. I sent one of my deputies to the house this afternoon to pick up those scrubs. He just called me from there. They're gone. Disappeared into thin air."

"That's because I have them here at my house, Mort."

"You? Why do you have them? They're potential evidence in a murder investigation, Mrs. F."

I kept the pique out of my voice as I said, "I'm well aware of that, Mort," and I went on to explain how Elliot had put them on and that I'd convinced him to change into something else. "What's important," I added, "is that I have them here in a clean plastic bag. Can you send a deputy to my house to pick them up?"

"Sure. I'll have him there in twenty minutes."

"I'll be waiting."

"But what about my question?"

"What question?"

"About your take on it. You've been spending a lot of time at Cliff Cooper's home, if you can call that mausoleum a home. You're usually pretty good at picking up leads, you know, scraps of information, with the way you use them in your books."

"I'm afraid I have to disappoint you, Mort, but the only thing I've picked up were the scrubs. If I'd found out anything else, you'd be the first to know."

"Well, maybe you can give me a hand with something else, then."

"Whatever I can do to help, I will. You know that, Mort."

"I want to interview those old ladies who live across the street."

"The Conrad twins?"

"Yes. A couple of people told me Cliff was sweet on one of them. I spoke on the phone with the other sister a little while ago, and she nearly bit my ear off. But she agreed I could stop by tomorrow. I thought maybe if you were to go there with me, they'd be more likely to open up and not take offense at my questions."

"You want me to accompany you when you interview them?"

"If you wouldn't mind. I think it would be helpful."

I looked around my kitchen and thought of the chores I'd put aside. Then I thought about the book sale and all that remained to do before it took place.

"All right," I said.

"You're the best, Mrs. F. I'll pick you up tomorrow morning at nine."

"I'll be waiting. Love to Maureen."

My tea had gotten cold, and I brewed a fresh cup and savored a few sips before picking up the phone again. I had just begun to dial when the front doorbell rang. I hung up the phone and hurried to answer it. When I looked through the peephole, I saw Evelyn Phillips staring back. "Evelyn, I just picked up the phone to call you," I said when I opened the door.

"Thought I'd save you a dime. Or whatever it costs these days. May I come in?"

"Please do."

"You know, of course," Evelyn said, stepping into my living room.

"Know what?"

"That Cliff Cooper was murdered."

"Yes, I just heard."

"Who told you?" Before I could respond, she said, "Or maybe it's more accurate to assume that you've known all along."

"You're entitled to assume anything you want, Evelyn," I said coldly.

"Sorry if I offended you."

"Would you like some tea? I just made myself another cup."

"Do you have chamomile? I don't like to have caffeine after lunch."

"I think I can rustle up some chamomile tea."

Evelyn followed me into the kitchen, where I rummaged in my cupboard and pulled out a box of mixed herbal teas. "You're in luck. This is my last chamomile tea bag."

"I didn't mean to accuse you of lying, you know, Jessica. I just meant that you have this close relationship with Seth Hazlitt and our sheriff, and you probably knew about Cliff Cooper the minute they did."

"Let's just say that I learned about it

through normal channels, Evelyn. Is that why you called earlier?"

"Yes. But I'm having trouble getting people to call me back. So I decided to do what I did as a journalism student and put feet on the ground, as we used to say. Seth Hazlitt's nurse refused to interrupt his office hours for me, but I'll try him again later. I left my photographer in his waiting room. I told him to call me when Seth is available. I'm hoping he can also get me a good shot for the front page."

Seth wasn't going to be happy being ambushed in his own waiting room.

"I wasn't sure you'd be home," Evelyn continued. "I hear you've been spending a lot of time up at the Spencer Percy House, and I was prepared to track you down there if necessary."

"I'm spending a lot of time there because I'm trying to get Cliff's books in order for a book sale to benefit the library. It's going to take place on Halloween."

I slid a cup of hot water in front of Evelyn along with a saucer holding the tea bag. "Do you take milk or sugar?"

"This is fine as it is," she said, dunking

the tea bag in her cup. She had already removed a reporter's pad and pen from her pocket and had them lined up on my kitchen table.

I settled in the seat across from her, resigned to talk about Cliff, but hoping to distract her as much as possible. "Cliff was a book collector extraordinaire," I said. "I don't think he ever got rid of a book after he'd read it. There were thousands of books in his library."

"I thought of him more as a hoarder than a collector, if you don't mind my calling a spade a spade. Eve took me through that house, and if I were she, I'd have junked everything."

"The contents of the house don't belong to her, Evelyn. Cliff's grandson, Elliot, is his heir. I imagine he'll need to tell Eve what he wants to keep and what she can 'junk,' as you say. Elliott already gave permission for us to hold the book sale. Do you think you can find some space in the **Gazette** to give us a little promotion?"

She picked up her pen. "You're holding it on Halloween. Isn't that kind of a busy day?"

"It was the only weekend date we could agree on that didn't conflict with activities by the library and the Friends of the Library."

"The library has its Halloween Parade that day, you know."

"I'm hoping the library director, Doris Ann, will agree to have the parade on the grounds of the Spencer Percy House. That way it would get lots of parents of young children to the sale. Charlene Sassi has offered to hold a cookie sale to benefit the library, too. It promises to be a fun event."

"Okay. Okay. I'll put something in the paper after I run the story on the medium."

"The medium?"

"Yeah. Arianna Olynski. She invited me to watch the filming of her show. She says she's a good friend of yours."

"I wouldn't go that far."

Evelyn shook her head. "It looks like the **Gazette** is going to be camped out at the Spencer Percy House all month, what with the medium, your book sale, and my lead story, of course."

"Your lead story?"

"The murder of Cliff Cooper. What do you know about it?" she asked.

"Nothing. You probably know a lot more than I."

"I find that hard to believe, considering your reputation for knowing, well—for knowing everything that goes on in town."

"That's flattering," I said, "but hardly true."

The sound of a rock ballad emanated from Evelyn's pocket. A man's voice sang, "You know it hit me like a hammer." She pulled out her cell phone. "That's Huey Lewis and the News," she said, indicating her call music. "It was the only news reference I could find." She pressed a button, and the music stopped. "Evelyn Phillips here. Okay, stay with him. I'll be right there." She gathered up her pen and pad. "Seth has emerged from hiding. I have to run. Thanks for the tea, Jessica. I'll call you later."

Saved by rock music, I thought as I closed the front door behind Evelyn. Poor Seth. But at least I didn't have to duck her questions. I took my teacup into my office and sat at my computer. The rest of my phone messages could wait. The problem was that while sitting in my quiet home office was satisfying, I couldn't get my brain to cooperate.

I'd found Eve Simpson's behavior toward Elliot unnecessarily harsh, although I understood her need to clear out the house, including a new occupant, as a precursor to showing it to prospective buyers. Even so, she was days away, maybe longer, from having the house in shape, and she could have allowed Elliot a bit of slack until after the funeral for his grandfather. Selling the Spencer Percy House was going to be a challenge no matter what, considering its overall condition, as well as its reputation for being haunted.

That latter stumbling block was silly, of course—unless you happened to believe in ghosts. I'd found it surprising how many people in town had actually come to accept that a spirit occupied the house. I suppose it's a testimony to our ability to become immersed in a rumor and have our imagination override our intellect. While I don't personally believe in ghosts any more than I believe in extraterrestrial aliens, I'm not so closed-minded as to definitively rule out the possibility that they exist.

To my surprise, I dozed off in my chair, until the arrival of Mort's deputy woke me.

"Thanks, Mrs. Fletcher," he said when I handed him the plastic bag containing the green scrubs. "What do you think of Mr. Cooper's murder?"

"Very sad."

"Yeah, I know, but it has folks buzzing around town. We sure get a lot of murders in Cabot Cove, don't we? Well, I'd better get back before the sheriff starts looking for me."

We have had more than our share, I thought. Even one murder was one too many as far as I was concerned. I hoped this one would be solved quickly and things would calm down.

That turned out to be wishful thinking.

Chapter Twenty

"I really appreciate you doing this, Mrs. F.," Mort said as he held open the door of the patrol car parked in front of my house.

"Happy to help, Mort, only I don't think it's really necessary to have me accompany you to interview the Conrad twins. They're nice people."

"I'm sure they are, but since you know them pretty well, I figured having you along would put them at ease." He laughed. "People tend to get uptight being questioned by law enforcement, especially when it's a murder that's being investigated. It's not like they're suspects or anything, but I'm told they were close to Mr. Cooper and might have some insight into why he was killed."

Mort had called Lettie and Lucy to arrange

to meet that morning. While I thought my presence was more likely to put our sheriff at ease than to reassure the Conrad sisters, I had to admit, to myself at least, that I was curious to hear what they would say about Cliff Cooper and their relationship with him. We had talked a lot about Cliff's relationship with his son and daughter-in-law, and to a certain extent with his grandson, Elliot, but how Cliff's neighbors fit into his life was more a matter of speculation on my part. They hadn't divulged any intimacies in their relationship to me.

Lettie answered the door and invited us inside. Judging from the surprised look on her face when she saw me, Mort hadn't told them that I'd be with him. But she didn't say anything. We were ushered into the living room, where Lucy sat by the window, her Christmas tree quilt wrapped around her knees.

Mort took out the pad he used to make a report. "As you may have heard," he said, reading his notes, "'the Cabot Cove Sheriff's Department is investigating as suspicious the death of one Clifton Cooper, age eighty-three, who resided at...'" Mort recited his boilerplate introduction, and looked up uneasily. "It's customary to interview witnesses individually," he said, "so I'll have to ask one of you to leave temporarily. I know it's an inconvenience, but it's standard procedure. If you object, we'll have to invite you to police head-quarters for the questioning. I thought this would be a more pleasant environment for both of you."

"Is Jessica going to leave, too, or is she an official interviewer?" Lettie asked.

"Unofficial," I said. "The sheriff asked me to participate since I'm a friend of yours and was a friend of Cliff's."

"That's if it's okay with you," Mort said. "Wouldn't want to put you on the spot if you'd prefer to be interviewed without her present."

"I've got nothing to hide," Lettie said, "but I want to know why we're considered 'witnesses.' We weren't at the hospital when Cliff died."

"Merely a technical term," Mort said. "We're talking to all the deceased's friends and acquaintances to get the lay of the land, so to speak."

"You mean to find out if he had any enemies?" Lettie said.

"That, too," Mort said.

"Is Elliot or Beth here?" I asked.

"No," Lettie said. "They've gone into town to make arrangements for tomorrow's funeral. I mentioned that you were going to be here this morning, Sheriff, but they said they were sure you'd track them down when you wanted to talk with them. Isn't that right?"

"It would have been handy if they'd been here. Saves wear and tear on the patrol car, but, yes, I can talk with them another time."

Lucy, who'd said nothing beyond hello, picked up her quilt and walked to the door. "I have things to do in the kitchen," she said. "I'll be there when you need me."

Mort and I sat on the couch; Lettie took a ladder-back chair from a corner and placed it across the coffee table from us. "What do you wish to know, Sheriff?" she asked, a challenging expression on her angular face.

"Well," Mort began, "maybe you can fill

me in a little about your friendship with the deceased, Cliff Cooper."

"You mean my sister's friendship with Cliff Cooper," she said.

"Weren't you friends with him as well?" I asked.

"We were neighbors nigh onto forty or fifty years."

"Yes, but you were also familiar with details of his life, of his relationships with his family. That makes you more than simply an acquaintance," I said.

"I guess you could say we were friends of a sort, but it was really my sister he was interested in. I was just along for the ride. He'd probably have been just as happy if I hadn't been around."

"Okay," Mort said, "why don't you tell us about your sister's friendship with him?"

"Don't you think you'd be better off asking **her** that question?"

"I'll get to that," Mort said. "Right now I'm asking **you** the question."

"Well, what do you want to know?"

Lettie was becoming agitated.

"Why don't you tell the sheriff about Lucy's friendship with Cliff," I said, hoping to smooth the waters.

"It was more than friendship," Lettie said. "He was courting her. He asked her to marry him, and she agreed."

"She did? Then why did they never marry?" I asked.

"Because I put my foot down and said no."

"**You** said no?" Mort said, mirroring my reaction.

"What did Lucy say when you told her you were against their getting married?" I asked.

Lettie looked at me. "You probably think it sounds selfish, don't you?"

"I'm not in your shoes, Lettie. I don't know what you were thinking. Why did you oppose their marriage? Didn't you like Cliff?"

"Oh, I liked him well enough as a neighbor. Liked his wife, too. When she died, we brought him casseroles and such like neighbors always do. Like lots of women in town did, for that matter. He was an eligible bachelor. Not bad-looking, with a big house and his own business. Plus, his son, Jerry, was going to go off to college in a few years."

Not a very romantic assessment, I thought but didn't say. To me, Lettie always appeared to be the practical twin, so her opinion of Cliff as a prospective husband was not surprising.

"Was Cliff interested in marrying Lucy many years ago, when Jerry still lived at home?"

She shook her head. "No. He didn't start to court her until after Jerry and his wife took off for parts unknown. We helped him out a lot when Elliot was a tyke, watching the boy until the babysitters arrived, things like that. I think that's when he took a shine to Lucy. For a while, I thought I was the one he was interested in, but no, he wanted the prettier one. Always that way, isn't it?"

"But you're twins," Mort said.

"All identical twins will tell you that people always like to say one is prettier or handsomer than the other, as if that's the only way they can tell us apart." She looked out the window with a view of the Spencer Percy House across the road, and was silent.

"You were going to explain why you didn't want Lucy to marry Cliff," I reminded her.

Lettie shook her head as if I'd just interrupted a dream. "It **was** selfish on my part, I admit. She was willing to marry him but not to live in that monstrosity of a big house with all those rooms to clean. Cliff didn't have a lot of money, you know, only the property over there, the house and barn."

"Did she want him to sell the house?"

Lettie snorted. "I wish. No, she invited him to live in our house. Can you believe it?"

"That wasn't good?" Mort asked.

"Good for him maybe. Good for her. But what about me?" Lettie was working up steam. She glared at me. "I'll bet you think Lucy is the sweet one. I've heard that my whole life. But let me tell you, she might seem to be the sweet one, but she always got her way. My fault. I let her get away with it because it was no skin off my nose. Besides, everything was peaceful as long as she thought she was in charge. I've always been content to let her handle the household finances and write out the shopping list based on what **she** wanted us to eat. Then I did the cleaning and shopping."

"Who cooked?" I asked, trying to move Lettie off her complaints about her sibling. It seemed a logical question even though it had nothing to do with Mort's inquiry into Cliff Cooper's murder.

"We both do, although I make the main dish and do all the baking." A smile crossed Lettie's face. "She does make cookies every now and then," she said. "I've always gone along with what she wants; I don't care what we eat as long as we don't go hungry. I don't like confrontation, although people who know us find that hard to believe." She paused, wiping away a tear. "I feel as though I'm betraying our most intimate family secrets."

"Whatever you say stays right here," Mort said. "Isn't that right Mrs. F?"

"Of course. Lettie, I have a question if you don't mind."

"If I did, it's a little late," she said.

"Was there anyone aside from you and Lucy who got close to Cliff?"

"Virtually no one," she replied. "There was that nurse when Elliot was a baby, but I put an end to that. I told him she was just after his money. He laughed and told me he didn't have any."

"Maybe that's why he wanted to move in here," Mort suggested.

"If that was the case, he would have been using Lucy and her feelings for him."

"Did Mr. Cooper have any enemies?" Mort said.

"Knew you'd get around to asking that," Lettie said. "Aside from me stepping in between him and Lucy? No one that I knew. Frankly, he was a loner, like his son. That's where Jerry got it from. That's why, after he retired from carpentry, all Cliff did was read. Maybe there's someone in town who has a complaint about his work—you know, the door came off a cabinet or a step was loose. Ask around."

"That's exactly what we're doing," Mort said.

I was pleased that he'd deflected Lettie's sarcasm instead of responding with anger.

"Anything else?" she asked. "I've said all I wish to say."

"No, ma'am," said Mort. "Would you please ask your sister to come in now?"

A long period passed before Lucy entered the room, and I assumed that she and Lettie had had a conversation before she joined us. She took the chair that Lettie had vacated, smoothed the quilt over her lap, and smiled. "Lettie says that I'm free to say anything about our family. I hope she didn't reveal too many secrets."

"Not at all," Mort said. "She did say that you wanted to marry Cliff Cooper and have him move in here with you and your sister."

She nodded demurely.

"But Lettie was against it," I said.

"Yes, she was."

"That must have been difficult for you, being in love with him," I said.

Lucy hesitated before saying, "I have to admit that I really didn't love Cliff. He was a kind man and so well-read, never without a book in his pocket. Not that he was a snob about books, mind you. He liked the popular novels as well as history and philosophy. I liked him a lot. But I didn't love him."

"Then why did you want to marry him?"

"It's complicated. I've never been married. It would have been nice to experience that once, to be called Mrs. Cooper instead of Miss Conrad. I'm not so modern that I would have kept my maiden name."

"Is that the only reason?" I asked.

"No. That would have been very selfish of me if that was the only reason. I thought we could all take care of one another as we got older. That's not such a bad idea, is it?" This time a few tears came from Lucy, which she wiped away.

"Is there more to it than that, Lucy?" I asked.

"There is, but you mustn't say anything to anyone, especially Lettie. Promise me, Jessica."

"Our conversation is completely confidential," Mort said.

I agreed.

Lucy's eyes met mine. "All right. I'll tell you. I've been feeling myself starting to lose my faculties and—I just hope that you never experience this, Jessica. It's so distressing."

"Everyone has forgetful moments, Lucy," I said, "even young people."

"Mine are different, though. I don't have them all the time—at least I hope I don't—but when I do, they're bad. It isn't just, 'Where did I leave the keys?' It's more, 'What is this cell phone doing in the refrigerator?' And I keep forgetting things." She clutched the quilt to her chest and sighed.

"Go on," I said. "Is there more?"

"What?"

"You were telling us why you wanted to marry Cliff," I said.

"I was? Oh, yes. I thought that if Cliff moved in with us, it would be security for Lettie, company and help for her when I could no longer manage our affairs and needed caring for. Lettie's mind is still sharp; she remembers everything; every little thing I've ever said to her. She throws it back at me when she gets mad. She'll tell you she's the easy one, but I've been walking on eggs around her since we were children. Mama tried to protect me, told me to get some backbone and stand up for myself. I try. I'm not always successful. Lettie will let me do what I want, but then she'll fume and fuss, and eventually she'll explode. Well, she got her way. Cliff didn't move in. He got sick instead. At the end of his life, he was so pale and so frail, he didn't even want me to visit him in the hospital."

"He did say he wanted you to remember him as a healthy man, not how he looked in illness," I said.

"People think women worry over their looks, but I think men are worse. I didn't care that he was grizzled and weak. I just wanted to tell him how grateful I was that he cared for me, and how he'd been a wonderful friend and neighbor and an even better grandfather to Elliot."

"Was he a good father to Jerry?" I asked.

"Who?"

"Jerry, Cliff's son," I said.

"Oh, right. Yes, he was a very good father, although Jerry never appreciated him."

"What kind of relationship did they have, Cliff and Jerry?" Mort said, following up.

"You'll think this is funny, but Jerry was the one who got Cliff reading all those books."

"Why is that funny?" I asked.

"Well, it isn't actually funny at all. Jerry called his father names, said he was uneducated and ignorant."

"Jerry said that to Cliff?" Mort asked.

She nodded. "Isn't that awful, belittling the man who raised you, who paid for your college education? Yes, Jerry said that to him. He was an awful boy, even if I've defended him to Lettie. Once Jerry left for college, Cliff started reading everything he could get his hands on. He wanted to be able to have an 'intelligent conversation' with his son, he said. I told him he was already an intelligent man, but he felt he had to have book knowledge and kept it up even after Jerry was gone."

"Did Cliff have any friends other than you and your sister?" I asked.

"He knew just about everyone in town, but he mostly kept to himself. That's why I felt it was important to be close to him, so he would have someone in his life who cared for him."

"Tell me about the day Cliff died," Mort said. "Had you seen him that day?"

"He left specific orders that I was not to visit him. And that nasty nurse was only too happy to make sure I knew it. She's wanted to marry Cliff since Elliot was a baby. I was horrified when I learned that Carolyn, of all people, was his nurse on the evening shift. I knew he didn't like her— not romantically anyway—but a sick man is vulnerable. She was there to comfort him, make him feel wanted and loved. There was little I could do about it."

"What about your sister?" Mort asked. "Did she visit him?"

"Lettie? Heavens, no. She was never close to him the way—the way I was."

"Lettie told us a few minutes ago," I said, "that she was against your marrying Cliff and having him move in here."

Lucy gave her answer some thought before replying. "We fought over that, I'm afraid. I understood her objection, but her attitude left me with a sour taste in my mouth. I was trying to protect her." She pressed her fingers to her lips. "Of course I never told her that. I don't want her to worry about me. She will, you know. We've been sisters since before we were born. All we have left in the world is each other."

When Mort didn't raise another question, I did.

"You're sure that Lettie never visited Cliff in the hospital?"

"Don't you think she would have told me if she had?" She shrugged and gazed up at the ceiling. I was sure she was evading the question.

I didn't feel that I was in a position to challenge Lucy at that juncture, but the hospital aide's description of one of Cliff's visitors fit Lettie to a tee. The aide's description of the younger woman placed Beth at the hospital, and while she'd denied being there at first, I'd gotten her to admit that she had, in fact, visited Cliff. From what she'd said, she was there on the day that he was killed, and Beth had possibly placed Lettie there as well. I'd promised Beth that I wouldn't say anything to her great-aunts, and I would keep that promise. But I would inform Mort before he or one of his deputies questioned the young woman. Beth had lied about visiting Cliff, and I found it odd that she had seemed to be planning a visit to Sitka, Elliot's new home, even before she supposedly learned that he'd broken his engagement to another woman. Was she intending to woo him back? And was she being honest when she said Cliff had been sleeping at the hospital and that she had left immediately?

We talked for a few more minutes before Mort announced that we were leaving. Both sisters accompanied us to the door, and Lettie said that she hoped that Mort and his investigators would soon identify the person who'd killed Cliff Cooper.

"We'll do our best," Mort assured her.

I wasn't about to leave without asking Lettie an obvious question, but couching it in such a way that it wasn't a direct confrontation.

"What was Cliff like when you visited him in the hospital, Lettie?"

"Visited him?" Lettie said haughtily. "I never visited Cliff." She turned to Lucy. "Did I, Lucy?"

It was obvious from Lucy's expression that she wasn't comfortable being called upon to confirm or deny it. She simply said, "You already said you didn't," and disappeared back into the house.

Chapter Twenty-one

We'd had a run of lovely weather on coastal Maine for a few days, but on the Sunday morning of Cliff Cooper's funeral, the skies darkened and a steady rain began to fall. Seth called to ask if I planned to go. He'd routinely attended the funerals of his patients in years past but had begun cutting back recently. "At my age, if I go to the funeral of everyone I've ever seen professionally, I'll never get out of the cemetery." When I told him that I intended to join the mourners, he decided to accompany me, which worked out not only because he provided company, but because he'd be driving to the church and the graveyard. I love my bicycle, but not in the rain.

Cliff hadn't been a member of any

organized religion, so the attorney for the estate, Fred Kramer, had recommended to Elliot that he arrange for a simple observance following the regular service in the local Unitarian church. Burial would be in a small nondenominational cemetery in the northeast corner of town, in the plot next to his wife, Nanette, Jerry Cooper's mother. It took some searching, but the attorney had come up with a copy of the deed to the plot that Cliff and Nanette Cooper had purchased many years ago. Thankfully, they'd been thinking ahead, something far too few people do.

"Do you think the weather will keep people away?" I asked Seth as we drove to the church.

"A little rain shouldn't determine whether people celebrate the life of a friend. If they're afraid to get a little wet, then they weren't friends in the first place."

As we pulled into the parking lot adjacent to the church, I was pleased to see that a number of cars had preceded us. We popped open our umbrellas and joined the line of other mourners heading for the entrance. Once inside, we deposited our umbrellas in stands and entered the worship area. I spotted the Conrad sisters sitting in a front pew. Next to them were Elliot Cooper and Beth Conrad. Seth and I joined Mort and Maureen Metzger on the opposite side of the aisle. Mort had exchanged his sheriff's uniform for a blue suit and tie.

"Surprised to see you here," Seth said to Mort in a whisper loud enough for me to hear. "Did you know the deceased?"

"Met him once or twice," Mort whispered back. "Actually, I just figured I might pick up on something to help the investigation."

"Can't imagine what," Seth said.

"You never know," Mort retorted.

"If you say so," said Seth, sitting back as Reverend Lucinda Yates, a young minister who'd only recently been assigned to the Cabot Cove church, stepped behind the podium and welcomed everyone.

"As sad as death is," she said, "we gather to celebrate the life of a fine man, Clifton Cooper, a longtime member of this community, whose skills as a carpenter and craftsman made wonderful contributions to the homes and lives of many here. While he was building a life for himself and his family, he also built some of the best bookcases in Cabot Cove."

She waited until the murmurs of recognition subsided before introducing Beth Conrad, who read a poem, Longfellow's "A Psalm of Life," from a book she'd brought with her. I loved the lines:

> Lives of great men all remind us
> We can make our lives sublime,
> And, departing, leave behind us
> Footprints on the sands of time

Then the minister launched into an abbreviated recap of Cliff's life. It was a straightforward presentation until she reached the point when Cliff had taken over the raising of his grandson, Elliot. She talked of the daunting challenge he'd assumed in raising a small child alone, the financial and emotional strain it put on him, and how he'd risen to the challenge. She looked to where Elliot sat with Beth and said, "Elliot Cooper has some words to say about his loving grandfather." There was a rustle of movement as people sat up to get a better view.

Wearing a gray sport coat and red tie, which I assumed he'd borrowed for the occasion, a clean-shaven Elliot strode confidently to the podium, carrying sheets of paper on which he'd written the notes for the eulogy. He cleared his throat and smiled at those assembled.

"I haven't seen many of you for a long time, so I want to take this time to thank you for coming to celebrate the life of my grandfather, Clifton Cooper," he said. "He would have been tickled to see so many familiar faces here. He was a modest man, not one accustomed to a lot of attention, except, so I've been told, when my grandmother, Nanette, died, and Grandpa Cliff became an eligible bachelor. He got quite a bit of attention then." He paused to smile at the wave of laughter. "Even though I've moved away from Cabot Cove, I want you to know that I loved my grandfather very much, and I'll always be grateful for the sacrifices he made for me for all those years. We were two generations apart and had our differences, as you can imagine.

As I got older and smarter—or so I thought—we got into some heated arguments, but that was because I was a stupid teenager who didn't know better. I'll bet there are some people here who can attest to that." Elliot smiled. "I see some nodding heads. I hope I'm a better man now, but when I was a youngster, I was really upset when Grandpa Cliff sent me off to boarding school. But do you know what? It was the best thing he ever did for me, and while I didn't know it then, I know now just how difficult it was for him to make that decision."

His voice breaking at times, he spoke for another ten minutes, never referencing the manner in which his grandfather died nor speculating on why someone would want to kill him. Those who had come to the funeral expecting to be entertained by dramatic references to a murder—and I'm sorry to say there may have been a few with that purpose—went away disappointed. Those who came to mark the passing of a gentle, private man were rewarded with proof of Cliff's most successful undertaking, the rearing of his grandson. There were even a few sounds of sniffling in the pews. Lucy Conrad held a handkerchief tightly in her fist, frequently raising it to her cheeks. Her sister sat next to her, staring into space, Lettie's only reaction to Elliot's words the occasional pursing of her lips.

At the conclusion of the service, we left the church and headed to our cars for the procession to the cemetery. The casket carrying Cliff Cooper was placed in a hearse, and a limo containing only Elliot and the driver followed.

Among those watching as the hearse pulled away was a woman I recognized. I excused myself to Seth and approached her.

"You're Carolyn, aren't you?" I asked her. "You were Cliff Cooper's nurse."

She stiffened. "That's right. And you were one of the privileged few allowed to visit him. Theresa told me you'd tracked her down at the hospital."

"She's a very bright young woman. I've been hoping to speak with you, too."

She scowled at me. "If you think I had anything to do with Cliff's death, think again. I did everything to help him get better, including chasing away people who were upsetting him. Like you. If you didn't like it, too bad."

"Cliff wanted me to be there, but I'm sure you were only trying to protect him. I didn't take offense."

When I didn't respond negatively to her rudeness, Carolyn seemed to relax a bit.

"Look, I've already talked to the police. They said Cliff was murdered; I don't believe it for a minute. That probably came from one of the Conrad twins, because I kept them away from Cliff—at his request, I might add."

"But you don't know if they managed to see him when you weren't on duty."

"There were strict orders on file. The guards had been alerted."

I didn't tell her that I'd managed to elude the guards. Instead I said, "It was a lovely service today, wasn't it?"

She nodded but didn't reply.

"It must be gratifying to see what a fine young man Elliot Cooper is."

"Cliff was a good man, if stubborn. I don't see any reason why Elliot wouldn't have turned out well."

"Lettie Conrad said you were one of the nursing students who helped take care of Elliot when he was a baby."

"I'm sure she didn't have anything good to say about me. She and her sister went after Cliff from the moment his son and daughter-in-law ran off, but they didn't know anything about taking care of babies. They probably only wanted to add his property to theirs."

"But you **did** know about babies."

"I helped raise six brothers and sisters. I sure knew a lot more than they did."

"Lettie said you were interested in Cliff, too."

"I'll bet she did. I would have been a good mother to Elliot, but Cliff wanted to raise the boy by himself. Heaven knows why, but he did."

"So you left."

"I didn't see any point in sticking around, pining after a child and a husband I couldn't have. Does anyone think that's a motive for murder?"

"I can't imagine they would."

Seth tapped me on the shoulder. "Excuse

me, but if you want to go to the cemetery, Jessica, we have to leave now."

I thanked Carolyn for talking to me. She shrugged her shoulders and walked away without replying.

A smaller group of us than had attended the funeral stood at the hilltop graveside, umbrellas raised, while Reverend Yates delivered some parting words. Elliot stood between Beth and Lucy Conrad, their faces grim, windblown raindrops mingling with tears on their cheeks. Lettie was not with them.

Tim Purdy had been at the church and also came to the cemetery. He stood next to Eve Simpson, whose unhappy face, I thought, was more a reflection of having to stand in a rainstorm than any sad feelings she might have had for the late Cliff Cooper. Mort and Maureen Metzger stood with Seth and me.

"Pick up anything of use in your investigation?" Seth asked our sheriff.

"Maybe."

Maureen asked me, "Are you and Seth going back to the Conrad sisters' house after this, Jessica? I baked a batch of my special raspberry swirl cookies for them."

"I'm sure we'll stop in there—Elliot is living with them for the time being—but I doubt we'll stay for very long. He must be exhausted, and I'm sure all this has put a strain on Lucy and Lettie as well."

As Maureen and I talked, and others began leaving the graveside, I happened to look across the cemetery and was sure I saw Eve Simpson's handyman, Tony Tonelero, standing beneath a gnarled willow tree. He wore a yellow slicker and a tan rain hat.

"Excuse me," I said to Seth and Maureen, and started in his direction. What was he doing here? Hadn't I heard Eve say she was going to hire another man to work on the Spencer Percy House? As if wanting to avoid me, Tony turned quickly and walked away, disappearing behind an ornate mausoleum erected by one of Cabot Cove's notable families. By the time I caught up to where I'd last seen him, he was nowhere in sight. I couldn't see anyone walking down the hill wearing a yellow slicker. Although I couldn't be certain Tony had spotted me coming toward him, I was convinced that he'd kept his distance and made his exit to avoid speaking with anyone. But that was irrelevant. The real question on my mind was, why had he bothered on a soggy, rainy Sunday to come to the burial service of a man he never knew? I considered pursuing him but thought better of it. I didn't want to leave Seth standing alone in the rain, nor did I want to slog through wet grass that needed mowing.

"Where did you run off to?" Seth asked when I rejoined him and we headed for his car.

"I saw the handyman that Eve Simpson hired to do repairs on Cliff Cooper's house."

"So?"

"So," I said, "why was he at Cliff's funeral?"

"You'll have to ask him."

"Which is what I'd intended to do if he hadn't left so quickly."

Seth held the car door for me and came around to take the driver's seat. "Maureen said the Conrad sisters are hosting a gathering on Elliot's behalf," I told him. "We should stop by to pay our respects."

"I don't mind stopping there for a short visit, but we've been 'paying our respects' all morning, and I'd like to get in an hour or two in my office this afternoon. I still have to take care of the living."

"I promise we'll only visit a short time. But if you need to leave and I'm not ready, you go. I'll find a ride. I'm sure there will be lots of people available to drop me off at home."

It turned out that Lettie had skipped the graveside service to go home to prepare for guests after the funeral. When Seth and I arrived, there was an array of cookies, cakes, and pies as well as coffee and tea for those who came to pay a condolence call. Most funeral-goers had decided not to take them up on their hospitality, and I was happy that Seth and I were among those who did afford them that courtesy.

"It was a lovely service," Lucy said as I shared a cup of tea with her.

"Yes, it was, Lucy. I think that Cliff would have been pleased."

"And Elliot, poor, dear Elliot, spoke so eloquently."

"Eloquently **and** emotionally."

"I like to think that Cliff was listening to every word."

"He would have been very proud of Elliot today," I said. "Where is Elliot, by the way?"

"I don't know. He hasn't returned from the funeral yet. Nor has Beth."

I looked out the window at the Spencer Percy House across the street. A light was on in one of the upstairs rooms.

At that moment Eve Simpson arrived.

"I hate these sloppy days," she said, shedding her fashionable raincoat and shaking her head. "No matter how hard you work to look nice, the rain undoes everything you've accomplished."

"It's good for the crops," Seth muttered.

"If you're a farmer," Eve said sharply. "I'm not."

"I think you look lovely," Lucy said.

"You're a dear," Eve replied, accepting a cup of tea from her.

"How are things shaping up with the renovations?" I asked when Lucy had moved away to talk with the other guests.

"Slow, frustratingly slow. That handyman I hired seems to take his own sweet time getting things done. He's back on the job, thank goodness. I was getting ready to throw up my hands. Speaking of getting things done, Jessica, when will the rest of the books be packed up and moved out?"

"The sale is taking place next Saturday," I answered. "As you know, I haven't had a lot of help sorting Cliff's library. It's a daunting task, but we're almost there. I'm hoping to finish up tomorrow. What do you hear from our favorite medium, Arianna Olynski, also known as Agnes Pott?"

"She's a kook, Jessica."

I had to laugh at her directness.

"She's supposedly going to videotape an interview with Elliot Cooper, but she put it off until Evelyn Phillips can come and watch. Evelyn's doing a front-page article about her. I just hope Aggie remembers that the whole purpose of her being here is to rid the house of ghosts, not talk about them haunting the place. I've had exactly one query from a prospective buyer, and I'm eager to move this property off the market."

"Maybe Aggie's show will help sell it," I offered.

"Or scare everybody away," was Seth's

analysis. "Haunted house indeed!"

We stayed another twenty minutes before announcing that we were leaving.

"It was very generous of you to invite Elliot to stay here and to host this reception for him," I told Lettie.

"Thank Lucy. It was her idea."

"I will," I said. "Where is she?"

"She went to lie down. Said she had a headache. I think it's because she saw that nurse Carolyn at the funeral."

"Did you speak with her?"

"Ayuh. She came right up to me and said, 'Now, no one's got him.'"

"Oh, how awful. Did Lucy overhear her? Did you say anything back?"

"I don't have time for her. I just turned away."

Elliot and Beth walked in just as Seth and I were on our way out. We complimented Elliot on his eulogy and Beth on the poem she chose to read.

"Did you notice it was from Henry Wadsworth Longfellow?" Elliot asked.

"I did, as it happens. And I noticed that her book doesn't have a hole in the middle of it."

Elliot laughed. "I think Grandpa Cliff would have loved the irony."

The rain had let up; it was now more of a mist that had settled over Cabot Cove. Seth and I walked toward his car.

I looked across the road at the Spencer Percy House.

"Spare me a few more minutes?" I asked.

"If you wish."

I took his arm, and we crossed the street to the house where Cliff Cooper had lived with his wife, Nanette, and after her death had raised their son, Jerry, by himself— and had also brought up his grandson, Elliot, the same way. The light I'd seen in an upstairs room was off now. We walked up the gravel driveway toward the small barnlike structure in the rear. As we approached it, I saw Tony Tonelero's black motorcycle resting against the side of the building beneath an overhang that kept it dry. Raindrops on its surfaces glimmered, however; it had been used recently.

"I'll never understand people riding on those darn things," Seth commented.

"And they probably wonder why you feel that way," I said.

The door to the barn was only partially closed. I widened the gap and peered inside. "Tony?" I called out. There was no response. I pushed the door fully open, and we stepped through it. Although it hadn't been home to animals for a century or more, the barn still maintained most of the original structure from when it was built, with a center aisle and bays on either side that had at one time been stalls. Although it lacked the familiar barnyard smell, there was the aroma of raw wood and sawdust, testimony to its use as a woodworking shop.

"What are we doing?" Seth asked.

"I thought maybe Eve's handyman was here," I said, folding my umbrella and leaning it against the wall. "I wanted to ask him why he'd attended Cliff Cooper's funeral."

"A man has a right to attend a funeral, Jessica."

"But he never knew Cliff. Eve hired him after Cliff died."

"Maybe he's someone who likes cemeteries and funerals, or maybe he needs something to do on a Sunday morning."

"On a very **wet** Sunday morning," I said.

I ventured past one of the stalls in which there were a table saw and other machines useful to a carpenter. Beyond it was an area that probably had been a tack room when the barn was first built. It seemed out of place to be in a barn now. It was set up like a makeshift bedroom. There were a cot made up for sleeping, a small night table with a lamp attached to a long extension cord, a portable radio, and a stack of a dozen books. A rod had been crudely attached to the wall, where clothing dangled from wire hangers. A black motor-cyclist's helmet sat atop a legal-size banker's box on the floor in a corner.

"I suppose this is where the handyman Eve Simpson hired lives," I said, angling my head to see if I could read the titles of his books and wondering whether Tony had taken them from the boxes in the house.

"What are you doing?" a man's hard voice asked.

We turned to face Tony Tonelero.

"I hope you don't mind us being here," I said, quickly moving away from the door.

"This is Dr. Hazlitt, a friend of mine."

Tony nodded.

"We were visiting across the street. The Conrad sisters had some refreshments for those who attended Cliff Cooper's funeral."

Another nod from the handyman.

"You must have gotten wet riding your motorcycle to the cemetery," I said.

"I'm used to getting wet," he said. "Is there something you want?"

"No, nothing," I said. "I just was curious why you were at Mr. Cooper's funeral."

His face grew red. "I don't see that where I go on my day off is any of your business."

"You're correct," I said.

He grunted and turned his back to us. "I have work to do."

"I thought you said it was your day off," I said.

He whirled around. "Lady, do I have to explain my every move to you?"

"It isn't necessary to be rude," I said, taking Seth's arm. "We'll leave you alone to get it done."

"Aren't you ever afraid riding on that big bike out there?" Seth asked him.

"No."

"I've treated too many motorcycle accident victims. Those things are dangerous."

"No problem if you know what you're doing," Tonelero mumbled.

I yanked on Seth's arm. I wasn't in the mood for a debate on the perils of riding a two-wheel motorized vehicle.

But after we'd crossed the road and gotten into Seth's car, I said, "He rides a motorcycle."

"Appears that way, the fool. And in the rain as well, a double fool."

"Theresa, the nurse's aide at the hospital, told me that Cliff Cooper had had a visitor, someone carrying a motorcyclist's helmet. I thought her description matched Elliot, but Elliot arrived well after Cliff died, and his helmet isn't black."

"And now you think it may have been this fellow?" Seth said as he put the car in gear and pulled away.

"It seems strange to me that he was at the cemetery, but I can't imagine why he would have been at the hospital visiting a man he'd never met before," I said.

"There were other people in the hospital at the same time Cliff was there," Seth said, stopping to allow a gaggle of geese that had decided to cross the road to make it safely across.

"Yes, but Theresa talked about a motorcyclist visiting Cliff. How many people in Cabot Cove do you know who ride motorcycles?"

"Too many, Jessica."

"I only know two—personally, that is: Elliot Cooper and Tony Tonelero."

The final member of the gaggle of geese made it to the other side of the road.

"Know why a goose crosses the road in front of cars?" Seth asked.

A joke from Seth Hazlitt?

"Why?" I asked.

"I wish I knew," he said as we continued on our way.

Chapter Twenty-two

Seth dropped me off at home, and I quickly discarded my damp clothing in favor of a comfy gray and white sweat suit and slippers. I checked messages on the answering machine and saw that Arthur Bannister, my bookseller friend from New York City, had called. He said that he'd arrived in Cabot Cove and was staying at the Blueberry Hill Inn, owned and operated by my friends Craig and Jill Thomas.

"You made it," I said after I'd been connected to his room.

"Not a bad trip, considering the weather," he said, "but I prefer riding around in New York City, as insane as it is. The drivers are crazy, but all the traffic keeps down the speed."

"I'm just glad that you're here, Arthur.

Why didn't you let me know that you were coming?"

"Didn't know how long it would take me to get here, and I used the ride up to stop at some antiques shops and bookstores along the way. Made a little busman's holiday out of it."

"Do you have dinner plans?"

"I was hoping that you were available."

"Which I happen to be. However, I spent the morning at a funeral and need a little time to unwind."

"I'm sorry to hear that. No one close to you, I trust?"

"Actually, the service was for the man whose books I want you to see. Give me a few hours to catch up, and I'll tell you all about it tonight. You have my address?"

"I've already punched it into my GPS. Neat little device, and the woman giving directions is good company."

We firmed up a time for him to pick me up, and Arthur bid me **"Hasta luego."**

I called Peppino's restaurant to make a reservation, tidied up my office, and started to empty the dishwasher, but my thoughts kept going back to bumping into Geraldo

Tonelero in the barn. He certainly was a strange fellow, speaking in an almost incoherent mumble and avoiding direct eye contact. Not that his personality mattered. As long as he did what Eve Simpson was paying him to do, his lack of social skills was irrelevant. But I'd been meaning to look him up ever since Eve had hired him, especially since I suspected she still hadn't asked for references.

I switched on my computer and waited for the screen to come to life. A Google search failed to turn up the name Geraldo Tonelero with an address in a town down the coast, which was where Eve said he'd come from. I checked a page of images but found no Geraldo Tonelero, either senior or junior. Nor did his name show up under Tony Tonelero or on any of the pages rating the work of local Maine artisans and tradesmen. Of course, he could have used a company name for his business, and I could be looking up the wrong name. I only hoped he hadn't seized on Eve's predicament as an opportunity to enrich himself. On the other hand, if he was a criminal with plans to make off with

Cliff's valuable carpentry equipment, he probably wouldn't have stuck around this long. Frustrated, I turned off the computer.

Arthur arrived at the appointed time, and I took a few minutes to show him around my house before heading out for dinner.

"So this is where the famous Jessica Fletcher creates her spine-tingling masterpieces," he said as we stood in my office.

"This is where Jessica Fletcher hides from the world while she tries to make sense out of murder and mayhem," I said.

"Which you never fail to do," he said.

I smiled. "I do enjoy a flatterer, even though I know that you're just buttering me up for something. What is it?"

"Ah, she sees right through me," Arthur said to the ceiling. "But we'll get to that later. Shall we go share a repast?"

"I've been looking forward to it all day."

And I had. Arthur Bannister was an old-school gentleman with a classic education. He held a doctorate in languages, and would have made a superb professor had he stayed in academia. Instead, he devoted his remarkable mind to collecting and selling books, because, as he always put it, "Books are never rude, even if some of my customers are." Overweight and with a salt-and-pepper beard that refused to be tamed, he was also meticulous in his dress and habits—some said foppish. He was fond of bow ties and wore a neon yellow and red one this evening with a matching handkerchief in the pocket of the double-breasted blue blazer that was wrapped around his sizable frame. I caught the aroma of some citrusy cologne that he wore and thankfully didn't overdo. On occasion I have met gentlemen who douse themselves in a heavy fragrance, their scent overpowering all else and making it difficult to sit near them in a restaurant and enjoy the food.

We drove downtown and settled at a table in Peppino's, an Italian restaurant that had become a favorite of mine since it opened years ago. Arthur had been a lover of the aperitif Campari for as long as I'd known him, even though its bitterness was an acquired taste to be sure. He ordered it on the rocks; I opted for a glass of white wine.

"So," he said after we'd been served and

been given menus to peruse, "what's new in the world of Jessica Fletcher?"

I started off by telling him how the book organizing was going. "We're close to finishing," I said, nearing the end of my account. "There are thousands of them, most of them boxed up in Cliff Cooper's library. The sale is next Saturday. Doris Ann, our librarian, agreed to hold Cabot Cove's annual Halloween Parade on the grounds of the Spencer Percy House. The building is reputed to be haunted, so the date is appropriate. We should get a good crowd, weather permitting."

"How exciting."

"I have to admit that I did not put aside first editions for you, but I've culled some books that I thought you might be especially interested in, although you're free to look at everything."

"I'm really not expecting to find anything of great value, Jessica. Frankly, I've used your book sale as an excuse to get out of the city for a few days. I've left the shop in the hands of my new assistant and only hope that he doesn't burn the place down in my absence."

"I hope so, too," I said. "Cliff Cooper, the gentleman whose books we're selling, recently died. He was a book collector only in the sense that he never let any of them leave his possession. His interests were truly eclectic when it came to reading. We found books ranging from esoteric philosophy to potboilers. Ever hear of a writer named Graham P. Hobart?"

My mention of Hobart caused Arthur to straighten in his chair and lean on the table. "You have Hobarts in the collection?"

I couldn't help but laugh. "Yes," I said. "Do they interest you?"

"They do. They do."

"You must know the covers are gruesome, a real throwback to the early days of noir fiction. And the titles! One more lurid than the last."

"Sounds as if you've read them," he said.

"I haven't read any of them. I just keep coming across them every time I turn around."

"I want them all," he said.

"All?"

"Yes. I probably shouldn't tell you this, Jessica, but there is about to be a Hobart renaissance."

"I can't imagine why."

"He was an unappreciated master of the genre, a recluse and psychopath whose warped imagination took him into the darkest aspects of our existence. I have a friend at a publishing company who wants to reissue all Hobart's novels. If it weren't Sunday night, I'd call him at his office and break the happy news."

"I'm so pleased that your trip here will be fruitful," I said. "Shall we order?"

Arthur was his usual talkative self during dinner, and I played the role of good listener, which I find easy to do. He regaled me with stories of his special purchases—a collection of guides to being a successful housewife, owned by a gentleman who'd been married four times, and a set of taxidermy instructional manuals that sold out the first day Arthur put them on a shelf. "I can't imagine what animals that customer is hunting in lower Manhattan. Rather, I can imagine but don't think I really want to know."

I told him about Cliff's obsolete atlases, and he surprised me by saying, "You know, those fetch a pretty penny. People buy them to tear apart, then frame the maps and sell them separately. Old maps are very popular."

"I never thought of using an outdated atlas that way, although I do love to read a map."

"You do? I thought you don't drive."

"I don't, but I remember how much fun it was to serve as navigator when my late husband, Frank, was behind the wheel. I'd spread the map of Maine on my lap, follow our route with my finger, and alert him to the turns coming up." I smiled at the memory.

"I'll bet you loved telling him how to go."

I laughed. "I did, especially since he was so good-natured about getting instructions from a backseat driver with no experience whatsoever."

"Those big paper maps are not as readily available as they once were. They're being replaced by GPS systems and programs on your smartphone that only show you small sections of your route. As convenient as they are, they don't give you the big picture that a large map can provide."

"Or the opportunity to investigate alternate routes or side roads to your destination."

"Exactly," Arthur said as our dessert plates were cleared. "And speaking of opportunity, any chance I can see the Hobarts tonight?"

"They're boxed up in Cliff's library at the Spencer Percy House."

"Can we go look?"

"Now?"

He adopted a little boy's pleading expression.

"I suppose we can," I said. "No one is there at this hour, and I have a key that the real estate agent gave me. But promise me we won't be long. It's been a tiring day."

He agreed, and after saying good-bye to Peppino's father-and-son owners, we got in Arthur's car and headed for the Spencer Percy House. It occurred to me as we drove up the driveway that I might be invading the handyman's privacy again. But how likely was it that he'd be working late on a Sunday night? Chances were he was in his cubbyhole in the barn, reading one of the books on his night table.

Arthur looked up when we exited his car. "Amazing how many stars you can see out in the country."

"When you live in the city, the lights on the ground obscure them," I said. "It was one of my reasons for deciding to move back home to Cabot Cove from New York. I wanted to see the stars again."

When we approached the house, it was dark except for two lamps that Eve Simpson had put on timers, based upon my suggestion. I have lamps on timers in many rooms in my house, a sensible security step I'd been practicing for years. I inserted the key in the front door and stepped inside, with Arthur following.

"Hello," I called out, figuring if some-one was there, I wanted to alert them to our presence. I didn't want to be mistaken for an intruder. Too many times the arrival of an unexpected guest provokes an equally unexpected response.

"You talked about this place being haunted," Arthur said. "Are you expecting a spectral reply?"

"Certainly not. The haunting is simply a

rumor that's gotten out of hand."

"You don't believe in ghosts?" he asked as we entered the library.

I turned on the ceiling fixture. "No, I don't believe in ghosts."

"Oh, my," he said, his eyes lighting up when he took in the rows of boxes neatly marked with their category names. "I'm going to have a good time here."

"Not tonight, however. We're here for one thing, remember?" I picked up the carton containing the Hobart novels and handed it to him. "Come with me to the kitchen. It'll be easier to look at them there."

"And you'll get me away from temptation. Is that what you're thinking?"

"Unfortunately, there are more books in the kitchen." I led him down the hall.

"You should keep an open mind about ghosts, Jessica," he said from behind me. "They're very real. In many cultures, Halloween is followed by All Saints' Day and All Souls' Day, **el Día de Todos los Santos** and **el Día de los Muertos**, honoring those who have gone before us, both children and adults. Many peoples around the world are convinced that departed souls are still with us."

"I'll take your word for it," I said. "I'm not up for a debate." I switched on the overhead light and directed him to the kitchen's metal table. "This is the only unoccupied space on this floor," I said, putting down my shoulder bag. "All the other surfaces are piled with boxes of books."

Arthur looked around the crowded room at the stacks of corrugated cartons lining the walls. "I'd hardly call this space unoccupied," he said, smiling.

"These are the ones that haven't been sorted yet. The house's deceased owner kept books in the basement as well as the library. The handyman who's working on repairs kindly packed up the ones downstairs, saving me the trips up and down."

"A true gentleman."

"I was grateful for the help, but I'm fairly certain he didn't group them by category. That's work left to do. Not to mention that there were several legal-size boxes containing family papers. I don't see those, though. Maybe they're still on the shelves."

Arthur placed the box containing the Hobart novels on the kitchen table and eagerly began pulling them out, holding each one at a distance to admire the sensational cover. "Ah, yes," he said, "from the master himself."

"He really was that good?" I said, looking over his shoulder.

"Good in a literary sense? No. But there was—how shall I say it?—there was a level of perversion that emanated from his own warped personality." He withdrew from the box the copy of **Betrayal**. "How much are you asking for these?"

"I have no idea, Arthur. Make an offer. The money is going to the Cabot Cove Library."

"A worthy cause. Let me think about it overnight. Can I take these with me?"

"I suppose so, only—"

"I'd hate to leave them here and find out in the morning that someone has walked away with them."

"Then by all means take them with you."

"Think there may be any more downstairs?"

"I don't know. I haven't been downstairs

since Tony boxed up what was on the basement shelves."

"Who's Tony?"

"The handyman I told you about, Tony Tonelero."

"Tonelero? He must have a Spanish barrel maker in his family's past."

"If you say so."

"I'd love to take a peek downstairs, Jessica. Do you think you can accommodate me one more time? I'd hate to miss out on another Hobart if it's just sitting on a shelf waiting for me to discover it."

"I'm really tired, Arthur. Can't it wait until tomorrow? Besides, it's almost impossible to see down there—there's so little light."

"Didn't your letter to me ask if I would talk about book collecting at the library?"

"Are you bribing me?"

"Just offering you an incentive."

"All right, Arthur, but I'm only doing this to benefit the library."

"They will be thrilled with my lecture. I promise."

I went to the door leading down to the basement. "Strange," I muttered to myself.

"The key is missing." I tried turning the knob, but the door was definitely locked. **Now, why would he lock the basement door and take away the key?**

"Problem?" Arthur called from where he stood, paging through one of the Hobarts.

"The skeleton key that used to be in the lock is gone."

"A skeleton key? Don't see many of those anymore. They used to open all the doors in these old houses." He walked over to where I stood, pulled a ring of keys from his pants pocket, and fingered through them. "See anything promising here?" he asked.

I shook my head.

"Is there a closet nearby with a key?"

"The hall closet doesn't have a key, and the front door has a more modern lock. I have to tell you, Arthur, I'm not about to go room to room upstairs looking for a key at this time of night."

He gave a great sigh.

"However," I said, "I do have the key to my back porch in my bag. I've been meaning to have the lock changed. It's not very secure. I can't promise it'll open this door."

He perked up immediately. "Let's give it a try. If it doesn't work, I won't complain, and we'll leave our exploration of the nether regions for tomorrow."

"That's a deal."

I went back to the kitchen table and groped around the bottom of my shoulder bag until I came up with the skeleton key. I handed it to Arthur.

Just my luck, or maybe just Arthur's luck, the key turned in the lock. "Voilà!" Arthur opened the door and the pitch-black basement loomed.

"Let me go ahead of you," I said. "I know where there's a string attached to a light down there, but it's a very dim bulb. And, Arthur, the stairs are not very sound. If you feel any of them beginning to give, please step back up. The last thing we need tonight is for one of us to get injured."

"I'll be careful."

I gripped the wooden railing and began my second descent into Cliff Cooper's basement. Arthur followed, his breathing audible. I stiffened at every creaking board, but thankfully the steps held. When

I sensed I was near the bottom of the staircase, I put out my hand and waved my arm, hoping to connect with the pull chain that illuminated the night-light. My fingers connected with a cord, and I gave it a sharp tug.

A brilliant light came on, its beam aimed at the wall of mostly empty bookcases.

"My goodness," I said.

"That's hardly dim light. I think I'll be able to see very well if I can get out of my own way."

"How strange," I murmured. "He said he would rig something so I could work down here, but then he packed up all the books for me. Why would he need such a bright light now?"

"Don't question good fortune, my dear." Arthur walked past me, his bulk casting a large shadow over the bookcases. He stopped in front of the middle one and reached out to the side support. "Looks like he plans to disassemble these," he said, making the empty bookcase rock.

"Why on earth would he do that?" I tried to see past Arthur's girth as he reached for a book.

"Well, here's one!" he said, grabbing up his prize. He turned toward the light, holding up the book so I could see its title, **Wall of Blood**, with an equally gory illustration on the front cover.

"I found only one down here," I said, frowning. "Arthur, do you remember any of other titles in the box upstairs?"

"I think so. You have **Betrayal** and **Masquerade.** Never read those. I saw **Taking My Revenge**—great cover on that one. And...I'd have to go upstairs to take a look."

"That's not necessary," I said, turning to study the empty bookcase. "Just help me move this, if you would."

"What are you doing?"

"I remember seeing that the wall behind this bookcase looked different. I thought it was the result of a water leak, but now I'm not so sure."

"Why would that matter at this moment?"

"It may not, but I have a hunch that it does."

Arthur and I shifted the bookcase back and forth, the bottom rails shrieking as the wood scraped against the concrete floor.

We pulled it partially free, and I squeezed into the space behind it, patting the cold wall. "I can't see in here," I said, peeking out at him. "Do you have your cell phone with you?"

"Of course. Do you need to call someone?"

"No, I need to borrow it. Mine is upstairs in my bag. I'm casting such a strong shadow with that light behind me, I can't see the wall."

Arthur patted his pockets until he found his phone and passed it to me. "What are you looking for?"

"I'm not sure." His phone was the same as mine, and I quickly found his flashlight and turned it on.

"Well, I'll be darned," he said, leaning around the side of the bookcase. "Never knew it could do that. You'll have to show me which buttons you pushed."

I ran my fingers, as well as the light, over the wall, the surface of which was smooth in the center and rough on either side. I kneeled down. At the base of the wall, just above the floor, the plaster had been chipped away, leaving a ragged hole.

Someone had started sawing upward from the hole, leaving plaster dust on the floor, but had only gotten as far as a foot and a half. I pushed my fingers inside the opening at the bottom, but the gap was too small for my whole hand.

"I wouldn't do that if I were you, Jessica. An animal may have made that hole. You don't want to get bitten."

I shone the light on the hole again. "The edges don't look like an animal ate away at them," I said, pulling at the crumbling plaster. "And animals don't know how to use a hammer or a saw. You don't see one of those nearby, do you?"

I heard him move out of the way of the spotlight. "No. No tools on the shelves. I would have no idea where else to look."

"That's okay. Let's see what I can do."

I stood up and kicked at the hole with the toe of my shoe.

"Have you been feeling quite right, Jessica?" His voice held concern. "Are you sure you want to do this tonight? I'm happy to return in the morning and look for more books then."

"I'm fine. I just need to enlarge this a

little." I took off my shoe and pounded on the cracking plaster with my heel.

"I'm sorry if I made you come out when you needed to rest, Jessica. Let me take you home."

"There!" I said, dropping to my knees again and ignoring the fragments of wallboard digging into my skin. I broke off more pieces, sweeping the shards away with the side of my hand. I leaned down, putting my face near the hole and trying not to breathe in the plaster dust I'd created. The light from Arthur's cell phone illuminated only a small area inside the wall, but it was enough. "Oh, good heavens. I was afraid of this." I sat back with a cough, brushing the dust from my hands.

"What were you afraid of, my dear?" He was humoring me now and must have thought I'd lost my mind.

"I'm all right, Arthur; really I am."

"Let me help you up, then." He extended his hand.

"Not yet," I said, reaching into the widened opening, my fingers gently patting the floor behind the wall.

"I remembered the names of the other

Hobarts, Arthur."

"Yes, Jessica. What were they?"

I pulled my hand out of the hole and opened it, showing him what I held. "Those books were **Buried Sins** and **Hidden Grave**," I said.

"And what do you have there?"

I looked down at my palm. "A bone, Arthur, a human bone."

Chapter Twenty-three

The flashing red, white, and blue lights on police cars and an ambulance lit up the Spencer Percy House like bolts of lightning, eclipsing the starry sky Arthur and I had admired, and casting eerie shadows as they bounced off windows, trees, and the front of the barn. Emergency vehicles had raced to the scene after I'd called the sheriff's office from Arthur's cell phone, but they'd come silently—no need for sirens when the victim was already dead.

Arthur and I had met them at the front door, and we talked in the hall. I introduced my guest to Mort.

"What were you doing here so late, Mrs. F? It's Sunday night. Not exactly your usual working hours."

"I may be able to explain, Sheriff Metzger,"

Arthur said. "I convinced Mrs. Fletcher to allow me an advance look at the books that are going into the sale next weekend."

"And you happened to find a body?"

"Well, no. I mean, I asked to see if there were any more Hobarts in the basement."

"Hobarts?"

"A soon-to-be-in-demand author." Arthur paused. "I'm not sure how to explain this." He looked at me helplessly.

"We went downstairs to see if there were any more Hobarts in the basement," I said. "Tony—that's the handyman Eve hired—had boxed up all the books that were on the shelves and taken them up to the kitchen for me."

"So you went downstairs looking for books even though you knew all the books had been brought upstairs?" Mort gave me a skeptical look.

"In a way. But I also knew a few boxes with personal papers hadn't been brought up, so I thought maybe a book or two might be in among them."

"And did you find what you were looking for?"

"Actually, yes," Arthur said, holding up

Wall of Blood for Mort to see.

Mort grimaced when he saw the cover. "That's disgusting. Why do you want to read stuff like that, Mrs. F?"

"I don't read them," I said.

"They're not my cup of tea either," Arthur put in.

"Yet you went into the basement looking for books by this author?"

"They're very scarce," Arthur said.

"For good reason," Mort grunted.

"Mort, let him explain."

"I believe some collectors will pay well for them," Arthur said. "We already have six of the author's titles. He only wrote seven."

"But they're irrelevant to what we found," I said.

"What **you** found," Arthur said, still clutching **Wall of Blood**.

"Okay," Mort said, pulling a notepad and pen from his uniform pocket, "you and your friend here were looking for books. When you called, you told the dispatcher that you might have found a dead body in the house. **What** body?"

I handed him the bone and explained

where and how I'd discovered it. He rolled his eyes as he had me drop the bone into a plastic bag.

"I don't know, Mrs. F. You've been involved in some weird events before, but this one tops the list. If this turns out to be a bone from some squirrel or raccoon that got stuck in the wall and died, I'm not going to be a happy camper."

"I understand," I said, "but it looks to me like a human bone."

"All of a sudden you're an expert on bones?" he said.

"I'm not an expert on anything, Mort, but it would have been irresponsible for me **not** to have called."

"Yeah, you're right, Mrs. F.," he said. "Sorry. I'm a little on edge tonight."

He directed several of his men to fan out and search the property.

"There's something else you should know," I told our sheriff. "As we were coming upstairs from the basement, we heard the roar of a motorcycle engine outside. It sounded like it raced down the driveway and away from the house." I then told him about Eve's handyman who lived, at least temporarily, in the barn.

"Do you think this Tonelero character's midnight ride could be connected to what you found, Mrs. F?"

"I couldn't say, Mort. I didn't hear anyone walking around upstairs when Arthur and I were in the basement, but that doesn't mean he wasn't here. Then again, his departure may just be a coincidence. He might be visiting someone and have plans to return later."

"At twelve o'clock at night? That's pretty late to be paying a social call, don't you think?"

"It would be for me, but younger people go out late at night all the time."

"Maybe, maybe not, but I'm considering him a person of interest. When we find him, we'll ask about his **social life**."

Mort issued an all-points bulletin to be on the lookout for the handyman and his motorcycle, and decided that Arthur and I had little more to offer. "This house is a potential crime scene," he said. "You'll have to leave."

"The **basement** is a potential crime scene," I said, hoping he wouldn't take offense at my interjection. "Can't Arthur and I remain in the library, or maybe the kitchen, while you conduct your investigation?"

"I suppose so," he said. "Just stay out of everyone's hair."

He instructed two deputies to check out the basement and report back. As they left, Seth Hazlitt walked into the kitchen. "Why did I know I'd find **you** here?" he said.

"Why are **you** here?" I asked.

"I'm here because every time you find a possible murder victim, the medical examiner is out of town. I'm 'it' again. Do you know who it is downstairs that you discovered?"

Mort turned to me. "Yeah, Mrs. F. I didn't ask you that. Who **did** you find—**if** it's a person?"

"No idea," I said, which wasn't entirely true. While I couldn't swear whom the bone belonged to, I knew that there was a body behind the wall.

The deputies Mort had sent downstairs reported back that they saw the hole, and that there seemed to be some bones, but they couldn't tell whether they belonged to a human being.

"Want to take a look, Doc?" Mort asked. "I figure you know human bones when you see 'em." He handed Seth the plastic bag with the bone in it.

Seth held it up to the light and gave it back to him. "It appears to be a navicular bone, but I'd like to see more."

"Navicular, huh? What kind of bone is that?"

"The navicular is a bone of the foot."

"Not from a raccoon, huh?"

"Not unless it was a five-foot-tall raccoon with human feet."

Mort cocked his head at me. "Well, let's go see where you found it, Mrs. F."

I led our little troop of Mort, Seth, and the deputies downstairs to the basement wall that still entombed a body. The deputy who'd been there earlier had moved the bookcase out of the way, and the brilliant light Tony had set up now fully illuminated the wall, making it easier to see the section that had once been breached and sealed up again.

Seth pulled on a pair of latex gloves and

squatted next to the opening that I'd enlarged. He put his hand inside and withdrew another bone, turning it over in his palm. "You may want to get your techs down here," he said to Mort.

Mort used his walkie-talkie to call for crime scene specialists. "Bring an ax," he added to his instructions.

We returned to the kitchen to wait for the technicians to arrive and disinter the body. I was wide-awake now, the morning's funeral a distant memory.

Arthur wandered in from the library, holding a book. "Look what I found, Jessica."

"What do you have there?" Mort asked.

"It's a 1952 edition of Hemingway's **The Old Man and the Sea**. Even has a dust jacket, although it's a little ragged. This will sell well in an auction."

"Yeah?" Mort said. "How much is it worth?"

"A couple of hundred at least," Arthur replied. "Depends on the day of the auction. These things vary. But if there are more goodies like this in those boxes, I may be able to give the Cabot Cove Library a sizable donation on top of what you make from the general sale."

"I'm glad to hear it," I said.

I'd been thinking about the upcoming book sale and wondering what the discovery of the body would do to our need to complete the task of getting the books out of the house and ready to sell. The Spencer Percy House would become an active crime scene; Mort and his people wouldn't appreciate our getting in their way. Would I have to postpone the sale yet again?

Three technicians arrived a half hour later and clumped down the basement steps. They carried a suitcase full of the usual crime scene equipment, plus a body bag, hatchet, and an electric tool they called a Sawzall. Mort gave me permission to join them, and we watched while they set up additional lights, aimed at the wall from different angles than the spotlight Tony had installed. The crossing and bounced beams of additional lighting effectively canceled out the shadows thrown by people working the scene.

"If you're going to stay here, you'd better wear one of these," a tech said, handing

Mort and me paper masks. "Taking apart a wall can get pretty dusty."

A photographer dropped a ruler next to the hole I made and took a series of pictures, while his colleague began a sketch of the basement, measuring the walls and floor, and noting every object in sight, including the bookcases, Tony's light, and the decrepit dehumidifier, source of the supposedly ghostly noise that had scared off some people hired to fix up the house.

"Got anything to put these pieces in?" a tech asked, holding up a chunk of wall he had removed.

"There may be one or two empty boxes still in the library," I said.

Mort sent his deputy upstairs, and he returned with a box to hold the debris.

"Will the wall material be subject to forensic examination?" I asked.

"Not sure, but I'll save it just in case," Mort said, standing next to me with his fists on his hips. "Sorry if I doubted you, Mrs. F."

"That's all right, Mort."

"I should have learned by now to trust your instincts," he said as the tech started to saw again. Mort raised his voice. "Maybe your instincts will tell you—and you'll tell me—who we're taking out of the wall."

I had to shout to be heard over the noise. "I'd rather wait to see what the techs find, in case I'm wrong."

Mort shouted back. "I won't hold it against you if you're wrong."

"I think it may be a woman," I shouted.

The tech paused in his sawing, and Mort asked in a normal voice, "What makes you think that?"

"I couldn't find anyone who had seen her leave the house."

"Who never left the house?"

"Marina. Marina Cooper."

"Who is she?"

The answer came from behind us. "She's my mother."

Elliot, who'd apparently been there long enough to have overheard our conversation, stood halfway down the stairs, his face pale, his hair standing up where he'd nervously run his fingers through. "I think I'm going to be sick," he said.

Chapter Twenty-four

"I saw all the lights outside the house, and I knew something bad was happening. The deputy wouldn't let me in even after I told him it was my house, so I went around to the side and climbed in the window I've been using since I got back from Alaska."

"I was wondering how you made it past the police," I said.

Elliot and I sat at the metal kitchen table, a cup of tea in front of me, hot chocolate for him that I'd managed to dredge up, while Mort's crime scene technicians finished disinterring the body of Marina Cooper.

"There's a man in the library poking through all the boxes," Elliot said.

"That's Arthur Bannister," I said. "He owns a bookshop in Manhattan specializing in first editions. I was hoping he'd find some valuable books in your grandfather's collection that could be auctioned off to raise money for the town's library."

Elliot took a deep breath and nodded. "Maybe something positive will come out of all this," he said halfheartedly, rubbing his face with his hands. "You know what I don't understand, Mrs. Fletcher?" he said, his voice cracking. "She was dead my whole life. I never knew her, never knew anything about her, never even knew anybody who would tell me about her. She was nothing to me. So why do I keep crying?" Big tears slid down his cheeks, and he wiped his eyes with the sleeve of his checkered shirt.

I put my hand on his arm and said, "You were just a baby when you came to live with your grandfather, too young to remember what life was like with your parents. This is your mother we've found, not some stranger. Even though she wasn't in your life growing up, she is an important part of who you are."

"When I started school and realized other kids had parents—not just a grandfather—I remember being angry and lashing out at

Grandpa Cliff. I scoured the house looking for something about them, but he told me that he threw away all the old papers." He managed a small laugh. "This from a man who never threw anything away. You've seen what it's like."

I nodded.

"I was sure they would show up someday. I was certain that they hadn't been killed — only lost in the Amazon. Once, when I was reading one of the **National Geographic** magazines, I found a picture of the two of them together, my mother and father, stuck between the pages. I'm sure it was them — who else could it have been? — even though I could barely make out their faces. He was wearing one of those pith helmets, and she had a blue and green striped scarf over her head. I never told Grandpa Cliff I found it. I kept it hidden from him. It had been taken with one of those Polaroid cameras, so the picture was pretty faded. It was under my pillow for years until I woke up one morning and the picture was completely white, no image left at all."

I was glad that Elliot was comfortable speaking with me; he needed to tell someone about his feelings and experiences. For all the wonderful things Cliff had done for Elliot, he never encouraged the boy to talk about his parents and how it felt not to have a mother and father. According to Elliot, his grandfather hadn't told him about his father, about Jerry's youth, or how and where he'd met Marina. When Elliot would raise the topic, Cliff would dismiss it or distract him.

"I guess that's why I became something of a wild kid. I bragged to the other kids that because I didn't have parents, I could do whatever I wanted. I was planning to travel around the world." He shook his head. "Of course, the first place I landed in my great exploration of the globe was Alaska, and darned if I didn't put down roots as fast as I could." He looked up at me suddenly. "Do you think my father's body is hidden behind another wall?" he asked.

I shook my head. "The owner of the local taxi service remembers driving your father to Boston where he was to catch a flight to South America."

"So he may have died in the jungle after

all."

"It's possible," I said, "but your grand-father said he received a note informing him that both your parents were killed by the tribesmen they'd gone to study in Colombia."

"And you think that maybe it was my dad who sent the message?"

I shrugged. "Perhaps," I said, "but I can't say for certain."

Mort came into the kitchen. "Mrs. F., can I see you for a second?"

"Of course."

I followed Mort into the hallway off the kitchen.

"The guys have just taken the rest of the body out of the wall. They found a string tied around the plastic sheet that held the body."

"Yes?"

"There was a note attached."

He pulled a clear plastic bag from his pocket and smoothed it so I could read what was on the paper it contained. The message read: "This is my daughter-in-law, Marina Cooper. I killed her. Do not blame her husband, my son, Jerry." It was signed "Cliff Cooper."

"What's that?" Elliot asked, coming up behind us. "If that was with my mother's body, don't I have a right to see it?"

"Yes, son. I guess you do," Mort said, passing the bag to Elliot.

Elliot took it, his hand trembling. He held it for a moment, then handed it back to Mort. "My whole life has been a lie," he said. He looked at me, his eyes at once blazing with anger and filling with tears. "Remember all those nice things I said about him this morning? I take them back. He was not the man I thought he was. How could he have carried on a normal life"—he waved his hand toward the basement door—"knowing he killed my mother, the wife of his son, the mother of his grandson? He pretended everything was normal. He went to my school conferences. He took me shopping for shoes. He taught me how to use tools. He discussed books with me, philosophy, and history. Who **was** he really? **Who was he?**"

I put my hand on Elliot's arm. "You've had a big shock tonight," I said, gently steering him back to the kitchen. "The police still have a lot of investigating to do. Things aren't always what they appear to be at first. Please remember that. Cliff loved you more than anything or anyone in the world. His whole life revolved around you. Let's wait and make sure all the facts are in before we judge him."

"I think I'd like to go to bed now. Is that okay? This is too much to process all at once. Finding my mother's body and then learning that my grandfather was her killer."

"Of course. Is there anything I can do for you, Elliot?"

"No, thanks. I'll be okay. I just want to be alone for a while. I'll be across the street if you need to speak with me again, Sheriff."

"You go rest," I said, and Mort nodded his agreement.

"Will you tell Aunt Lucy and Aunt Lettie in the morning? I don't think I can face them with this news."

"I'll tell them," Mort said. "I have to interview them anyway."

I followed Elliot to the door. He put his hand on the knob and looked back at me. "I saw her again tonight."

"Who?"

"The lady in the white robe, the one who used to tell me stories. I dreamed about her, and the dream woke me up. I knew something was different. When I looked out the window and saw the police cars, I couldn't get here fast enough."

"You think it was your mother in the dream?"

"I know it was."

It was nearly three in the morning before I got home and crawled into my bed. Exhausted, I expected to fall asleep instantly, but instead my mind churned with the events of the day: the funeral service for Cliff Cooper, the surprise of seeing Tony Tonelero at the cemetery, Elliot and Beth's late arrival at the sisters' reception, the brief confrontation with the handyman in the barn, Arthur's arriving and wanting to see the Hobarts, and, most unsettling, the discovery in the Spencer Percy House basement.

When he drove me home, Arthur had insisted that it must have been the noir author who'd inspired me to examine the wall behind the bookcase. "The titles of his books hinted to you that something was there to investigate. You say you don't believe in ghosts, Jessica, but it looks to me as if the spirit world was guiding you, whether it was Grant P. Hobart, Cliff Cooper, or Marina Cooper herself."

I'd dismissed Arthur's speculations, saying, "I'll admit the titles of the books inspired me to search for Marina's body, but I'm not ready to credit a ghost with being an informant in a murder case."

But as I lay in bed, I began to wonder why it had taken so long for the history of the Cooper family to intrigue me. Was it simply the questions no one else had bothered to pursue? Cliff had been a valued and accepted member of the community, admired as much for his skill as a craftsman as for his devotion to his grandson. Had we all misjudged him? Had we all taken him at face value and allowed a murderer to live out his days among us?

And if we had, who had murdered the murderer?

Chapter Twenty-five

The phone rang at eight thirty the next morning, rousing me from a deep sleep.

Seth Hazlitt's voice came over the line. "I figure that since I'm up examining the body you discovered, you won't mind being awakened to hear the results."

I struggled to sit up on the edge of the bed, running a hand through my tousled curls to smooth them even though no one was there to see me. "What have you learned?" I asked, reaching for the pad and pen I keep on my bedside table.

"Of course, it's too early in the post-mortem to confirm that the deceased was indeed Marina Cooper, no matter what the note says. But I can say that the skeleton belonged to a woman, probably late twenties is my best guess, dressed in a white nightgown or what's left of one. No evidence of arthritis; the cranial sutures have not completely fused, relatively little wear of the so-called wisdom teeth."

"How did she die? Was there any indication?"

"Oh, yes, a very obvious one."

"Don't keep me in suspense, Seth. What was it?"

"There was a clear fracture of the skull. I'd say death was caused by blunt force instrument trauma to the right frontal lobe near the cerebral cortex."

"Someone bludgeoned her to death."

"Precisely. And now that I've completed my preliminary examination of the remains, and reported the initial observations to both the authorities and to my good friend, Mrs. Fletcher, I am going to take myself off to surrender to this aging physician's fatigue."

"You must be exhausted."

"I'd already retired for the night when Mort called about your **find**."

"Unfortunate timing," I said. "You deserve a good sleep, Seth. Thanks for giving me your conclusions. Oh, did Mort Metzger say anything about whether they've located the handyman, Tony Tonelero?"

"No. I just gave our esteemed sheriff the same news I'm giving you. Go back to sleep."

The phone clicked in my ear.

Go back to sleep?

Impossible!

I'd just put on my slippers and robe, and was on my way to the kitchen when the phone rang again. It was Eve Simpson.

"Jessica," she said, "this is terrible, the worst sort of news."

"Yes, it was a tragic discovery," I said, assuming she was referring to the murder. She was, but not in the way I expected.

"What will this do to my getting the house ready for sale? I drove past it this morning. There's that vile yellow tape strung across the driveway, and two police cars and officers are stationed to keep everyone away."

"It is an active crime scene, Eve."

"But what will I do?"

"You'll have to speak with the police about it," I said.

Eve wasn't the only one with a pragmatic

response to the discovery of Marina Cooper's body. It had crossed my mind that my discovery of the body might also impact the book sale. I'd ordered the tent in the event of rain, but holding the sale, even a small part of it, in the Spencer Percy House was likely to be out of the question. Would Mort and his officers even allow us to erect the tent on the property? I made a mental note to ask him about it.

Our exasperated real estate agent ended the call, freeing me to reach the kitchen and get coffee going. Now fully awake, or close to it, I used the wall phone to call Mort Metzger's office.

"Hello, Mrs. Fletcher," the dispatcher on duty said.

"Good morning. Does the sheriff happen to be there?"

"Oh, no, he's over at the crime scene. Shocking, isn't it, finding a body like that. He said that you were the one who discovered her, poor thing."

"Yes, it certainly was shocking," I agreed.

"Can I give Sheriff Metzger a message from you?"

"No, thank you. I'll catch up with him

later."

My final comment reflected a decision I made on the spot. I'd go to the Spencer Percy House and hope to steal some time with Mort.

After a banana, a cup of coffee, and a hurried shower—and a call to Arthur Bannister at the Blueberry Hill Inn to tell him where I'd be—I ordered a taxi and soon stood in front of what by now had become an emerging tourist destination, judging from the group of people congregated outside the crime scene tape. Notably absent from the crowd were Elliot, Beth, and the Conrad sisters. I approached the officer at the foot of the driveway. "Is Sheriff Metzger here?" I asked.

"He's inside, Mrs. Fletcher."

"I really need to speak with him."

The deputy spoke into the walkie-talkie clipped to his shoulder, and a minute later Mort emerged from the house. He waved to me, and the deputy lifted the yellow tape for me to duck under.

I waited for Mort to make his way down the driveway. "Why am I not surprised to see you here this morning?" he said, dark circles around his eyes and a hoarse voice testifying to his lack of sleep.

"Are things going all right?" I asked.

"We're winding down our investigation," he said. "I spoke with Doc Hazlitt earlier. It's a clear-cut case of murder, no doubt about that."

I didn't mention that Seth had already told me the result of his examination of the body. Although he hadn't made a definitive identification, I was certain that the homicide victim was Jerry Cooper's wife, Marina. "Are you going to ask Elliot for a DNA sample to confirm the victim's identity?" I asked.

Mort nodded. "Good suggestion, Mrs. F., but it's already on my agenda. He wanted me to break the news to the ladies who live over there, but from the looks of this place"—he gestured at the onlookers—"I imagine they have a pretty good idea that something big has happened."

"Have you found the handyman that Eve Simpson hired?" I asked.

"If I didn't know better, I'd think that you were wired into our police communications system," he said. "I heard only five minutes ago that he's been picked up at a down-state motel. Local police there did their job. I told them to bring him here. I want to interview him away from the station house. Sometimes official surroundings make people clam up."

As Mort and I spoke, Arthur Bannister pulled up in his car, parked across the street, and hurried over. His appearance preceded that of Evelyn Phillips and her photographer, who arrived and parked farther down the road. Evelyn trotted up the road, just as the truck belonging to Arianna Olynski pulled in behind her car. Boris jumped out, camera on shoulder, filming the scene.

Mort spotted Evelyn and said, "You'll have to excuse me, Mrs. F. I'm in no mood to speak with the press or some crazy ghost chaser."

"May I come inside with you?" I asked.

Mort sighed. "Yeah, I suppose so. No damage can be done now that we've completed our work." He eyed Arthur. "You, too?"

Arthur gestured toward me. "I'm with her."

"Come on, then," Mort said.

Arthur ducked under the crime scene tape as Evelyn yelled to the sheriff, "I need to speak with you!"

Mort walked swiftly to the house and led us through the open front door to where the crime scene techs and Mort's deputies were in the process of packing up.

"Can you find a few minutes to talk?" I asked.

"Just a few."

We settled in the library where Arthur perused the small number of books left on the shelves while I addressed my concerns to Mort. I told him of Eve Simpson's call and her distress at not being able to continue fixing up the house for sale. I then raised the issue of the book sale.

"I know that you don't want people traipsing around in the house," I said. "I've ordered a large tent. Is it all right if we have the sale but confine it to the tent outside?"

"I don't see why not," he said.

"But we will have to let people come into this room to remove all these boxes. Okay?"

He nodded. "Anything else, Mrs. F?"

"You mentioned that Tonelero is being brought back here for questioning. I'm curious about what he knows about the body in the basement. Someone had started sawing a hole in that wall. I don't know who else it could have been but him."

"That's what I want to ask him. We collected some tools in the barn to test for plaster dust. Maybe he was just curious about what was behind the wall. Maybe he got scared when he had an idea of what it was, and took off. But he's not a suspect. Cliff Cooper did us all a favor by leaving that note."

"Doesn't it strike you as odd that Cliff would specifically say in the note that his son Jerry **hadn't** done it? I mean, if he'd simply taken the blame, its purpose would be clear."

"I think your creative juices are acting up, Mrs. F., if you don't mind my saying so."

"I suppose you're right, Mort. It's just that—" I turned to Arthur, who was still perusing books. "Last night, Arthur, you said that Tony must have had some barrel makers in his family's past."

"That's right."

"I didn't pay attention to it then, but I've been thinking about it since."

Mort scratched his head. "Why, Mrs. F? What do you care about the handyman's family?"

"Arthur, I'm not fluent in Spanish, but you are. Does his name, Tonelero, mean barrel maker in Spanish?"

"Right you are," Arthur said, not taking his attention from the book he was examining.

I looked at Mort. "And another name for barrel maker in English is 'cooper.'"

"Cooper? No kidding?" Mort said. "That's funny."

"Cooper," I said, "as in the name Cooper."

"I'm not sure I see where this is going."

"He calls himself Tony, but he introduced himself to me as Geraldo, pronouncing it **Heraldo**."

"Heraldo?"

"Yes, Spanish for Gerald. And the nickname for Gerald is Jerry. Mort, I think Tony Tonelero is Cliff's son, Jerry Cooper, the husband of the woman in the basement."

"Whoa, slow down," Mort said. "Cliff

Cooper's son was killed in South America."

"And so was his son's wife, Marina—supposedly! But the note says the woman in the basement is Marina Cooper."

It dawned on me that I'd never shared with Mort what had come out of my conversation with Dimitri, the taxi driver, who'd driven Jerry Cooper to the Boston airport. I rectified that by recounting it for him.

When I finished, he said, "So you're saying, Mrs. F., that Marina Cooper never went to South America."

"That's right. She never went anywhere except behind the wall in the basement, her head bashed in."

"By Cliff Cooper," Mort said.

"**If** you believe the note he left."

"Why wouldn't I?"

It took me a few seconds to gather my thoughts. "It's possible, Mort, that Cliff Cooper's note means exactly what it says, that he killed his daughter-in-law, Marina, and was concerned that if the body was found, his son, Jerry, her husband, would be accused of the murder. On the other hand—"

"What, Mrs. F? You're not going to challenge my nicely solved case, are you?"

"We have to consider the evidence, Mort. Cliff might have left that note to protect his son in the event the body was ever discovered. What if he sent Jerry off to South America to get him out of harm's way, to shield his son from facing the consequences of having killed his wife? Then he buried the body in the wall and built bookcases to cover up the crime?"

"I don't know, Mrs. F. That's an interesting what-if sort of thing, like what you write in your murder mystery books. But I have an open-and-shut case. If you doubt it, you'll have to show me evidence to the contrary."

"I only wish I could, Mort. Maybe when you question Geraldo Tonelero and ask him if he really is Jerry Cooper, things will become clearer. In the meantime, thank you for indulging my speculation."

"That goes for me, too," Arthur said. "I never thought when I came to this sleepy little town that I'd be an eyewitness to a real-life murder mystery."

We were interrupted by a deputy.

"Sheriff," he said, "Ms. Phillips from the **Gazette** is outside, howling like a banshee about seeing you. She's threatening to bring a lawsuit against the town and keeps talking about some freedom of something act and—"

"Yeah, yeah, okay," Mort said wearily, standing and stretching against a pain in his back. "Go tell her I'll give her ten minutes, no more."

"She also says she wants to talk to Mrs. Fletcher," the deputy added.

"I'd rather not," I said.

"Good," said Mort. "Let's keep your what-if thinking between us, at least for a while."

"You have my word," I said.

"And that goes for you, too," Mort said to Arthur.

"Me?" Arthur said, placing his hand on his heart. "These lips have never been more sealed."

"Does he always talk like that?" Mort whispered to me.

"Like what?"

"You know, sort of, well, sort of artsy-like."

I smiled but didn't respond.

"I'll be speaking with those Conrad sisters after I get rid of Ms. Phillips. I promised Elliot I would. Will you come with me?"

"If you like," I said. "Go talk to Evelyn."

"Okay, but don't leave."

"I'll be around."

When Mort left, Arthur came up to me. "So," he said, "let's hear it."

"Hear what?"

"Your thoughts on what's happened. Let's say you're writing a murder mystery with this as the plot, you know, with the body in the basement."

"Fiction is very different from reality," I countered.

"It is? I've read your books. They may be fiction, but they reflect real life. People get murdered all the time."

"Unfortunately," I said. "Would you excuse me, Arthur?"

"Where are you going?"

"I want to take a look in the barn at the rear of the property."

"Oh? What's back there?"

"It's where Cliff Cooper had his workshop, and where the man I think is his son,

Jerry—masquerading as a handyman with a Spanish name—has been living."

"Mind if I tag along?"

I hesitated.

"I gave you the big clue, didn't I?"

"Yes, you did."

I'd have preferred that he didn't accompany me, but there was no reason for him not to. "Come along," I said.

We left the house through the rear kitchen door, crossed the yard, and entered the barn. I switched on lights installed in the ceiling beams and went to the tack room where the handyman had been living. As I stood at the door, I couldn't help but wonder what had motivated him to return to Cabot Cove with his assumed identity, and to attempt to exhume the skeleton of his ex-wife. He'd been confident that no one would recognize him, and for good reason. His son, Elliot, had been just an infant when he'd left, and certainly couldn't remember what his father looked like. Even so, Tonelero had kept out of Elliot's way, telling Eve he was taking the day off when Elliot arrived, and lurking in the cemetery at his father's funeral, rather than take the chance that someone might remember him.

Jerry Cooper had lived his teenage years and young adult life as a quiet, introverted young man who rarely mingled in society. Few in town knew him well. Some twenty-five years later, he looked nothing like the young man whose face Tim Purdy had circled in the picture of the Explorers' Club at Cabot Cove High School. College had brought him his only social contact in the form of a perplexing relationship with a young woman whom he married but hid away from the community. Had having a child pulled them apart? What could have precipitated the blow that took Marina's life and sent Jerry into hiding?

And why had he returned?

I went to the bunk he used as a bed and surveyed the books on the makeshift nightstand. Then my eyes went to a far corner shrouded in shadow. One of the boxes I'd seen in the basement containing family papers and photos sat there, its top open, some of its contents spilled on the floor.

"Who lived here?" Arthur asked.

I gave him a capsule account of the family history and said I believed it was Jerry Cooper who'd returned to the home where he'd grown up.

"He was married to the woman in the basement?" Arthur asked.

"Yes."

"So who killed his wife and buried her behind the wall, the father or the husband?"

"That's what I want to find out. The note says it was Cliff. But is that true?"

"How can you prove otherwise?"

"I'm not sure, but this box may help me."

We dragged the box over to the bunk bed. I sat on the edge of the bed and randomly pulled out materials from the box. I quickly rifled through it, not looking for anything in particular. There were letters and notes written by Cliff Cooper, copies of handwritten estimates given to potential customers for his carpentry services, a school paper on the Amazon authored by a teenage Jerry Cooper, his name in an awkward scrawl at the top of the page. I was about to return the items to the box when I retrieved the letters that

Cliff had written. This time I examined them more closely.

"What's captured your interest, Jessica?" Arthur asked.

"These," I said. "If I'm not mistaken, I can—"

I was interrupted by a commotion from outside. There were multiple voices, and the slamming of car doors.

"Sounds like something's happening at the house," Arthur said.

I picked out several of the papers and put the top back on the box. "I think I have what I need," I said. "Let's go."

I led us from the barn to the kitchen door and to the library where two officers wearing uniforms from another town flanked the handyman, his hands cuffed behind his back.

"I'll take custody of him," Mort told the police. After an exchange of paperwork and Mort's expression of thanks, the two officers who'd delivered Tonelero left, replaced by two of Mort's deputies.

"I'd like to know what this is all about," Tony said angrily. "Can't a man take a ride on his motorcycle without being hassled by the police? Release me now, right now, or get me a lawyer. What crime do you think I committed?"

His little speech contained more sentences than I'd heard the man put together since I'd first encountered him in the cellar of the Spencer Percy House.

"I think you know the answer to that," Mort said. "It's about your murdered wife who was buried behind a wall in the basement."

"I'm not married, and I don't know anything about anyone buried in the basement. Take these stupid cuffs off me."

"Oh, come on, Mr. Tonelero—or should I say Mr. Cooper?"

"Call me whatever you want," he said, his voice having taken on a tone of uncertainty, "but get these off me."

"Not until we have a little talk. You say that you know nothing about your dead wife?" Mort asked again.

I could almost see the wheels turning in the head of the man I knew as Tony. He pursed his lips, gave me a nasty smile, and said, "I'll bet you think you have the whole thing figured out. I knew you were trouble from the first time I saw you."

"Leave Mrs. Fletcher out of this," Mort said. "Just tell us when you knew about the woman in the basement."

"When? I knew about it from the beginning. Believe me, it was a shock when he did it."

"When **who** did **what**?" Mort asked.

"When my old man—my father—told me what he'd done. It was devastating, that's for sure. I felt like my whole life was over."

"Your father told you that he'd killed your wife?"

"That's right."

"Why did he kill her?"

"He didn't like her, never did, from the minute I brought her home. Thought she was after his money. Said he caught her stealing from him and let her have it."

"Who buried her behind the wall?"

"He did. Who else? He said he'd get rid of the body and told me to get out of town. That's when he came up with the story that Marina and I left for South America. I thought he was right, that I'd better go or be accused of the murder if anyone discovered it."

As he wove his story, I sat quietly, clutching the written materials I'd brought from the barn. I was dying to ask questions of my own but managed to stifle the urge. This was Mort's show, and he would have been angry if I'd interfered.

"Didn't you read the note my father left?" Cooper asked.

"The note?" Mort said. "How do **you** know about the note?"

Cooper responded, "He showed it to me."

"Oh, really?" Mort said. "He bashed your wife's head in, wrote the note to get you off the hook in case the body was discovered, and buried her in the basement."

"Right, Sheriff. That's exactly right."

"Mort, I—"

Mort turned to me. "What is it, Mrs. F?"

"I don't mean to interrupt, but I'd like to know why he returned to Cabot Cove and decided to exhume his wife's body."

The man I now knew as Jerry guffawed. "Do I have to answer questions from a hack writer?"

Mort immediately came to my defense. "Watch who you're calling names. This woman knows a lot about this case."

Buoyed by Mort's faith in me, I said, "I'm asking because I knew your father as a decent, caring man. I find it hard to believe he was a murderer. Why **did** you come back and start to dig your wife's remains out from behind the basement wall?"

Jerry looked to Mort, who said, "Answer her."

"If you must know," he said, "my father called me from the hospital. He said he was dying, was putting the house on the market, and giving the proceeds to my son."

"Your father knew where you were?" I asked.

"I told him just before he went in the hospital." He snorted. "Matter of fact, I thought that's what made him sick. Then I saw something in the local newspaper about the famous Spencer Percy House being up for sale, stupid stuff about it being haunted and all. And I thought, okay, they need help, and I need to get in there."

"The Cabot Cove paper?" Mort said. "You've been living here all this time?"

"I live down the coast."

"Local papers often pick up stories from neighboring towns," I put in. "You said you needed to get in here. Eve never questioned that you knew there was a room in the barn where you could stay. But when you first got here, you moved into your old room upstairs instead—didn't you?—the one you shared with your wife. Her blue and green striped scarf is still in one of the dresser drawers."

"How do you know what belonged to my wife?"

"Elliot found a photograph of the two of you. Marina was wearing that scarf."

"That's not all we found upstairs," Mort put in.

I rushed on before Mort could bring up the green scrubs. "The most important question is why did you feel it necessary to get rid of Marina's body if your father left a note confessing to having killed her?"

Jerry glared at me. "I didn't want a new owner to discover the body and start raising questions. I thought that if I got rid of the body, I'd be doing us all a favor— me, Elliot, my father, and whoever bought the place. It was wrong. I can see that now.

But remember that my father was the killer. He did it. He left a note admitting it. You just said so. Did you hear that, Sheriff?"

"Your father didn't write that note," I said firmly. "**You** did. And I'm willing to bet you were the one who walled up the body, not Cliff. You wanted another chance to hide your crime because you were afraid if Marina was found, no one would believe that Cliff was capable of such a brutal killing. And you were right. I don't believe it."

Another guffaw. "Yeah, my father was a real good guy. That's what you think. He built those bookcases to cover up my 'shabby workmanship.' That's all he knew. A hammer and nails. He read all those books and never got any smarter."

"Here," I said, handing Mort the papers I'd brought from the box in the barn.

"What's this, Mrs. F?"

"Examples of Cliff Cooper's handwriting. And examples of a young Jerry Cooper's handwriting. I'm not an expert in handwriting analysis, but I think if you consult a professional, you'll learn that the handwriting on Cliff's letters is vastly different from the handwriting on the note found with Marina's body. And since we have samples of Jerry Cooper's handwriting, too, I'm sure that an expert will be able to verify who really wrote that note."

Mort redirected his attention to Jerry. "What about that?"

"You listen to her?"

"Most of the time," Mort replied.

"Are we finished now? I want these cuffs off."

"I have one more question," I said.

"Go ahead, Mrs. F."

"You say that your father called you from the hospital, Mr. Cooper."

Jerry sneered at me. "Mr. Cooper is my father. That's not my name anymore."

I ignored his comment. "What prompted you to visit Cliff at the hospital?" When he didn't respond, I added, "An aide saw someone carrying a motorcycle helmet enter his room. Your father was suffocated to death by someone who visited him. Was that person you?"

"Now wait a minute. I didn't kill him. I didn't kill anybody. Tell her to shut up." He glared at Mort.

There were so many other questions I wanted answered, especially why Cliff Cooper, knowing that his son had killed his wife, had allowed Jerry to bury Marina behind the wall and then had lived with that knowledge for so many years, all while he was bringing up Elliott. While I'd never considered Cliff capable of violence, his love for his son made him a criminal anyway; it made him an accessory to murder.

But I didn't get to ask that question, at least on that day, because Mort said, "Mr. Cooper, Tonelero, whatever name you want, I'm instructing my deputies to take you to headquarters where you'll be charged not only with the bludgeoning death of your wife years ago, but with the murder of your own father as well."

Cliff's son struggled to get free, but the deputies maintained their grip on him and led him from the house. I handed Mort the written materials from the barn and slumped in a chair. Arthur Bannister applauded. "You not only write murder mysteries," he said gleefully, "but you also solve them."

"Not all the time," I said. I turned to Mort. "We need to go see the Conrad twins and Elliot. As painful as this will be, I know he'll want to learn the outcome of your investigation, Mort."

"You're right, Mrs. F."

"Poor guy," Arthur put in.

"Yes," I said. "He gets his father back, only to lose him again."

Chapter Twenty-six

Mort, Arthur, and I stepped through the front door of the Spencer Percy House and were confronted by not only Evelyn Phillips and her photographer, but also Arianna Olynski and Boris, who filmed the crowd, which had now grown to at least forty onlookers. Behind the yellow tape, Boris swiveled and aimed his camera toward us as I scanned the faces in the crowd in search of the Conrad sisters, their great-niece, Beth, and Elliot. They weren't there.

The medium waved her gold-topped cane, trying to attract my attention. "Jessica, over here."

Instead, I turned to Arthur.

He took my hand. "I'll excuse myself now," he said. "I don't expect to be included with you and the sheriff in your further investigations. And don't worry. I won't reveal what I know. But I do hope you'll satisfy my curiosity later on."

"Thank you, Arthur. I appreciate your discretion. I promise I'll call you when this is over."

As Mort and I started across the street, Evelyn rushed to block our path. "Sheriff, you never mentioned an arrest earlier."

"We didn't make one earlier."

"I saw your deputies take Eve Simpson's handyman away in handcuffs. What is going on?"

"I'll be happy to fill you in, Ms. Phillips," Mort said, "once I've wrapped things up."

"Wrapped **what** things up?" She turned to me. "Jessica, you're holding back on me, too. You can't deny the public access to the news."

"Excuse us," Mort said, stepping away in the direction of the Conrad house. "There'll be a press conference," he said to Evelyn over his shoulder.

"When? What time? Jessica! I want a statement from you, too," Evelyn snapped.

"The sheriff is in charge," I said, following

him. "I have nothing to say right now."

"What about later?"

I nodded as I hurried to keep up with Mort's long stride. "Later," I said.

I understood Evelyn's annoyance. Despite her occasional bouts of brashness and aggressiveness, she was a good person, a professional who worked hard to give Cabot Cove a responsible, accurate newspaper. I would have been happy to fill her in on what had transpired in the house but knew I couldn't, at least not yet. But I would have to keep my promise of "later."

There was no crime scene tape around the Conrad sisters' house, nothing to keep the curious from following us up their front path. But Mort waved over one of his deputies, and the young man discouraged anyone from getting close to us.

Lettie had already opened the door. "I can see something's going on. Was that the handyman I saw taken away? We never met him."

"He probably was trying to avoid you," I said. "Did you recognize him?"

She didn't answer my question, instead

saying, "Beth called this morning to ask what I knew."

"And what did you tell her?" I asked as we stepped over the threshold.

"I said that I knew nothing."

Lucy sat on a chair with her quilt wrapped around her knees. Looking up briefly when we entered, she smiled sweetly and said, "I knew you'd be coming."

Lettie waved us into the living room. "Elliot's still sleeping. Or at least he's pretending to be. I looked in on him, but he turned his back to me. Are you going to let us in on the secret, Sheriff?"

"We need to have a talk," Mort said.

"Well then, sit down." She turned to her sister. "Lucy, get them some of your cookies."

"That's not necessary," I said before Lucy had time to put aside her quilt. "This is not a social call."

Lucy nodded and sat down again.

"Elliot asked us to talk with you this morning," Mort said. "I wish he'd come down now."

"I'm letting him sleep. I'll tell him whatever you need him to know later," Lettie said.

"Don't you think he should hear this for himself?" Lucy asked.

"No!"

Lettie took the high-back chair while Mort and I settled on the sofa.

"Last night," Mort began, "Mrs. Fletcher found a suspicious hole in the basement wall of the Spencer Percy House and called in the police to investigate."

"You were always so clever, Jessica," Lucy said. "I was telling Lettie that just the other day. Wasn't I, Lettie?"

"Be quiet, Lucy, and let the sheriff speak," her sister said.

"We called in a forensic team to take down the wall and found the body of a woman behind it. There was a note identifying her as Marina Cooper."

"Elliot's mama," Lucy whispered as she picked at the stitches in the fabric on her lap.

Lettie sat rigidly in her chair, her eyes looking out the window at the big house across the street. "I've heard some of the rumors," she said. "What else did the note say?"

"How did you know the note said anything more?" I asked.

Lettie shrugged.

"It was signed by Cliff Cooper, who confessed that he'd killed her," Mort said.

"Oh, but he didn't, of course," Lucy said.

"Lucy!" Lettie looked angrily at her sister.

"Well, it's true, Lettie. Cliff wouldn't hurt a fly."

"You both knew about that body, didn't you?" I said, the truth dawning on me.

"No!" Lettie said. At the same time, her sister said, "Yes."

"Lucy! Go get cookies. Do it now."

"All right, Lettie. No need to yell." She smiled at Mort and me. "I'll only be a few minutes. I'll make some tea, too." She tossed her quilt on the seat of her chair. It slid to the floor, and I leaned over to pick it up. It was a traditional pattern of repeated Christmas trees.

Lettie snatched it away from me, folded it, and placed it back on Lucy's chair. She frowned at us. "She's losing it. She doesn't know what she's saying."

"But is it true that you both knew that Marina Cooper's body was in the house all these years?" Mort asked.

Lettie's nostrils flared, and she struggled to get the next words out. "Marina was a thief. Jerry found out and killed her. Cliff swore us to secrecy, and we've kept his secret all these years. I guess since he's dead, it doesn't matter anymore, does it?"

Mort pulled a notepad from his pocket. "I wouldn't say that."

I sat forward. I saw Elliot sitting on the stairs eavesdropping, but I asked the question anyway. "Is that why Lucy didn't want to move into Cliff's house if they got married—not because it was messy, but because she knew there was a body buried in the basement?"

Lettie shrugged. "It didn't matter. She wasn't going to marry him anyway."

"Because you didn't want her to," I said. "You told her that."

"This is my house, too, my home. Didn't I have a say in it?"

"You certainly had a right to raise an objection. When you voiced your concern, how did Lucy respond?" I asked.

"She said I had my own room and asked what I was complaining about. But there's only one bathroom. I like my privacy. My whole world would have been turned topsy-turvy."

"It certainly would have changed your relationship with your sister. You couldn't allow that, could you?"

Lettie chewed her lip and looked at me earnestly. "I'm glad you understand, Jessica. Lucy's always thought that whatever she said would go, but this time I wasn't going to let her get away with it." She looked down at her rough hands, hands that chopped the wood for the fireplace, hands that fixed the torn screen door and changed the batteries in the smoke alarms. She was a strong, capable woman.

"When Cliff was in the hospital, did you try to convince him not to marry her?"

Lettie's eyes widened. She glanced at the sheriff. "Didn't I already tell you I **never** visited Cliff in the hospital?"

"Yes, you did tell us that, but I don't believe that's the truth."

"Are you accusing me of lying? That makes me very unhappy, Jessica," she said, shrugging her shoulders and raising her chin. "I've **always** prided myself on being a truthful person."

"You may usually be a truthful person, Lettie, but right now your body language is giving you away. I would have expected you to get angry when I accused you of lying."

"Well, I am angry. I'm just trying to be polite."

"Politeness is not the usual response of someone accused of being dishonest. Even if that were not the case, I have two witnesses who saw you at the hospital. Witnesses, Lettie. That's how I know you're lying when you claim that you never visited Cliff there."

Lettie said nothing.

"Do you want to tell us about it?" Mort asked.

"I was only there a few minutes. You must believe me."

"We believe you," he said. "Go on. What happened?"

"I saw that nurse go into his room, carrying a pile of laundry. I waited until she'd left. I didn't want to see her. I'd only get into an argument with her."

"Why would you argue with **her**?" I asked.

"Because I knew she was trying to take Cliff away from Lucy."

"But if you didn't want Cliff to marry Lucy, why would you care if he was attracted to another woman?"

"I didn't want him to hurt her. It's all right if she's mad at me. I'm used to that. But he's not allowed to hurt her. I wouldn't put up with that."

And maybe you didn't want him to be comforted by Carolyn either, I thought, but didn't express it. Instead, I said, "All right. The nurse left his room. What did you do then?"

"He was lying in bed. I asked him where he thought he'd go when he got out of the hospital. And he says, 'Lucy wants me to move in with you.' And I say, 'Over my dead body.' And he laughs and says, 'That can be arranged.'"

"**If** Cliff said that, he was just baiting you, Lettie."

"Well, it worked. I got angry." She sat nervously wringing her hands. "I didn't go there intending to kill him. That's what you thought, right, Jessica?"

Mort took a deep breath next to me, but I kept my eyes on Lettie.

"I'm sure you didn't intend to kill him. What happened when you got angry?"

"I told him that I wouldn't tolerate sharing my house with a stranger. And he said, 'It's only Lucy's name on the deed, not yours.' And it's true, Jessica. She must have told him."

"Told him what?"

"My mother always said I knew how to take care of myself, but Lucy didn't. So she left everything to her, the house, the furniture, everything, to her alone. She could throw me out at any time."

"Lucy would never throw you out, Lettie. You know that."

"But she could. She could."

"Is that when you took the green uniform and held it over Cliff's face?" Mort asked.

"Yes! That's right. Carolyn had left the pile of folded laundry on a table. I just grabbed what was on top and pounced on him. I was just trying to scare him at first, but then I don't know what happened to me. It was all those years of being the 'other' one, not the pretty one, not the nice one. I just pushed and pushed until he stopped fighting me."

"And then what did you do?"

"I got scared. I stuffed the clothing in my bag and left his room. I saw Carolyn down the hall. I don't think she saw me. Then out of the corner of my eye I noticed another nurse pushing a cart. I saw my chance to escape and banged into it like it was an accident, and flipped it over. Everyone started to scream. People were running from everywhere, picking up the pills and papers. I was able to sneak out the door."

"And went home?"

"Not at first. I went to Cliff's house. I had the key."

"What did you do there?"

"I just walked around, talking to him in my head, trying to explain that I didn't r eally mean it, asking him to forgive me."

"Is that when you put the scrubs in the upstairs drawer?" Mort asked.

She gave a soft laugh. "Cliff had so much junk in the house. I knew that Miss Simpson was going to get rid of everything, so I thought no one would ever find them."

"But I did," Mort said, pocketing his pad.

"I know what it was about, you know," she said softly, "Lucy and Cliff."

"What was it about, Lettie?" I asked.

"She wanted to be able to say that she was a married woman while I was still a spinster." She shook her head slowly. "Lucy has always tried to one-up me ever since we were little. My mother favored her. Mama was so obvious in her preference for Lucy that my father tried to balance things out. But he died young, and I grew up with Lucy always getting everything she wanted, and I was left with—well, with the leftovers. She kept insisting she would marry him. I had to put a stop to it."

Lettie seemed to brush away tears, but I didn't see any moisture on her fingertips. She put out her hands to Mort. "You can arrest me now."

I put my hand on Mort's arm. "Not just yet," I said.

Lucy walked in carrying a tray, her face set in a placid smile. "Here are the cookies. Did you finish telling them, Lettie?"

"Yes, Lucy. You don't have to protect me

anymore. I told them I was at the hospital."

"Of course you were. We both were."

"No, Lucy. It was only me. Don't you remember? I told you all about it. That's why you think you were there. I'm going to go into town with Jessica and the sheriff, now. You stay here."

"Doesn't anyone want any tea?"

"No!" Lettie yelled. "Let's go, Sheriff."

"I'll have a cup of tea, Lucy."

"Oh, thank you, Jessica." She set down the tray on the coffee table and pulled her chair closer, laying the quilt over her knees. "How do you take it, Jessica?"

"I can pour for myself, Lucy," I said, picking up a cup. "Tell me, how did Cliff look when you saw him in the hospital?"

"Oh, he looked just awful, Jessica. He was suffering so."

"Did you bring him a present?"

"Oh, yes! How did you guess? I brought him my quilt."

"You don't have to talk to her, Lucy," Lettie said. "I already told them what they need to know."

"Keep quiet," Mort said, "or I'll have a deputy take you outside."

"Lucy?"

"Yes, Jessica?"

"How did you know that Cliff was suffering?"

"He told me so. Said he was at death's door and just wanted to die."

"And you wanted his suffering to end?"

"Oh, yes, no one should have to suffer at the end of their life. He said he was ready to go."

"So, did you help him, the way you helped Amos?"

"Who the heck is Amos?" Mort asked.

"Our cat," Lucy said to him. "He was so old and in pain. We had to put him down."

"And that's what you did for Cliff?" I asked.

"He didn't mind. I used my quilt." She patted the green quilt with the Christmas trees. "I'd made it especially for him."

"Didn't he struggle against you?" Mort asked.

"Not very much. It was almost peaceful. He wanted to die, and I wanted to help. I kept telling him that over and over." She took a cup for herself and poured in tea.

"Where was Lettie all this time?" I asked.

"She was in the corridor, watching out for Carolyn." She giggled. "Carolyn never could tell us apart." Then her expression turned serious and her tone confiding. "Lettie said she would say that **she** did it, but I don't think that's right. I did it, and I want to take the credit. That's only right, isn't it, Lettie? This way, if they put me in jail, I'll be taken care of the rest of my life and not be a burden to you."

"Oh, Lucy." Lettie was crying real tears now.

"But how did she know about the scrubs?" Mort asked me, cocking his head toward Lettie.

Elliot, who'd been listening from the stairs, came into the room. "I told them. You made such a fuss over the scrubs, Mrs. Fletcher, I thought they must have had something to do with my grandfather's death."

I didn't add that Mort had inadvertently confirmed our suspicion that the scrubs had been the murder vehicle when he'd asked Lettie if she'd used the green uniform to kill Cliff. It didn't matter now. And I was sure that when the DNA test results came back on the material, there would only be mine, Mort's, and Elliot's easily discernible, and perhaps the DNA of whoever had worn them years ago.

Lucy looked up at Elliot. "I'm sorry you never came home to see your grandfather again, but I'm so happy you're here now. We've always loved you. You were part of our family, you and Cliff and Beth and Lettie and me."

Elliot nodded, but his lips were pressed together and his eyes were shiny with tears. "Sheriff," he said finally, "I have a favor to ask."

"Go on."

I thought he was going to ask something about Lucy or Lettie, but instead he held up his cell phone and said, "Beth left me a message. The news is all over town. I'd like to come with you and meet my father."

Chapter Twenty-seven

The day of the book sale arrived and the sky was a brilliant blue. Early in the morning, workers from the local party company came to erect the tent. They set up tables on which the boxes of books would be displayed and unfolded the chairs for the volunteers assigned to each table. When the crew members learned that the event was a fund-raiser for Cabot Cove Library, they donated the cost of the equipment rental and promised to return with their families to browse the books.

Shortly after the tent went up, a large contingent from the Friends of Cabot Cove Library, led by Elsie Frickert, ferried the boxes from inside Cliff Cooper's house to the many tables outside and set up signs printed by Beth Conrad that credited downtown merchants who had sponsored tables.

The **Gazette**'s photographer was on hand to shoot our preparations. Evelyn Phillips promised to stop in later to cover the event for the paper. She'd made peace with me after I'd given her a statement about Cliff's murder and finding Marina's body, giving credit to Mort's detective work and his arrest of the responsible parties.

Charlene Sassi arrived with her two assistant bakers and spread a bright yellow tablecloth over one of the tables, on which they placed platter after platter wrapped in pink cellophane.

"What do you have there?" I asked, coming over to admire the colorful display of baked goods.

"Wait until you see," Charlene said, grinning at me. She removed the cellophane from one of the platters with a flourish. On it were stacks of cookies in the shape of books, their titles spelled out in pink icing.

I read off some of the names. "**Moby-Dick** by Herman Melville, **Pride and Prejudice** by Jane Austen, **The Godfather** by Mario Puzo. **Carrie** by Stephen King. Oh, my goodness! You have **The Corpse Danced at Midnight**."

"By J. B. Fletcher," Charlene added. "Of course, we couldn't ignore our homegrown famous author."

"May I buy a cookie now?" I asked.

"Nope! You'll have to wait for the start of the book sale. But I have a few extra 'books' put aside for you."

"Charlene, you're wonderful."

"**You're** wonderful for organizing this event. I can't wait to hear your friend's lecture this afternoon on 'Collecting Books for Fun and Profit.' I have boxes of books in the basement that my parents left me. Might be a treasure there I don't know about."

Since Mort had thoughtfully taken down the yellow crime tape, I had arranged with Arthur Bannister to give his lecture in Cliff's library. We had folding chairs set up, and the shelves were now free and thoroughly dusted. Elliot had given Eve permission to empty the upstairs rooms, and Herb, the junk man, promised to make a donation to the library after his tag sale of the usable items he carted away.

"It's not perfect," Eve said after touring the house that morning, "but I think my buyers will be able to see the potential. I have an appointment today. Cross your fingers for me, Jessica."

"I will."

"Elliot and Beth want a quick sale, but I warned them it might be hard, considering the history of the house. Most people don't want to live where a murder took place, even though Aggie swore that her sageing got rid of all the negative energy."

Our medium had finished filming her show earlier in the week. She was disappointed when Elliot decided not to participate, but with Eve's permission she had wandered the rooms of the Spencer Percy House, talking to the spirits she said were still in residence. I both looked forward to, and dreaded, what her finished video would look like.

Mort had put the Conrad twins under house arrest, at least until the court decided how to deal with them. Attorney Fred Kramer was planning a "not guilty due to diminished capacity" defense for the murder charge against Lucy, and he was hoping to gain a dismissal of the obstruction of justice charge both sisters faced. He'd already looked into a health-care facility willing to take both women after Lettie vowed she'd never leave Lucy's side.

Elliot met his father in jail, but the father and son found they had little to say to each other. Jerry, who had escaped prose-cution for so many years, had signed a full confession once he realized that the evidence was stacked against him.

And Elliot announced that he and Beth were planning to return to Sitka together, something she said she had dreamed would happen. It represented the only truly happy ending in the whole murderous mess.

I looked around the library, remembering the thousands of books Cliff Cooper had read in his effort, perhaps, to obliterate the memories of the unhappiness in his life. I turned and spotted a book that had somehow been left behind. Perhaps it had fallen when an overloaded box had been carried outside, or perhaps it had lain there all along, unnoticed. I stooped down and picked up the slim paperback. A cool breeze brushed my cheek. I turned the book over to see the cover illustration. It showed a brilliant sunset under the title, **Vindication!**

By Graham P. Hobart. His seventh and final book.

My entire body suddenly felt chilled, and I quickly walked from the library and out into the sunny day, where I recognized many friends and neighbors browsing the thousands of books Cliff Cooper had collected. Children in their colorful costumes—little witches, ghosts, and goblins—were lining up for the Halloween Parade. Our event was going to be a big success.

I turned to gaze up at the Spencer Percy House. It looked just as it had in the old photograph I'd found in Cabot Cove Library's Local History Room, complete with a woman's face in an upstairs window. I blinked in surprise, and she was gone. But I could have sworn that before she disappeared, she'd raised her hand to wave at me.